VIRTUE AND VALOR

COLLETTE CAMERON

SOUL MATE PUBLISHING

New York

VIRTUE AND VALOR

COLLETTE CAMERON

Cover Design by Rae Monet, Inc.

Published in the United States of America by
Soul Mate Publishing
P.O. Box 24
Macedon, New York, 14502

ISBN: 978-1-61935-983-3

ebook ISBN: 978-1-61935-853-9

www.SoulMatePublishing.com

Also by Collette Cameron

CASTLE BRIDE SERIES

Highlander's Hope
The Viscount's Vow
The Earl's Enticement

HIGHLAND HEATHER,
ROMANCING A SCOT SERIES

Triumph and Treasure
Virtue and Valor

To my little sisters

Jody Georgette and Holly Minette.

Ladies of incredible grace,

fortitude, and creativity.

You hold a special corner of my heart.

Acknowledgements

I've grown so much as a writer in this, my fifth full-length novel and eighth titled work, because of one incomparable critique partner, SH. Her willingness to share everything she's learned helped me drastically hone my writing skills—something I hope I do with each new work.

Chapter 1

London, England
8 September 1818

"There's nothing for it." Yancy tipped back his tankard and enjoyed one last bracing pull of dark ale. "It's off to Craiglocky at first light. Unrest between the clans has escalated steadily since I visited there in July."

His companion, Lucan-Rochester, Duke of Harcourt, offered a non-committal grunt.

Yancy scratched his nose and frowned. "Peculiar, that. In recent years, tribal disputes are rare, even in the Highlands."

"I am certain you are not overly distressed at the summons." Harcourt gulped the last of the coffee he'd been nursing between sips of brandy. "You may be Bartholomew Yancy, Earl of Ramsbury and an English lord by birth, my friend, but you've displayed a distinct penchant for certain things Scottish."

Yancy glowered, sending a silent warning.

Harcourt grinned, completely unabashed. "Come now, admit it. You've been sniffing about Isobel Ferguson's skirts for the better part of a year."

Damn. Will he not let the matter go?

Nonetheless, a stab of expectancy flooded Yancy.

Anticipation always preceded a visit to Craiglocky Keep. Its laird, Ewan McTavish, the Viscount Sethwick, hailed as one of Yancy's closest chums, and Isobel, Sethwick's sister, *was* of particular interest.

Possessed of a lively intelligence, she had matured into a magnificent beauty. Graced with cocoa-colored hair, streaked with creamy highlights, her eyes mirrored the shade of a tropical sea at sunset, and her peach-tinted lips . . . well, he'd give his earldom to taste their dewiness.

However, she loathed him.

None, but God in heaven, knew why. Until last December, they had gotten on famously, and he had been certain she harbored a distinct *tendre* for him.

Holding his tankard, Yancy fingered the smooth rim.

Charming, biddable, and educated, Isobel possessed every attribute a quintessential countess ought to, and he'd been of a mind to pay his address. Until she gave him the cut direct at her sister's Christmastide ball.

A rakish gleam entered Harcourt's eyes. "By-the-by, how is your pursuit of the fair Scots lass progressing?"

Tempted to ignore the taunting, Yancy instead lifted a shoulder and feigned nonchalance. "She treats me as if I am a sore-laden leper or the devil himself."

Harcourt threw back his head and roared with laughter, causing several patrons to turn and stare in their direction.

Yancy stopped caressing his cup, a dismal substitute for the silken, ivory skin he yearned to trace his fingertips across. "The last time we met, I actually sniffed beneath my arms and blew my breath into my hand fearing an unpleasant smell might be the cause of her aversion."

Another robust burst of mirth from Harcourt followed Yancy's disclosure. "Poor sot."

Yancy crossed his legs and returned his mug to the polished table. Tapping his buff-covered knee with slightly ink-stained fingers, he relaxed against his chair and turned his thoughts away from the vixen who had him at sixes and sevens.

Scanning White's dining room, he acknowledged several acquaintances with a slight inclination of his head.

The club bustled tonight, a sort of pleasant male hubbub. A steady stream of London's finest arrived for an evening's entertainment or to escape the company of demanding females. An occasional guffaw interrupted the low murmur of voices and the clinking of silverware against dishes.

Laden with the aroma of food, candles, and the stench of men doused in cologne or in need of bathing, the air hung thick in the room.

Nasty habit that, drenching oneself in scent in an attempt to cover noxious body odors. Personally, Yancy enjoyed a good daily soak in the tub.

Upon spotting Sir Gwaine MacHardy entering the cardroom, he grimaced. "MacHardy's arrived."

"Why the bore hasn't been banned from White's altogether, I do not understand." Harcourt's clasp on his snifter tightened until his knuckles glowed white, and he shot the stout Scot a glare intended to lay MacHardy flat.

"Nor do I." Elbows resting on his chair's arms, Yancy tapped his fingertips together. "I do wonder why he's admitted, especially since he's blatantly contemptuous of the English."

"Awfully smug prig for a feudal baron." Harcourt pushed his coffee cup to the edge of the table, his dark gaze impatiently roving the room. "Where's our waiter?"

"You drink more coffee than anyone else of my association. Sleep less than any of them too," Yancy observed matter-of-factly. Hence the need for copious amounts of the bitter brew, which Harcourt claimed helped keep him alert. "The practice cannot be good for your health."

Cynicism wrinkled Harcourt's brow. "Are you pointing a finger at me? You, who confessed last week that you overindulge in spirits more often than you ought?"

"No, I'm simply making an observation." Resting his head against the plush chair, Yancy eyed his friend.

Impeccable, as always, in his usual all-black togs, his blond hair neatly brushed, and his face smooth as a lad's, Harcourt lounged in his seat. His gray eyes, the whites red-tinged, didn't hold their customary wicked gleam.

Returning Yancy's appraisal, the duke's lips swept into a mocking smile. "What?"

"You look like bloody hell, Harcourt. Late night?"

Yancy chuckled, fully aware of Harcourt's mistress's reputation and her insatiable carnal appetite. After all, he had introduced her to his friend, though Yancy hadn't sampled her charms himself.

That was one rule they, and their friends, strictly abided by; no sharing of women or sampling the same wares. The practice created too many complications and the potential to brew conflict amongst the rogues.

Friendship before females—always.

The comrades had lived by that motto until six of them had gone corkbrained and fell head-over-arse in love. So much for oaths of friendship. The pledge had been tossed aside with as little regard as a smelly, moth-eaten sock.

Chuckleheads.

True, his friends seemed blissful as mice in a full larder, and the women they had chosen as mates proved quite exceptional. Nonetheless, Yancy wasn't such a slowtop he didn't realize his friends had stumbled upon something exceedingly rare in their unions.

From his observations, most leg-shackling appeared tolerable at best and, far more commonly, altogether torturous.

Now, only he and Harcourt remained unencumbered by wives, except Yancy's infernal obligations demanded that he acquire a countess. Every time he reluctantly contemplated selecting a spouse, Isobel's lovely face hovered around the fringes of his consciousness.

He'd never desired the damnable title. The Earls of Ramsbury who held the honorific before him hadn't been noble men he proudly claimed as relations or whose footsteps he gladly followed in.

Since inheriting the earldom, the one concession he refused to make pertained to his form of address.

Devil it, he had been known as Yancy since Eton. The rest of the world could call him Ramsbury, or Honey Sop, or Flitter-Mouse for all he cared. However, to his closest friends and those he held dear, he would forever be Yancy.

Harcourt yawned behind his hand, his signet ring glinting from the candles nestled in the silver candelabra centered atop their table.

Yancy crooked an eyebrow. "Have you slept at all?"

The duke motioned for a waiter to refill his cup.

"No, I haven't, not that it's any of your business." He covered his mouth and yawned widely again. "I severed my association with my mistress last evening. She had become too demanding and untrustworthy."

"She didn't take receiving her *congé* well, I gather?" Yancy gave a lopsided smile. "Precisely why I refrain from such cumbersome entanglements. Dashed nuisance that, having to coddle and appease manipulating females."

Though a few, like his mother—God rest her tormented soul—made the best of her circumstances without complaint. Mother had filled her life with an excess of scripture, cats, shopping, and rich foods. The latter of which sent her to an early grave at a mere seven and thirty and corpulent to the extreme.

Harcourt snorted and combed a hand through his hair. "Not well at all. I was compelled to call for a physician to administer drops to calm her hysteria. Why she thought I wouldn't object to her sharing her favors with three other men while under my protection is beyond me."

Grimacing, Harcourt shut his eyelids and pressed two fingers there. "I wasn't miserly with her either. A greedier woman I've never met."

Vulnerability registered on his face for a flash, then vanished. For all of his affected aloofness, Harcourt possessed a sensitive soul.

Yancy grasped the first thing that sprang to mind and pointedly changed the subject. "Did I ever mention Cecily ensconced herself and that niece of hers at Bronwedon Towers a mere week after I inherited the title? Without my knowledge or permission, I might add."

He flicked bits of dried wax off the table. Too bad he could not rid himself of his stepmother and her niece as easily.

"Then my dear stepmother dared to call herself the dowager countess and went on a spending spree that would shame the Prince Regent."

Harcourt *tsked*. "The nerve."

Brushing a waxy flake from his pantaloons, Yancy scowled. "And she had the pluck to assure the merchants I would cover her bills."

He pinched the bridge of his nose against the ache thinking of Cecily and Matilda always caused. They'd been thorns in his side since his father married Cecily. Thank God, at seventeen, he had been off to university shortly thereafter.

"I put a quick stop to that, I'll tell you." He dropped his hand to his lap. "Told the merchants I refused to pay a single groat of her debt. Nipped her expenditures faster than clippers to a rosebud, I did."

Harcourt released a throaty chuckle. "For certain, she's been a trial to you."

"Indeed." Yancy heaved an exaggerated sigh. "Did she ever fly into the boughs over that last bit. Her screeches rang in my ears for days."

"Cannot abide a harpy," Harcourt murmured sympathetically.

For the past two years, Yancy permitted Cecily to reside at Bronwedon Towers during the summer months, which meant he avoided the estate like the seventh level of hell.

Even worse, Cecily's niece, Matilda, had attempted trysts with him the last three times they'd been under the same roof. A doubt didn't exist that, despite having just seen her seventeenth birthday, the chit was no virtuous miss.

Curling his lip, he grimaced at the memories of Matilda's wagtail ways and Cecily's constant harping. "Visions of that harridan are what have kept me content with casual liaisons these many years."

That and memories of Julia Cambrill—the voluptuous widow who'd captured his trusting heart at eighteen. She mauled it beyond recognition, and then, her hand on the arm of her latest conquest, had tossed his mangled heart at his booted feet.

A satisfied smirk on her face, she had publically mocked him. "I need a man, not a *boy*, in my bed."

Chapter 2

After ten years, the heat of Julia's humiliation still sluiced Yancy. A drink or two typically helped erase her gloating expression from his mind. Forgetting he'd drained the cup, he seized his tankard.

Confound it.

"You have the right of it, Yancy. No commitments to muddle things, even carefully contracted ones." Drumming his fingers on his thigh, Harcourt clenched his jaw for a moment. "Blast and bother, but females become emotional when they don't get their way. And spiteful too."

"I'll say." Yancy directed his contempt at his empty cup. *Spiteful and cruel.*

"Their histrionics and waterworks. Godawful." Harcourt rolled his eyes dramatically and shuddered before snatching his brandy and emptying the glass in one gulp. "I may never marry."

Their waiter approached the table bearing a laden tray.

"Most wise, Harcourt, if you can manage to avoid the trap."

Harcourt's countenance darkened. "I cannot, any more than you can, my friend. But I'm damned well taking my time, I tell you."

With a nod of thanks, Yancy accepted a crisp linen napkin from the servant.

Alas, Harcourt spoke the truth as fate had refused to spare Yancy the aggravation of matrimony. *More's the pity.*

However, with a countess as delectable as Isobel Ferguson in his bed, he might make do. *If* she thawed her comportment toward him. He didn't want a frigid ice-maiden between his sheets or beneath him either.

The servant placed plates overflowing with thick beefsteaks, boiled potatoes, carrots, and herb-seasoned asparagus before them.

Yancy sniffed in appreciation. His stomach answered with a rumbling growl. He hadn't eaten since breaking his fast early this morning.

After adding a basket of hot rolls and a dish of butter, their waiter filled the duke's coffee cup then dutifully added three lumps of sugar and a generous portion of cream. Lastly, he placed a bottle of claret in the middle of the table, along with two sparkling crystal goblets. "Shall I pour, Your Grace?"

The servant knew full well Harcourt preferred to uncork the bottle himself. Nonetheless, he respectfully made the same request every time he served the duke.

Yancy quirked his mouth into a droll smile.

The waiter's consideration always earned him an extra guinea—precisely why the cunning chap made the gesture.

"No, just leave the corkscrew." Harcourt took a healthy gulp of the coffee, then winced. "Confound it. You might warn a chap the brew is scalding."

The servant's bemused glance met Yancy's, and Yancy winked.

"Harcourt, it is always steaming hot. That's how you request the beverage served." Yancy waggled his fingers at the cup. "See those misty little tendrils curling upward? That ought to have warned you. They generally indicate heat."

"Do stubble it." Harcourt snatched up his fork and knife. "Burned my tongue. Shan't be able to taste my food now, and I'm ravenous."

His expression carefully composed, the waiter's lips twitched as he cleared away the empty tankard and brandy glass.

Yancy was of half a mind to offer the man a position. He had a feeling the young chap would liven things up amongst his entirely too-proper staff at Bronwedon Towers.

No, on second thought, the handsome servant would be too much of a temptation to Matilda.

"Will there be anything else, my lord, Your Grace?"

"Not at present." Yancy seized his eating utensils, eagerly anticipating slicing into the juicy steak. "Is there apple tart this evening?"

As much as he enjoyed a nice slab of meat, his true weakness lay in sweets and fancy pieces. He patted his stomach. Better watch that indulgence, or he would be nigh on to guts and garbage. A flabby cove he'd find himself all too soon, though sparring in the ring three times a week kept his stomach firm.

"Yes, sir, but Cook only has one pastry left. If you will excuse me, I'll cut you each a slice before it's all gone." With a quick bow, the waiter withdrew, leaving them to enjoy their food.

After opening the wine, Harcourt poured a generous splash into the glasses. The duke lifted his, gently swirling the port before he raised the wine to his nose and inhaled. He took a sip and nodded his approval. Running his finger round the rim of his goblet, he stared at the crimson liquid within.

"Yes, I do believe I shall follow your example for a bit, Yancy—restrict my dalliances to eager widows and demimondes. No innocents and positively no marriage-minded misses." A portion of his weariness faded from his countenance, replaced by a renewed spark of interest. "Why, *Le bon ton* is swarming with delectable females impatient to share their favors with a duke."

He winked. "And an earl."

"Quite so." Yancy reached for his wine.

If Harcourt suspected he contemplated marriage, his friend would taunt him unmercifully. Yancy had no intention of sharing that news until the cleric read the banns. Or mayhap he would skip the whole rigmarole and trot across the border to Scotland.

Scandalous.

Unless his bride happened to be Scottish.

Harcourt took a bite of potato, chewing thoughtfully.

"As for the Highlanders, Sethwick wouldn't have asked for your help if matters hadn't grown more urgent. As you know, he generally prefers to keep the English out of Scottish affairs." Harcourt pierced a carrot. "I shall accompany you. After all, it's my cousin who's at the center of this feuding. Lydia didn't intend to remain at Craiglocky this long."

"Damn ye, unhand me! He cheated *me,* not the other way around."

A commotion near the cardroom entrance drew the diners' attention. Amidst black oaths and dire threats, two burly footmen forcefully escorted a flushed and struggling Sir Gwaine in the exit's direction.

Yancy canted his head toward the Scotsman twenty feet away. Keeping his voice low, he murmured, "I do believe MacHardy's set a new record for being ousted. He couldn't have been in there more than ten minutes. Cheating again, do you suppose?"

Harcourt shifted in his chair. He raised his quizzing glass and inspected the baron toe to top. "Wish I had wagered on that. Always did prefer a sure thing. Once a cheat, always a cheat, I say."

The Scot jerked his head in their direction, his beefy jowls swinging below a scruffy auburn beard.

MacHardy's face grew redder yet, until his cheeks glowed puce. He narrowed his slate eyes to slits, sending Harcourt a venom-filled glower. Sir Gwaine's mouth worked silently, a drop of spittle on his unkempt beard.

Good God, was he having an apoplexy?

Tearing off a sizable chunk of his roll, Yancy buttered it, and through half-closed eyes, observed the Scot. "He heard you, Harcourt."

His arm draped lazily across the top of his chair, Harcourt's attention remained on the fuming Scotsman being herded to the door.

"Indeed. I meant him to." A challenge resonated in Harcourt's clipped words. "He has caused Lydia and her father no small amount of grief."

Teeth clenched, the baron strained against his captors' tight grips. "Bloody Sassenach."

"I say."

"Hold your tongue, short-arse."

"What insolence."

Harcourt spoke over the protests ringing round the room. "Wasn't your mother a 'bloody Sassenach,' MacHardy?" Scorn dripped from his voice. "*Tsk, tsk*. Such irreverence for your poor, deceased parent."

Eyes bulging, the Scot lunged, but the oversized footmen brought him up short.

"Ye be tellin' that cousin of yers, sequesterin' his daughter at Craiglocky be gettin' more Scots involved in our private disagreement." He wrenched ineffectually at the hands restraining him. "Lydia Farnsworth should have accepted me offer of marriage, the pernickety slattern."

More murmurs of outrage, much louder this time, echoed throughout the dining room.

"Hound's teeth!" Harcourt went rigid and tossed his napkin on the table. "I'll make him eat those words. After I knock what teeth he has remaining down his fat throat."

Holy hell.

Yancy sprang to his feet.

"Don't. The sot's foxed." He laid a staying hand on Harcourt's shoulder. "Be sensible. MacHardy's baiting you."

Angling his back to the struggling Scot, Yancy added, "Call him out, and although he's not a crack shot, he'll choose pistols. In the last six months alone, he damn near killed two men. Claimed weapon malfunction caused the guns' early discharges."

"Not likely, the sneaky bilge rat." Harcourt gripped the chair's arms, vengeance simmering in his eyes.

"True, but no one's proved otherwise." Yancy jutted his chin toward the Scot. "Ignore the bugger. He's already lost face tonight. Besides, didn't you give your mother your word you wouldn't engage in duels?"

His expression bland, Harcourt stared at Yancy for an extended moment then gave a dismissive shrug. "I did, and you are right, of course."

Yancy relaxed a fraction. Thank God, Harcourt had listened to reason.

The duke retrieved his napkin and addressed his food once more, pointedly disregarding Sir Gwaine. "So, are we to ride or take a coach to Craiglocky?"

His stomach coiled into a tight knot, dousing further enjoyment of his meal, Yancy returned to his chair. However, his attention remained riveted on MacHardy.

The Scot's reputation for depravity was well-earned. No female should be subjected to the fiend's degeneracy, most especially not a gently-bred woman like Lydia Farnsworth.

The brawny footmen dragged the cursing man the remaining few feet to the entrance then unceremoniously shoved him out the door.

The latch shot home with a firm *click*, cutting off his string of obscene epithets. A moment later, the entrance reverberated with a tremendous thump, followed by a muted howl of pain.

Yancy would wager his precious apple tart MacHardy had punched the stout, three-inch thick door. Likely, he'd broken a knuckle or two for his efforts.

"Good riddance." Yancy returned his focus to Harcourt. "You are going to leave all this"—he waved his hand in a circle—"for the wilds of Scotland?"

Harcourt sighed and flung his napkin aside.

"I have grown bored with all of this." He flicked his fingers in imitation of Yancy's gesture. "Besides, I am concerned about Lydia. She has almost been a sister to me."

His mouth swooped into a wicked grin. "And I cannot wait to see Isobel's reaction when she discovers you will be underfoot at Craiglocky for days, maybe weeks."

A memory of gorgeous marine eyes framed by thick dark lashes gazing at him with adoration flashed to Yancy's mind.

He needed something damned stronger than ale or wine to eradicate *her* memory. A mug or three of Scotch whisky—the fiery stuff Sethwick favored that plowed a path of fury to one's gut and oblivion to one's mind—ought to get the job done.

Who was he kidding?

He doubted he'd ever consume enough spirits to banish Isobel from his memory. What the devil had he done to cause her to spurn him?

By God, he would oust the truth this visit.

Yes, he would give Isobel Ferguson one last chance to come round. Hopefully, she'd realize what an opportunity he offered. If not, he would direct his attentions to the dozens of eager misses all too willing to warm his bed, if not his heart.

The notion perturbed him. He hadn't an iota of interest in anyone else. Isobel had captured his heart years ago. He'd simply have to redouble his efforts to win her over.

Yancy viciously stabbed his steak.

No naked-arsed Scot was going to win *his* lass's favor.

Chapter 3

Craiglocky Keep, Scotland
13 September 1818

Isobel bounded from her bed, sucking in a sharp breath as cool air hit her. Shivering, she dashed across her chamber, the stone floor between the hand-braided rag rugs biting cold beneath her bare feet. She threw open the heavy plum-colored velvet draperies and grinned.

Finally.

The vivid blue sky, an occasional puffy cloud in the distance, promised a day of sunshine and mild temperatures.

She nearly danced a jig. Instead, she bounced to warm her icy toes as frigid tendrils crept up her calves. The mornings had turned quite cold, and her maid had yet to come and light the fire.

A rather violent storm blew through three days ago, dumping an avalanche of rain upon the area. Several times a day, Isobel peered out a window, impatient for an opportunity to examine the face of the rock outcrop once the torrent ceased.

The cool, dark jade of the early morning forest paralleling the loch caught her attention.

The color of his eyes.

A tiny twinge of melancholy twisted her heart, dampening her bright mood.

For years, she'd girlishly mooned over her brother's good friend, Lord Ramsbury, admiring his dark hair, a shade somewhere between sable and whisky, and the way his tresses curled atop his ears. Many a time, she had sketched his almost straight nose and firm, Cupid's bow lips.

They often tilted into a teasing smile, revealing a row of white teeth—one, the tiniest bit turned—which added a charming, boyish element to his already too-appealing features. But his eyes, intellect gleaming in their depths, were what captivated her.

Framed by midnight lashes—no doubt the envy of many a lady—they were the darkest green she had ever beheld. Except for a narrow ring around the iris. That band gleamed smoky-gray, almost ebony.

Also funny and considerate and kind, he—

No.

She slapped her palm against the stone sill.

Isobel Ferguson, do not waste a single moment fantasizing about Yancy . . . Lord Ramsbury.

She'd never been anything more to him than the immature, younger sister of his long-time chum. Not to mention, Ramsbury was a deceptive blackguard.

Yes, but a deliciously handsome and rakish one.

Bah!

Rubbing her stinging palm against her stomach, Isobel whirled from the encasement. She rushed to her wardrobe where she rapidly donned her oldest gown, a soft Kersey wool.

At one time a rich Highland heather, repeated launderings had faded the cloth to a pale iron shade. Since she rode astride, a riding habit simply would not do. Neither could she mount and dismount a sidesaddle without assistance.

After slipping her feet into comfortable, though worn and scuffed half-boots, she collected a simple gray-brown cloak. A coarse cloth bag followed, along with a wide-brimmed straw hat and thick leather gloves. She dropped a pair of sharpened pencils, her sketchpad, a dagger, and a leather pouch of tools into the bag.

What else might she need?

A scented kerchief.

She always ended up with dirt smudges on her face.

By the time Maura, her nurse-turned-maid, arrived to wake her, Isobel stood ready to depart for a long-anticipated morning of archeological investigating.

After depositing a tray atop the oval table situated beside an arched window, Maura planted her hands on her ample hips and scowled at Isobel's attire. "Ye be dressed like a wench from the village. *Again.*"

She fairly hissed the last word.

Isobel chuckled and sank onto a straight-backed chair before the table. "It doesn't make sense to dress in finery, since I shall be clambering over rocks and scraping away bits of dirt and clay. No one except my family will see me in any event."

She lifted the cover from the food.

Ham, oatmeal, and bannocks with fresh butter and raspberry jam awaited her. "You know guests are not expected until this weekend."

Her sister, Adaira, the Countess of Clarendon, and her husband would arrive Friday or Saturday to celebrate their sister-in-law Yvette's birthday. Several other family members were also expected, including Yvette's cousins, Lord and Lady Warrick and Isobel's cousins, Lord and Lady Bretheridge.

Pouring a cup of tea, Isobel inhaled the heady scent. She added two lumps of sugar and a dash of milk before stirring the contents.

She adored the smell of hot tea. The scent reminded her of her childhood. Every morning, Mother had gathered the children around her for a cuddle and enjoyed a cup with them.

Lifting the hand-painted teacup to her lips, Isobel eyed

the disgruntled maid stomping about the bedchamber casting her astringent glances every now and again.

"Suppose this means ye be plannin' on wallowin' about in the muck too." Maura did exaggerate so.

Isobel pointedly focused her attention on the ceiling to keep from rolling her eyes.

"I do not wallow, as you know full well." She wiggled her free hand at the maid. "My hands and nails shan't even get dirty."

"Ladies do not collect rocks and *dead* things turned to rocks." Maura harrumphed and trundled her way to the rumpled bed. She shuddered dramatically. "It be unnatural, I tell ye. Creatures turned to stone. They be cursed. The same as Lot's wife in the Good Book."

"She was turned into a pillar of salt, not stone." Isobel suppressed a chuckle and spread jam over a roll.

"*Humph*. Stone. Salt. It makes no matter to me."

Maura patted the purple and white coverlet into place then adjusted a couple of pillows to her satisfaction. "A curse is a curse—like those Callanish sinners turned to stone for their heathen activities on the Sabbath."

"Maura, that's Superstitious drivel. The Callanish Circle was used to track lunar activity."

Clearly baffled, Maura pursed her lips and squinted at Isobel. "Loony activity?"

"*Lunar*. The path of the moon." Isobel smiled, pointing with a forefinger and drawing an arc in the air.

"The *sinner's-to-stone* business is nonsense. Simply a silly legend spread by the early Kirk of Scotland to discourage rites they didn't approve of."

Maura sniffed doubtfully before her focus shifted to the remaining food. "Ye goin' to eat any more?"

Isobel dutifully swallowed a few additional mouthfuls of oatmeal and ham. "Happy now?"

"Hmph." Maura's grunt resounded with disapproval as

she scooped Isobel's nightgown from the back of a chair.

Isobel drank the last of her tea. Dabbing her mouth, she rose. Keen to be on her way, she swept her cloak over her shoulders.

"At least take a hound and a knife with ye. And *dinna* stray too far." The servant made her way to the wardrobe. She opened the doors, and after shaking the plain, white gown, hung it on a hook inside. "Yesterday, while herding sheep by the tors, Fergus saw Highland travellers and other Scots he didn't recognize."

"I'll take Tira with me." Isobel collected her other things.

Maura faced Isobel. "Keep yer eyes sharp. I be tellin' the laird yer off pokin' about in those outcrops once more."

"Please do, and let Mother know, too, will you?" Isobel slid the bag's handles over a wrist. "Tell her I shall be back in plenty of time for luncheon. Is Sorcha making Scotch stovies?"

"*Aye* and strawberry tarts," the servant grumbled.

Isobel gave Maura a quick hug. "Not to worry, I have my dagger."

More for scraping away dirt than any need for protection, but Maura needn't know that.

The maid's sputtering recriminations about the propriety of hugging staff, and unaccompanied females trotting off to scratch about in the mud, followed Isobel as she left her chamber and headed for the stables.

Three hours later, she stretched her arms overhead to ease the dull throb in her back from crouching so long. Habit had her skimming the dirt. She froze, staring intently at the ground.

"Ah, I knew it."

Tiny frissons of excitement pricking her nerves, she scooped a coppery brown shard into her gloved hand. Turning the chip over, she brushed away the moist dirt clinging to the piece.

She held the sliver before her face. "Would you look at this, Tira? It's an arrowhead."

The charcoal-colored boarhound obediently poked her boxy nose near the flint and gave the tip a cursory sniff before turning away disdainfully. The dog nuzzled Isobel's cloak pocket then raised soulful eyes to her as if to say, *Is that all*? *You brought me all the way out here for an insignificant splinter of stone*?

Isobel chuckled and rubbed behind the dog's ears.

Tira's back leg thumped as she twitched in rhythm to Isobel's scratching.

"I didn't promise you a snack, my friend. Only a nice run, to stretch those long legs of yours."

She stopped petting the dog, and Tira snuffled her snout against Isobel's faded skirt.

"When we get back, I shall get you something tasty. I promise. I was in such a hurry to examine the cliffs today, I forgot your treat."

The hound did enjoy a buttery shortbread cookie or two—or six.

Several feet beyond the other side of the rock bed, Isobel's mare blew out a breath and swung her pale, gray head.

Isobel laughed. "No, Emira, I shan't forget to get you a carrot."

Rubbing the arrow head between her thumb and forefinger, she surveyed the crag. Many eons ago, a glacier had scraped and gouged its way across this scarred stretch of land. Rocks and boulders, ranging from coin-sized to mammoth stones larger than crofters' cottages, dotted the landscape.

Tempests washed dirt away from the precipices, exposing all manner of fascinating treasures. Isobel had unearthed a few shards of crude pottery and two more arrowheads inside one of the larger cave's openings.

The history behind the items captivated her. Primitive

peoples, quite possibly her ancestors, had occupied these lands at one time.

Ages ago, the barbarous Vikings had settled farther north and on the islands west of the mainland. Both locations were a good distance from Craiglocky Keep, which eliminated the Norse as the people responsible for the relics. The items in the caves hadn't been left behind by the gypsies venturing near Craiglocky's lands twice yearly, either.

The objects were far too old.

Petting Tira, Isobel scanned the large boulders intermittently edging the rock and cave-embedded cliff. Her attention whipped to a peculiar series of indentations.

"I think . . ."

She rushed to the bluff. Brushing her fingers against the slightly rough ridges of a rock, her heart kicked against her ribs. "Oh, look, a trilobite."

Her practiced gaze traveled the length of the overhang. "I would bet my sainted grandmother's Bible there are more here."

Isobel considered the caves' yawning black mouths.

"Possibly, in those as well."

Next time, she must bring a lantern to thoroughly explore them. Fingering the fossil, Isobel grinned. Imagine, at one time this area had been under water. Fossils of the strange sea creatures were quite common in Scotland, or so she'd read.

She'd discovered many fascinating facts and learned about many enchanting places from reading.

Then again, that was primarily what she did for entertainment and adventure.

Read. And read. And read.

And yearn to travel.

Somewhere. *Anywhere*.

Oh, to have a grand escapade of some sort—to see the pyramids or the Great Sphinx of Egypt. Or perhaps, something closer to home, like the Standing Stones of Callanish or the Ring of Brodgar.

Isobel gave a derisive snort and rubbed her itchy nose. The dirt smudged into her glove tickled her, and she sneezed.

Thirty miles.

The farthest Isobel had ventured from her birthplace, except for the house party at Adaira's last December and one at the Marquis and Marquesses of Bretheridge's a couple of years before that.

Tira barked and loped after a rabbit.

A pensive sigh escaped Isobel. "There's a whole amazing world out there, and I am stuck at Craiglocky Keep."

Not that she didn't love her childhood home. Of course she did. Nonetheless, she yearned to see undulating deserts or roaring waves pounding the surf instead of the Highland's sloping emerald hills dotted with fragrant purple heather and dolloped with creamy sheep.

"Wouldn't life be a mite more wonderful if I saw more of the world before I marry and have children?"

At nearly twenty, several marriage offers had come her way already. Thank goodness, her parents allowed her to choose a husband. Unfortunately, the Highlands rather limited the selection of possible candidates.

Though rugged, handsome Scots abounded, so far her many admirers only complimented her on her beauty. Not her desire to discuss politics, or her knowledge of various sciences, or her ability to speak multiple languages, or even her delight in solving complicated mathematical equations.

Her capacity to see something once, whether it be a map, diagram, or the contents of a book—practically anything, truly—and recall the information in nearly perfect detail, had been a delightful game when she'd been a child.

She had a voracious appetite for knowledge and scant patience for beaus whose interest lay in ogling her bosom or staring raptly at her face with an idiotic expression upon theirs.

Isobel could paper her bedchamber in the ridiculous poems and sonnets she had received. She'd been praised for her eyes— *the color of the morning sea*—and her skin—*as soft, satiny, and white as a dove's breast*—and her hair—*warm chocolate swirled with fresh cream.*

She had laughed outright at that ridiculousness, although she'd wondered what admirer had sent the anonymous note.

Pshaw. What twaddle.

She had a looking glass. Yes, she was pretty. All right, perhaps more than pretty, but what had outward appearances to do with a person's merit? She'd had no hand in the way the Good Lord formed her.

Her mind, her intelligence, her thirst for knowledge, those she did have some influence over. And not a single man beyond her kin had ever complimented her on those attributes. She wasn't altogether convinced that men, in general, weren't a mite jingle-brained.

No, that wasn't true. Lord Ramsbury had a sharp mind and quick wit. However, that jackanape was a devious knave. He'd played with her affections when he wasn't in a position to pay court to anyone.

Mayhap she deserved the blame for naïvely reading too much into his attentions. She had dared to hope he had a genuine interest in her, an unsophisticated Highlander, rather than the dazzling, proper English miss he was all but betrothed to.

Isobel knew better now.

Straightening, she scrutinized the area, seeking more artifacts. The caves she wanted to poke around in lay farther along the rock-laden wall. A little shiver tingled between her shoulders. Just imagine what she might uncover.

Shifting her focus overhead, a resigned huff escaped her. Almost noon time, if she calculated the sun's location correctly.

No exploring those caverns today. Lunchtime drew near.

She would barely get back to the keep in time to freshen and change into something more appropriate. Besides, she had promised she would finish embroidering a shawl as a gift for Yvette's birthday in a few days.

Isobel examined the tips of her tan sheepskin gloves. Her forefingers threatened to poke through the worn seam.

Again.

Her third pair in three months. The next glove order would be for six pairs.

She turned and then examined the horizon behind her.

Loch Arkaig glowed sapphire blue in the noonday sun; the brilliant rays, a dancing rainbow of diamonds, glistened atop its pristine surface. Nonetheless, the water remained frigid, especially where the forest rimmed the shore.

A few migrating cranes, virtually invisible in the reed beds, wandered amongst the boggier area against the backdrop of the original castle's charred ruins.

Tucking the arrowhead into her bag, she whistled for Tira. A few moments later, the dog came bounding from across the meadow bordering the cliffs.

After gathering her belongings, Isobel retrieved the mare, and mounted her. With a final sweeping glance at the area, she turned the horse toward the keep proudly standing at attention on the far side of the loch.

Fifteen minutes later, she trotted Emira into the south stables. Isobel inhaled the familiar scents of horses, hay, liniment, and leather. Her stomach rumbled and contracted, reminding her how little she'd eaten to break her fast.

Tira disappeared, no doubt eager to join her sister and brother in the gatehouse for their customary afternoon nap.

Craiglocky's head groom, Jocky, assisted Isobel to the ground. "Did ye find anythin' today, Miss Isobel?"

She smiled and nodded, untying her bag from the saddle. "Thank you, Jocky. I did. An arrowhead and a fossil."

Another stable hand appeared, prepared to unsaddle

the mare. Grasping the reins, he patted the horse's neck and turned her toward the other end of the stables.

"Wait, Conrad. I promised her a carrot." Isobel rubbed the mare's muzzle. "Will you see that she gets one or two?"

The lad ducked his head, his freckle-covered face blooming with color. "Be pleased to, Miss Ferguson."

"My, it's proving to be a rather warm day, after all." Plucking her bonnet from her head, Isobel welcomed the slight breeze wafting from the open doors. She tucked the hat underneath her arm before peeling off her gloves.

Striding to the stable's exit, she called over her shoulder. "Did anything occur while I was gone?"

"*Aye*." Jocky's enthusiastic grin exposed a missing front tooth. "Two fancy English gents arrived half an hour after ye rode out."

She stopped, turning halfway in his direction. "Lord Clarendon and Lord Warrick? Or was it Lord Bretheridge? I didn't think Adaira, Vangie, or Angelina would arrive until this weekend."

"*Nae* ladies be with them, Miss Isobel." Removing his sweat-stained hat, he wiped his beaded brow with the back of his hand. "And it *nae* be any of them lairds."

Isobel's stomach vaulted to her throat then plummeted to her scuffed boots.

Please don't let it be him.

Lord Ramsbury had been here in July, and matters had not gone well between them.

"No? Who then?" She swallowed convulsively.

Scrunching his brow and squinting, his eyes in concentration, the groom scratched his chest. "The Duke of Harcourt and the—"

"Earl of Ramsbury," said a much-too-familiar, melodious baritone.

Chapter 4

Isobel wheeled around and wound up planting her face squarely in a very masculine chest.

"Oh!" She leaped backward reflexively. Her heel caught on the cloak's hem, and she tilted at a precarious angle.

Simply fabulous.

She flailed her arms, and her possessions clattered to the stable floor. Lord Ramsbury rushed forward, grasping her shoulders just as her feet left the ground. Eyes locked on his, she seized his coat lapels, frantically trying to stay upright.

His eyes widened in alarmed surprise when he teetered toward her.

Too late.

Lord Ramsbury's solid form toppled onto her and mashed her into the rough wood. Eyes closed and surrounded by his sheer male essence, she waited for sharp pain to stab her. Tentatively, prepared to cease at the slightest discomfort, she wiggled her fingers and toes.

No pain. Nothing broken then.

Gads, how much did his lordship weigh? She tried to pull in a deep breath, but his weight bore down upon her chest.

She opened her eyes. Silky, whisky-colored hair tickled her nose. A clean virile scent, with a hint of sandalwood, hovered over him. He smelled wonderful, and she had the oddest urge to nuzzle her nose in his hair.

She sniffed noiselessly instead.

Mmm, heavenly.

Did he twitch the merest bit?

Lord Ramsbury's chest squashed her breasts nearly flat, and his lean hips were nestled between her thighs. For certain her backside and shoulders would sport a bruise or two.

Lifting her head, she winced. That hurt. She wriggled her fingers, attempting to poke him. Why didn't he get off? A gentleman would have, but he had already proved he didn't deserve that title.

She squirmed a bit then stilled instantly when a peculiar hardness pulsed against her womanhood.

His pocket watch must have fallen from his waistcoat and wedged between them. Isobel jostled harder, trying to dislodge him and his timepiece.

"Don't." He ended on a strangled groan.

He *was* injured. But how could he possibly be? She'd cushioned his landing. Splaying her fingers, she cupped his firm ribs and shoved with all her strength.

"Cease." His warm breath caressed her neck, sending sensations spiraling to her middle as she jostled him again. "Do not move."

Booted feet jarred the floor beneath her in an irregular rhythm. Jocky stuttered to a stop. "Miss Isobel, me lord, are ye—"

"Yancy, I want to sho—" Mouth wide open, Ewan gaped, looking much like a freshly caught brown trout.

Isobel peeked over the earl's shoulder, which now vibrated suspiciously. She jabbed him harder with her fingers.

He quaked more.

Was he ticklish? Turning her hands into half-claws, she scraped at his sides unmercifully.

A rich-timbred chuckle whispered against her neck, and the sensation was beyond wonderful. This wouldn't do at all. She needed Lord Ramsbury to withdraw before she flung her arms around his neck, hugged him to her breast, and planted kisses on his jaw.

"Get. Off. Me." She clenched her teeth as his bothersome watch poked her again.

All at once, she froze.

She knew exactly what prodded her nether regions. She had been raised around animals, for pity's sake. How could she have been so stupid to think his timepiece had slipped free?

No, his *thing* twitched against her.

"I do hope you have a damned good reason to be sprawled atop my sister, Ramsbury."

The steely edge to her brother's voice caused the hairs at Isobel's nape to rise.

Jocky and Ewan reached the earl in the same instant.

His lordship made a miraculous recovery, and in one agile movement, leaped to his feet.

Isobel sucked in a deep gulp of air, holding the breath suspended in her lungs. She bit her lip against the fit of giggles seizing her at the countenances of the three men peering at her.

Poor Jocky. His face as pale as fresh dough, he appeared on the verge of an apoplexy.

Ewan's face bore a ferocious scowl, his eyebrows drawn into a severe vee and his lips pressed into a disapproving line. He shot daggers at Lord Ramsbury with his wintry glare.

She levered into a sitting position, scooting her attention to his lordship last.

The jackanape.

His lovely mouth curved into a lopsided smile, and undisguised amusement danced in his jungle eyes. His gaze leisurely traveled the length of her, a visual caress that caused her skin to tingle and a flush to heat the angles of her cheeks.

Something flickered deep within his eyes, and his pupils dilated. His infuriating grin widened.

She could not tear her gaze away.

Did he know how he affected her?

Of course, he did. God help her, she was as vulnerable as a mouse before a snake.

What a ninny.

Look away.

Her dratted eyes refused to obey. Instead, they feasted upon the glorious male specimen before her.

Ewan shoved his way in front of Lord Ramsbury. After lifting Isobel to her feet, he stepped back. Holding her shoulders, he assessed her from head to toe. "Are you unharmed?"

She managed a nod.

He brushed her tousled hair from her cheek and picked a strand of straw from the tresses. "What happened? How did you come to be—?"

"I . . ." She sliced Lord Ramsbury a peek from the corner of her eye.

He regarded her, his head cocked to the side and that enigmatic smile on his too-perfect mouth.

"Lord Ramsbury startled me—quite by accident, I assure you. I became unbalanced and panicked, so I clutched his lordship's coat, which, unfortunately, resulted in us both taking a tumble."

Isobel refused to look into Lord Ramsbury's beautiful eyes. They turned her to warm pudding. Months ago she had resolved to no longer let him affect her.

Hiding her reaction, she cast her gaze downward. "Please accept my apologies, your lordship. I hope you weren't injured."

"No apology necessary." Why couldn't he have a high-pitched nasally twang instead of a deep, pleasant rumble for a voice? "I regret I could not save you the fall."

He brushed at his claret-colored coat sleeves, knocking bits of oat, hay, and dust from the tight-fitting fabric. The movement stretched the coat taut across the breadth of his shoulders. His had been no soft, pampered body atop hers. No, sinewy, sculpted muscles had melded against her softness.

A scintillating current jolted down her spine.

Stop it, Isobel Janette Moreen Ferguson.

He. Is. Not. For. You.

Quashing her reaction, Isobel angled her head, offering Ewan a contrite turn of her lips. A curl flopped onto her shoulder. She could already hear Maura's *tsks* of censure. Her old nurse still fussed as if Isobel were in leading strings.

"You may let loose of me now, Ewan. I assure you, I am not at risk of toppling over again."

In fact, her clumsiness was out of character, and such ineptness in front of Lord Ramsbury, wholly humiliating. Fresh warmth heated her cheeks. If only she could flee to her chamber and escape mortification's sting. What had possessed her to latch on to his lordship, yanking him down atop her?

A brooding expression on his face, Ewan released her and took in her rumpled appearance.

Poor Ewan. Always such a serious brother.

She gave him another stiff smile and made an attempt to straighten her drooping hair.

Ewan turned his regard to Lord Ramsbury. "And, why, pray tell, did it take you so long to remove your person from my sister?"

Isobel wanted to know that too.

She arched a brow, silently applauding her brother's question while surreptitiously inspecting the earl.

Disheveled umber hair gave him a rather dashing appearance. A gold, cerulean, and burgundy patterned waistcoat complemented the deep hue of his jacket.

Her gaze inched lower, taking in his buckskin breeches, and—

"Well, Ramsbury?" Ewan's voice cut short her scrutiny.

"I . . . that is . . ." Lord Ramsbury's customary grin

slipped. Concern, or perhaps chagrin, registered on his lean face. His posture tense, he bent his neck for a moment.

When Lord Ramsbury raised his head, entreaty had darkened his eyes to agate. "I most humbly beg your pardon, Miss Ferguson. My behavior is beyond reprehensible."

Isobel gaped, her stomach doing all sorts of peculiar antics. Who was this contrite, humble man? Drat, the gentleman proved much harder to stay indifferent toward. Laying a hand on her stomach tumbling over itself, she blinked, at a loss for words.

He met her perusal head-on.

The meshing of their gazes proved lovely and discomfiting at once.

Ewan made a rude sound in the back of his throat. His keen scrutiny swung between her and his lordship, before her brother's eyes narrowed in displeasure. He hunched his shoulders. "Yancy, so help me God."

The earl's gaze snapped to Ewan's. "Sethwick, I would be happy to speak with you regarding this matter. *In private*."

With that, Lord Ramsbury gave Isobel a stiff bow. "Miss Ferguson."

He turned and, gait rigid, marched from the stable. His behavior was most irregular.

And why was Ewan angry?

There wasn't a doubt he was beyond peeved. She studied him furtively. Fuming, actually. The half-moon scar on his face always turned white when he was in a high dudgeon. Surely, he must know nothing untoward had occurred between her and the earl.

Isobel nibbled her lip. The predicament had appeared rather scandalous though, had it not? A bit exciting, too.

Jocky stood a pace away, shifting from foot to foot, her possessions clasped in his gnarled hands. A hint of color had returned to his weathered face, although anxiety lingered in the deep folds.

She reached for her bonnet and bag, and he passed the items into her outstretched hands.

"Thank you, Jocky."

She looped the bag over one arm and tucked her bonnet underneath the other.

Nervously rubbing his palms on his coarse dun trousers, he bobbed his grizzled head. "Terribly sorry I be, Miss Isobel, that I *didnae* catch ye."

Not given to stoutness by any means, Isobel harbored no misconceptions regarding her size. Poor Jocky was five and sixty, if he was a day. Scarecrow thin and a good four inches shorter than she, he would have been flattened like an oatcake had he attempted to break her fall.

She gave him a reassuring smile. "Don't be. You couldn't have reached me in time, and my own ineptness caused the mishap. Except for my rumpled state, no harm's been done."

Other than the annoying ache at the back of her skull, and the more bothersome one between her thighs where she'd cradled Lord Ramsbury. That strange sensation flickered through her again. Her pride stung a morsel too, truth to tell. When had she become so ham-fisted?

"Glad I am to hear it, miss. If ye'll excuse me, I be checkin' on yer horse."

With a subservient nod, he hustled away, his bow-legged step reminding her of an oversized goose. More likely the dear man headed for his stash of whisky.

Ewan observed her intently the whole time. Rather disconcerting, that. Her brother possessed an uncanny ability to read people, which proved wholly perturbing when he directed his scrutiny at her. Especially, when he did so as her laird.

She schooled her expression into polite inquisitiveness and faced him. "Did you have something you wanted to say?"

If she didn't hurry, she would be late for luncheon. Sorcha had made Scotch stovies too. Her stomach gurgled, a loud, gnawing echo. Now, in addition to changing her gown, she needed to repair her hair and hastily wash before she appeased her hunger.

"You're sure you are unharmed?" Something more severe than worry tinged her brother's eyes.

She rose onto her toes and brushed a kiss across his angular cheek. "I'm fine."

Doubt registered on his face.

"I am not referring to your spill." He gave the stable a swift perusal. "Isobel, I am neither ignorant nor blind. I saw what passed between you and Ramsbury."

Firming her lips, she clamped her teeth on the inside of her cheek to stifle a groan of chagrin. Ewan had witnessed her making a cake of herself over Lord Ramsbury and recognized her infatuation. The knowledge rubbed salt into an already raw wound.

After all, she was the daughter with exceptional manners and poise. Or so she'd been told often enough. Until this instant, no one suspected she'd been attracted to, let alone half in love with, the earl for years.

Ewan took a step closer and hushed his voice. "I would be remiss if I didn't say something, my dear. I couldn't bear to see you hurt."

A horse nickered a few stalls away. Another answered with a soft snort and shuffle.

A fresh wave of mortification suffused Isobel. Even her loving brother recognized that she didn't—*couldn't*—measure up. Rustic Highland heather, such as she, fell beneath the touch of an earl who required a delicate English rose for a countess.

Pride stiffened her spine. Surely, Ewan didn't think she had serious designs on Lord Ramsbury, for heaven's sake. She hadn't set her cap for him; she knew her place.

Besides, his lordship had already selected his bride. Ewan must be aware Ramsbury all but knelt at the altar—

unless the earl had kept the information a secret from her brother.

She adjusted the bag dangling from her arm. “Please, Ewan, I am—”

He laid a finger on her lips. “Yancy’s not the man—”

Turning her head aside, she fought the urge to cover her ears.

A dog barked, followed by frantic clucking and children’s giggles. A smile tempted.

The bairns are trying to catch the hens again.

“What I mean to say is, do not harbor a *tendre* for him.” Ewan gave her a boyish smile and tweaked her nose. “I would hate to have to call out one of my dearest friends for breaking your heart.”

Deliberately quashing the pain that lanced her at his words, Isobel dredged up the last remnants of her dignity and raised her chin a notch. “I assure you, Lord Ramsbury is not now, nor is he ever going to be, the object of my affections.”

She swung away from her brother, intent on gaining her chamber and calming her bruised pride. A tall shadow angled across the stable entrance.

Lord Ramsbury stomped past.

Chapter 5

Yancy pushed away from the rough wall he'd leaned against until his ardor cooled enough to allow him a degree of decency. Stalking about with a stiff-as-a-fire-poker bulge in his britches was sure to cause a snicker or two.

Clan members milled throughout the courtyard talking in small groups or going about the various tasks required to keep a castle the size of Craiglocky running efficiently. Laughing children and barking dogs played together. Chickens clucked in alarm and scattered before him as he stalked across the bailey.

Isobel's words echoed in his ears over the clanging of metal in the blacksmithy lean-to twenty yards away.

Lord Ramsbury is not now, nor is he ever going to be, the object of my affections.

Succinct. Direct. Final?

God's toenails.

At Craiglocky merely hours and his quest to gain her favor extinguished like a spent candle with scant hope of rekindling the nub's flame.

He'd been marble hard the moment he landed between her soft thighs. The wool of her worn gown, molded gently to her body, revealed her womanly lushness. Only by remaining rigidly still had he been able to keep from embarrassing himself in his buckskins.

Then to have had Sethwick come upon them.

Yancy blew out a long breath. Damned awkward, that.

Did he stay sprawled upon the delectable form of Isobel

in full view of God and all, or stand and expose the hard bump in his trousers for the world to see?

The instant Sethwick detected Yancy's arousal, warning fire sparked in his friend's eyes.

Not that Yancy blamed him. If he had sisters as lovely as the Ferguson misses, he would hire an army to ward off the fawning bucks, irredeemable rakes, and lecherous rogues dangling about.

He knew full well which category Sethwick would place him in. Twisting his lips in derision, Yancy marched up the gatehouse risers, the click of his boot heels bouncing off the weathered stones.

He well-deserved Sethwick's opinion of him.

Yancy hadn't been a monk by any stretch of the imagination, though he had been careful not to father any by-blows. Nevertheless, he'd been openly contemptuous about the unpleasant institution of marriage.

Neither had he hinted to Sethwick that his sentiments had recently shifted regarding the parson's mousetrap, albeit compelled out of a sense of duty and not a shift in Yancy's personal philosophy.

At least that was what he kept telling himself these past months, whenever he contemplated matrimony and Isobel's exquisite face came to mind each time.

Pulling on his ear, he stifled a sigh.

Regrettably, the duties of an unwelcome earldom thrust upon him four years ago required him to marry. Other than a distant cousin somewhere in the wilds of America—if Dawson still lived— Yancy, alone, remained to carry on the Ramsbury title.

How it had come to pass that he, the sixth in line to the earldom, should have inherited, was stroke after stroke of implausibly bad luck for his predecessors.

The *ton* had heartily congratulated him on his good

fortune, but how did one count oneself fortuitous when six men had died in order for him to inherit the title?

Rather morbid and nothing to celebrate.

Nonetheless, he could no longer shirk his responsibilities to the earldom. This trip to Scotland was his last in the capacity of War Office Secretary.

He'd tendered his resignation to The Prince Regent, despite His Royal Highness's belligerent protests and proclamations that England would be inundated with spies and vulnerable to her enemies if Yancy *deserted his post*.

Plus, much to Yancy's consternation—or perhaps astonishment was more apt—he rather wanted to experience fatherhood. He blamed Sethwick and Warrick and their endearing offspring for that absurdity. No doubt Clarendon's would be equally precious when the babe arrived. Wasn't Adaira due soon?

"You look in a foul mood. Your ugly scowl would frighten the bravest of children away. That is, if they didn't expire on the spot, terror stopping their tiny, fragile hearts."

Yancy's attention jerked to Harcourt exiting the keep's entrance, pocket watch in his hand.

"As always, Harcourt, you are a veritable fount of fustian rubbish. Where do you acquire such drivel?"

"Such ingratitude." The duke snapped the cover closed then tucked the fob into the pocket of his silver and black striped waistcoat. "I came in search of you to tell you luncheon is about to be served."

Casting his friend a sidelong glance, Yancy continued to the open arched door where an impeccably clad, unusually tall butler stood at attention. "Why you and not a footman? I have never known you to run a servant's errand."

"I hoped to catch you in a compromising situation." Harcourt's teasing grin and wink belied his words.

Yancy issued an inarticulate sound, somewhere between a grunt and a snort. "You are too late. Sethwick already did."

"Truly?" The duke paused, giving Yancy a piercing look.

"Truly," Yancy answered, compunction coloring his words. "I don't know when I've been more thoroughly discomfited."

"Do tell. We've only been here a few hours. May I ask with whom?" Harcourt rubbed his palms together and waggled his eyebrows, an exaggerated leer contorting his face. "This ought to be most entertaining."

Yancy turned his back on Harcourt's needling. Gaining the entrance, he nodded at the majordomo. "Hello, Fairchild."

"Always a pleasure, Lord Ramsbury." Fairchild inclined his head. His gaze searched past Yancy. "Are Miss Isobel and Lord Sethwick far behind you?"

Yancy shook his head and glanced over his shoulder. No sign of them yet. "No. I should think they'll be along momentarily, however."

Harcourt chuckled and snatched a piece of straw off Yancy's coat. He dangled the golden length triumphantly. Humor cavorting in his eyes, he slapped an arm across Yancy's shoulders and hurried him away from the entrance hall. "Come now, spill everything. Then I shall tell you what I have learned."

Yancy waited until well out of earshot of the butler before speaking. After a thorough search of the passageway, and confident he wouldn't be overheard, he gave Harcourt an abbreviated version.

"Miss Ferguson stumbled. I tried to prevent her from falling. Instead, we both ended up on the stable floor. Sethwick found me, bum upward, with a raging erection atop his sister."

Harcourt's shout of laughter rang the length of the corridor and echoed off the hall ceiling.

Yancy grimaced. A muscle twinged at the back of his neck, no doubt the result of his little tussle with Miss

Ferguson, and he rubbed at the soreness. "That's the whole of it in a nutshell."

"Damn, I would give anything to have seen his face." Harcourt chuckled again and pounded Yancy's back. "And yours."

"I am sure you would." Yancy's tone was as dry as burned toast as he continued down the hallway.

Isobel's countenance remained etched in his mind.

Skin, milk pale, peachy-pink lips parted, turquoise eyes wide with confused wonder, and above all, wholly vulnerable.

He had never seen her hair partially unpinned before and had itched to spread his fingers through the silky, almond-brown tresses spilling over her shoulders.

How long was her hair?

Shoulder length? Waist? Hip? Longer?

She'd smelled amazing. Wildflowers and sun and a hint of lavender, or perhaps the musky essence had been heather. Her refreshing scent soothed and invigorated him at the same time.

His member pulsed.

Confound it.

Shutting his eyes, he conjured her image in his mind.

He started, and his eyes flew open.

Why had she been in the stables dressed like a servant? Had she been outside the keep's walls unescorted? Didn't Sethwick realize how dangerous that was at present?

Yancy gave a mental shrug.

Enough.

He would address the issue with Sethwick later. Harcourt hadn't sought Yancy out solely to indulge his perverse curiosity.

"Pray tell, what is so provoking you were compelled to look for me yourself, Harcourt?"

Drawing Yancy to a stop, the duke checked both ends

of the wide, stone hall. “Seems that gypsy caravan we saw north of the village Craig . . .”

“Craigcutty,” Yancy supplied.

“Yes, Craigcutty. I heard the gypsies spend a few weeks in the area each spring and fall.” One hand on his hip, Harcourt paused to watch a pretty maid hurry by, a coy smile on her lips. Harcourt’s gaze trailed her gently swaying backside until she disappeared around a corner.

Yancy cleared his throat. “The travellers?”

An unrepentant Harcourt shifted his attention back to him. “And, according to Sethwick’s cousins—”

“Gregor and Alasdair McTavish?”

“If they are the two blond giants, then yes. I cannot keep his family straight.”

Harcourt cast another swift glance around. “In any event, as I was saying, according to Sethwick’s cousins, his scouts have seen a great deal of activity between the Highland travellers and the Scots.”

“So? The black tinkers typically trade with the residents near their camps. I saw at least half a dozen Scottish Highland gypsies in the bailey when I arrived.” Yancy shrugged and another piece of straw floated to the floor. “There’s nothing unusual in that.”

Harcourt’s expressive eyes darkened, and he rested a shoulder against the wall. “Therein lays the mystery. The local Scots are indeed bartering and trading with the tinkers. So why, then, are Clauston clansmen lurking about?”

“Clauston? They’re remote Highlanders.” Yancy stared at Harcourt, and then frowned. “What are they doing this far south? The Claustons live at least five or six days’ hard ride from here.”

Harcourt gave a knowing smirk. “I’ll wager they aren’t after baubles or here to have their fortunes told or palms read.”

A trace of scorn colored his last words.

"I wouldn't scoff if I were you, Harcourt." Yancy leveled the duke a sharp look. "Many Scots, other than the gypsies, also claim to possess the second sight, including Sethwick's sister, Seonaid."

Harcourt's expression sobered. "True enough. I met her earlier. Took one look at me and said, 'You should consider drinking less coffee, and cold tallow candles are wonderful for treating eye injuries.' Then she smiled sweetly and swept from the room."

"You don't say? How irregular." Seonaid had never so much as hinted she discerned a thing about Yancy. Perhaps he was unreadable.

Harcourt shuddered, puzzlement crinkling his eyes. "Wholly unnerving, that. I don't like being read like a book, and that candle business . . . quite bizarre."

"Indeed." Hands clasped behind him, Yancy rocked back on his heels, deep in thought.

An extended silence reigned as he contemplated the information Harcourt had imparted about the gypsies. As for Harcourt's musings, well, who knew exactly what went on in that fair head of his? The man was an enigma.

"I expected the Blackhalls and the MacGraths to be lurking about." Yancy pulled on his earlobe. "After all, they're causing the disruption with your cousin's clan, and MacHardy's barony encompasses their lands."

Hell, the entire bumblebroth made his head ache. He rubbed his forehead while staring at a portrait of a fierce-looking Scot on the opposite wall. "This may be more complicated than I'd anticipated."

He'd have to extend his visit. That, he didn't object to at all; he'd have more opportunities to court Isobel.

MacHardy, on the other hand . . .

An uncouth Scot, nothing like Sethwick and his kin, MacHardy had earned a reputation as a troublemaker and a whoremongering cheat. A foul one too. From the stench lingering about his person, his substantial flesh and clothing hadn't encountered a droplet of water in a goodly amount of time.

The baron laid odds far too often in White's betting book, gambling on every ludicrous wager from the knot of a lord's cravat to the feather or ribbon colors adorning a lady's bonnet. Once, he had placed a bet as to the number of whiskers on Lady Clutterbuck's many chins.

There were five.

The man was a corkbrained buffoon. His tendency to dispute his losses had gained him the reputation of a hotheaded Captain Sharp. Yancy hadn't a single doubt the baron had fired early during the duels. The Scot was a blight upon the earth.

Voices echoed from the entrance.

Glimpsing Sethwick and Isobel crossing the threshold, Yancy narrowed his eyes. Turning on his heel, he strode purposefully in their direction, his boots beating a harsh staccato upon the stone floor.

Isobel's rough attire, and what the garments suggested about her whereabouts, troubled him. As a War Office representative, he had a duty to speedily solve the clan crisis while ensuring everyone's safety. Particularly, the well-being of strong-minded young misses capering about the countryside.

Head bowed, she made straight for the stairs.

"Hold there, Miss Ferguson." Yancy quickened his pace.

One foot on the bottom riser, she paused and swung her startled gaze his way. The closer he came, the larger her beautiful eyes grew. She ascended a couple of steps, sending her brother an alarmed look.

"Thank you, Fairchild," Sethwick said. "Please have luncheon delayed fifteen minutes. Isobel must change her gown."

"Very good, sir." Fairchild disappeared down the passageway.

Sethwick turned his attention to Yancy and raised a brow. "I know that expression. That's your War-Secretary-about-to-issue-an-order glower."

"How astute of you." Yancy forced his annoyance aside. "Until further notice, I would prefer no one"—he cast a sidelong glance at Isobel hovering on the stairs—"especially the women, leave the walls of the keep unaccompanied by at least one armed man. On second thought, make that two men."

"No." Isobel gasped and whirled to face Yancy full on. "You cannot—"

"*Aye*. I'm in agreement." His features thoughtful, Sethwick slowly nodded. "We need to discuss the situation after we dine. That's the reason I sought you in the stables. I have information I believe you'll find of particular interest."

He turned his attention to Isobel. "Shouldn't you be changing? We're late as it is."

"Yes, but . . ." She compressed her lips and clutched the folds of her cloak, obviously struggling for comportment.

"Ewan, you are the laird." Her color high, Isobel pointed at Yancy. "Are you going to allow him to dictate like that? Forbid us to leave the keep?"

Although he stood several feet away, Yancy sensed the frustration radiating from her. He hadn't seen this fiery streak in her before. Her faultless manners had kept this side well-hidden. He would bet his best French brandy he'd been right about her being outside the keep unaccompanied this morning. Why was she so upset she couldn't leave without an escort?

A nasty notion crashed into him.

Did she have a lover?

His stomach clenched almost as tightly as his fists. The urge to shake the truth from her—no, hunt down the man and pummel him—raged across Yancy's reason. In his mind, he'd all but claimed her as his, as irrational as he knew that was.

Who did she sneak out to meet?

He surveyed her coarse garb again. A villager? Or, devil take it, one of the Highland travellers? Taking a controlled breath, he attempted to curb his anger.

Sethwick needed to keep a closer eye on his sister. Perchance, Yancy would drop a hint into her brother's ear.

Sethwick approached the stairs. "Ramsbury is here in an official capacity at my behest. There are details regarding Lydia and the clan unrest you're not aware of."

"And may I assume, because I am a woman, I'm not to be apprised of those unpleasant details?" Arms folded, Isobel glared at them, one toe tapping an angry cadence on the stair. "To protect my delicate sensibilities, of course. Correct?"

Now she understands.

Yancy allowed a pleased grin. "Precisely."

He enjoyed a lingering appraisal as she stood fuming. Her arms, pressed below her breasts, jammed the full mounds upward. He tore his gaze away from the tempting, and wholly distracting spectacle. "Women shouldn't have to bother their lovely heads with politics, warfare, or clan skirmishes."

"Hell. Now you've made a mull of it," Sethwick muttered with a severe shake of his head. "I thought you had more sense than that, numbskull."

Yancy shot him a curious glance.

"I shall leave you to muddle your way out of this sticky mess, my friend." With a wave of his hand, Sethwick ambled along the hallway, calling, "Don't dawdle too long. I'm ravenous. We shall eat without you."

Isobel's regal features had settled into an icy mask of disdain. No hint of the adoration Yancy had once seen in her magnificent aqua eyes remained.

Devil it. He had made a grievous error.

She pursed her lips then tilted her head, much like an inquisitive sparrow. "Are you a wagering man, Lord Ramsbury?"

Though politely worded, and her tone the epitome of a gently-bred woman, the question rang rapier sharp, and he winced imperceptibly.

He met her gaze, accepting the challenge in the depth of her eyes. This could prove interesting.

"It depends, I suppose, Miss Ferguson, on the wager." He took her measure. "And who I bet against."

Her lips formed a small arc belying her barbed words. "Why don't you pick something, anything, you are confident your superior masculinity would result in an easy win against the fairer sex."

A stab of disquiet pierced him. What was she about?

She fluttered a dainty hand in the air.

"Cards. Chess. Fencing. Riding. Archery. Hunting. Fishing. Reading. Mathematics. Physics. Interpreting Socrates or Aristotle's work from the original Greek. *Name it*."

Yancy couldn't rip his gaze from her. Lord, but she was magnificent when enraged. Her eyes fairly spewed azure sparks. Could she really read Greek? Once more, he eyed her from her drooping hair to her scuffed boots.

Most intriguing.

He tried gauging her thoughts. Why was she so peeved?

Perhaps she did have a lover, and now she wouldn't be able to keep their clandestine appointments.

Annoyance pricked along his spine.

That would explain her adamant denial in the stable. Most inconvenient and wholly disappointing, if true. He would have to search elsewhere for his countess. He'd had his share of fast women warm his sheets and his blood, but taking one to wife invited cuckolding.

Isobel raised a perfectly arched brow and continued tapping the toe of one small foot on the stairs. “Well, my lord?”

Chess?

Yes, that might do.

He hadn’t been beaten since his days at Eton. In fact, he rarely found anyone who’d partner him. Naturally, he would be a gentleman and let her win the first game or two. Trouncing her soundly at the onset wouldn’t further his suit.

Not that he stood much chance of winning her over after her blunt declaration in the stables. However, he wasn’t ready to give up the race quite yet.

What was that verse his mother used to quote? Something nonsensical from the Bible about the race not being to the swift or the battle to the strong, wasn’t it?

A more subtle approach might prove more successful with Isobel. That remark he’d made about not worrying her pretty head had really worked her into a froth.

Yes, chess. That ought to appease her.

She continued to gaze at him expectantly.

Yancy flashed her his most charming smile, the one that generally caused ladies to flush or bat their eyelashes in seductive invitation.

Isobel, however, simply leveled him a bland stare.

“My lord?” Her tone indicated anything but respect and deference.

“I would be honored if you joined me in a game of chess, Miss Ferguson.”

Her pretty lips curled into a wide smile. “I had rather hoped you’d pick fencing. I would have enjoyed having a go at you with my sabre.”

“You fence?” A vision of her derriere in snug, white breeches sprang to mind. He really had become a lecher.

“After my parents allowed Adaira to learn, Seonaid and I insisted we have the same opportunity.” She turned and climbed the risers. The sway of her hips, even underneath the thick cloak, tantalized.

Isobel peered over her shoulder, a siren's smile on her lips. "I suppose it's only fair to tell you I've never lost at chess."

Confident little thing, wasn't she?

Yancy released a hearty chuckle. He quite liked this unconventional morsel of womanliness. "Surely when you first learned the game?"

"At seven." Isobel shook her head and more silky strands spilled from the loose knot. She gave him a falsely honeyed smile.

"No. Not ever, my lord."

She proceeded up the stairs, her voice floating back to him. "By the way, your lordship, if I win, I'm permitted to leave the keep without two escorts."

After Isobel disappeared from the landing, Yancy strode the length of the corridor, having forgotten he'd left Harcourt loitering in the hallway. Naturally, the lout stayed on and listened to every word Yancy exchanged with her.

Harcourt joined him as he made his way to the great hall.

"Miss Ferguson's never lost a match, and I don't recall the last one you didn't win." A fiendish grin tilted the duke's lips. He stopped to examine a suit of medieval armor. "Can you imagine gadding about in this? And would you look at the length of this blade?"

Yancy scowled, itching to plant his friend a facer if he didn't shut up. "Leave off, will you?"

"What size sword do you suppose Miss Ferguson fences with?" Harcourt blinked at him innocently.

"She fences with a sabre, but then you already know that because you rudely eavesdropped on our conversation." Yancy shot him another black glower.

"'Pon my soul, I'd like to have seen her have a go at you too." Harcourt ran his forefinger along the claymore displayed across the armor's chestplate then grasped the weapon's hilt. He fairly oozed glee.

"I know you'd rather see her impale me, but you'll have to be content with a simple chess game." Damn, but the sword Harcourt toyed with was enormous.

"Care to wager on the game's outcome, Ramsbury? I know you've had your eye on my pair of blacks." A shadow flitted across Harcourt's face. "Hound's teeth, I wish I was in London and could place a wager at White's. Nevertheless, this castle overflows with people. I should be able to get a nice bet running."

"Stubble it, will you? There will be no betting on the result." Yancy raked his hand through his already-mussed hair. "I'm in a deuced amount of disfavor with Miss Ferguson. She would be peeved beyond Sunday to know everyone bet against her."

He glanced above him, his gaze colliding with a serious-faced knight whose portrait hung from a silken ruby cord high above the armor. It seemed Sethwick's ancestors disapproved too.

"Who says I'll wager against her?" Harcourt smacked Yancy on the back and snickered. "No, I do believe I shall lay odds she'll be the one to finally bring you down on your marrow bones."

Marrow bones?

As if Yancy would be on his knees begging her pardon after winning. She had challenged him, blister it. What was he going to require of her when *she* lost?

A kiss from those luscious lips would do nicely.

To start.

Chapter 6

Her victory assured, Isobel stepped onto the landing. Did Lord Ramsbury linger below? She couldn't resist peeking over her shoulder.

Standing at the foot of the stairway, he stared at her, his brows slightly furrowed.

After her declaration, she swore he'd muttered, "Holy hell."

A thrill shot through her. By George, she'd flummoxed him. She found verbal sparring with his lordship rather invigorating, truth to tell.

Indulging in a triumphant smile, she rushed to her chamber, removing her wrap along the way. She charged into the room and, after tossing her cloak on an armchair, sat and removed her half-boots.

Maura emerged from Isobel's bathing chamber. "I've laid out yer dress."

She indicated a pink and jonquil gown draped across the counterpane. A lacy chemise and white stockings lay there too.

Bless Maura's efficiency.

"I've warm water waitin' for ye in the basin." The maid rummaged in a chiffonnier. She withdrew an ivory silk shawl fringed in pink tassels.

"Let's get you out of that thing." Maura's face scrunched in disapproval. Her gaze roved Isobel from her bare toes to her mussed hair.

"Ye've straw stuck in yer hair and dirt on yer face."

Maura plucked several strands from Isobel's tresses. "What have ye been doin', rollin' in the stalls?"

Close enough.

With the maid's help, Isobel made swift work of shedding her soiled gown. After a hasty wash, she hurriedly donned the clean garments.

Sinking onto the satin wood dressing table bench, she smoothed her eyebrows. No need to pinch her cheeks, as her confrontation with Lord Ramsbury had her color high. "Just gather my hair into a simple knot, please. I am terribly late as it is."

"*Hmmph.*" Maura quickly brushed Isobel's hair, removing the last vestiges of straw, and then after a couple of artful twists, pinned the hair in place.

"We have visitors, ye ken. That handsome Lord Ramsbury and another fancy friend of the laird's be here to settle the nasty business between the clans."

"I know. I came upon the earl in the stables." Yanked him to the floor atop her was more accurate. "The other gentleman is the Duke of Harcourt. I've met him once before."

Grasping the shawl Maura extended, Isobel whirled back to the dressing table. "Wait, I forgot perfume."

Arching a wiry, gray eyebrow, Maura's gaze traveled from Isobel to the cobalt vermeil covered perfume bottle. "Yer almost out."

Isobel draped the shawl around her shoulders. "Yes, I know. I'll order some tomorrow when I send the request to Edinburg for more gloves. Someday, I hope to visit Floris's in London and have a customized fragrance concocted there."

Almost to the door, she turned. "Maura, have you been to Edinburgh? I should like to venture there and see the Assembly Rooms and Arthur's Seat. Actually, there's a great many places I should like to visit."

The maid paused in straightening the items atop the dressing table.

"*Aye*, once when I was *verra* young. Before ye were born."

Her features softened and a dreamy expression settled upon her aged face. "I met me husband there."

"Your husband?" Isobel retraced a couple of steps. "You were married once?"

"*Aye*." Maura smiled sadly. "He drowned after a severe squall came upon his fishin' boat. We ne'er found his body."

Isobel traveled the remaining steps to the maid.

"I'm so sorry." She hugged Maura. "How awful, to have known that kind of tragedy so young."

"It happened over forty years ago, lass. As for Edinburgh, it be a lovely city. Ye would enjoy visitin' there."

Isobel offered a budding smile. Would she ever see anything of the world? Or would she spend all of her days in the Highlands?

Now very tardy, she made for the door once more. She seemed destined for poor behavior and doldrums today.

"I shall wear the sea green with the lace overskirt for dinner, Maura, and I would like a bath before we sup. As much as I enjoy hunting for relics, I do prefer being clean, and that hurried sponge wasn't altogether satisfactory. Besides, my hair needs washing."

"I'll say it does and—"

As Isobel swept from the room, saving herself from the rest of Maura's tart response, her fingernail caught on the shawl's fringe.

Bother.

She'd discovered the broken nail after dressing and had forgotten to file it. Several moments later, she entered the great hall to find everyone assembled as expected. The dogs—Tira, Arig, and Rona—raised their heads, their tails thumping in welcome.

Yvette smiled at Isobel before turning her attention to

Lydia, and Seonaid was deep in a discussion with Gordon Ross, Lydia's brooding uncle.

Lydia had been an enjoyable addition to the keep these past months, but a cloud of gloom seemed to hover about Mr. Ross. Though the man had less than ten years on his niece, he appeared much older. He rarely smiled, and his face usually sported a pinched expression, as if he were perpetually displeased or constipated.

His features brightened at Isobel's entrance. He graced her with a rare upward turn of his lips. The small act transformed his features into those of a rather striking man.

Hiding her emotions, as she'd been taught, she offered a weak, closed-lip smile and swiftly turned her attention elsewhere.

She feared Mr. Ross harbored a tendre for her. For the past several weeks he'd sought her company at every opportunity. She was fast running out of excuses to avoid him. A long-dead trilobite held more appeal than the stone-faced Mr. Ross.

Twice, he'd found her alone in the library, though thankfully, Yvette had come along each time.

Perhaps Isobel should confide in her parents. But what would she say?

Mr. Ross stared at her? He complimented her on her appearance and manners? He appreciated her talent on the harpsichord and admired her needlework? He made her feel as if great, hairy spiders crawled all over her?

Even now, Isobel sensed his intense perusal upon her. Undressing her. A shudder rippled her from shoulders to waist.

Securing her shawl tighter, she focused on the ancient weapons hanging on the far wall above the vast fireplace large enough for a grown man to stand upright within. She headed toward the hulking trestle table, easily seating thirty before extensions. Customarily an informal meal, diners gathered at the end opposite the dais for luncheon.

Father winked a greeting while listening to something Ewan said to the Duke of Harcourt.

"We were about to begin. Duncan and some of the others have engagements this afternoon." Mother's tone held the tiniest amount of censure.

Isobel cut a glance to Ewan's uncle, Duncan McTavish. He and his two sons, Gregor and Alasdair, had already filled their plates.

"I'm sorry to have kept everyone waiting. Please forgive me." She offered an apologetic smile.

Polite murmurs excusing her echoed round the table.

No point in defending her tardiness by telling them her lateness was caused by first rolling about on the stable floor with Lord Ramsbury, and later, arguing with his lordship in the entrance.

Her stomach growled once more.

In addition to the Scotch stovies Isobel had anticipated, an assortment of cold meats, cheese, fruits, pickled foods, and breads graced the tabletop. A sideboard displayed fresh tarts and other desserts.

Isobel, her skirts swishing softly in her haste, inspected the seating as she hurried across the floor. One chair, situated between the Duke of Harcourt and Lord Ramsbury, remained empty.

Yer bum's oot the windae, lass, as Grandmother Ferguson would say.

Perturbed, Isobel glanced away. She was stuck, pure and simple, with no way out.

One dratted vacant chair, right beside the one person she would rather eat feathers than sit next to. She couldn't very well plop herself at the other end of the table nor take her food to a chair by the vaulted windows either.

Perchance she should feign a headache and request a tray in her room. No, that wouldn't do. She seldom had headaches.

If she were to suddenly have one so severe she had to retreat to her chamber, she would rouse concern or suspicion, especially if she asked her food to be brought above stairs too. Before Isobel exited the hall, Mother would have sent for the physician or ordered Gregor and Seonaid to fetch their healing herbs.

Slowing her pace, Isobel released an acquiescent sigh.

Lord Ramsbury stood and waved away the footman who approached. His lordship pulled out the chair beside him, a satisfied grin on his mouth. "There you are. You'll be delighted to learn I've arranged for that chess game you requested—right after we eat."

Chapter 7

Yancy almost laughed at the lethal glare Isobel leveled him. Good manners prevented her from disputing the arranged game.

The woman approaching was nothing short of exquisite, yet he almost missed the disheveled sprite from the stables. Who was the real Isobel? This composed perfection waiting to take her seat, or the free-spirited, dust-covered girl lying beneath him and tickling his sides in the stable?

Silverware clattering drew his attention to the other side of the table.

One hand fisted beside his plate, Ross's gaze narrowed as Isobel gracefully made her way across the room. Interesting and annoying. Was everyone not kin to Isobel enamored of her?

Yancy didn't pretend he wasn't delighted she'd be seated next to him. He offered Ross a sideways smile, just short of gloating. Determined to be his most charming self, Yancy intended to woo Isobel into regarding him more favorably, despite their shabby start earlier.

She avoided meeting his eyes and slid onto the chair.

"Thank you."

"Your gown is most becoming, Miss Ferguson." Yancy pushed her chair in.

"It's kind of you to say so."

He caught a whiff of her heady perfume. His damned body reacted predictably. Sporting an obvious bulge in his pantaloons, he hastily sought his seat.

He was worse than a buck in the rut around her, and

he shouldn't be. He was no wet behind the ears milksop pursuing his first conquest. That had been Julia. The thought of her doused his ardor faster than icy water separated fighting dogs.

"I am looking forward to the chess game." Harcourt helped himself to a generous portion of meat before selecting two kinds of cheese to add to his full plate.

Isobel made an odd noise and took a quick sip of her wine.

Harcourt peered around the huge hall. "Are we to watch the match in here?"

Yancy shot him a quelling glance.

"No, Your Grace. The chess set is in the parlor. It's quite old. The game belonged to Ewan's great-great grandfather." Isobel took another sip of wine then set about filling her plate. "And I assure you, the match will not be worthy of an audience. I shouldn't want to bore you or the others. No one need feel obliged to attend."

"On the contrary, I am certain the contest will prove highly diverting. I'm quite looking forward to it." Harcourt perused the diners. "As is everyone else, I'm sure."

"I know I am." Yancy smiled, pretending not to see the troubled look Isobel sliced him.

"*Aye*." Dugall nodded, sending a shock of black hair over his forehead. "Me sister's trounced me every time I play her."

"I distinctly recall Yancy beating me soundly at Oxford." Sethwick paused in buttering a piece of bread. "And I've never seen Isobel lose. It should be a spectacular display."

"I'll say," Yancy muttered beneath his breath. He swallowed an oath as sudden pain lanced the back of his hand resting on his thigh.

His gaze leaped to Isobel.

She blinked at him, an innocent smile framing her lush lips.

By George, the vixen had pinched him. Hard. In an hour, he would have a bruise to prove it.

Alasdair reached behind his mother sitting between her sons. He prodded Gregor's shoulder. "Ye want to lay odds on who wins?"

Nodding, Gregor stuffed half of a pickled egg into his mouth. Chomping happily, he wagged his eyebrows at Ross.

Ross's lips thinned further, and he sneaked a covert glance Isobel's way.

Yancy's estimation of the dour Scot plunged farther south.

"You'll do no such thing." Though she smiled, Lady Ferguson's voice was firm.

"Really, you two." Kitta's vexed gaze moved between her sons. "Must you compete over everything?"

"*Aye*, Mother." Alasdair shook his shaggy head and grinned. "Since we shared your womb and the great lummox forced his way out first."

Yancy's amusement faded.

He'd bantered like that with Randolph, his older brother, before the Peninsular War had robbed Yancy of his best friend seven years ago. Now, he made do with Harcourt and the other rogues' antics. However, since they'd married, his chums had become downright stodgy.

See what matrimony did to a fellow?

"Gentlemen before giant-arsed gollumpuses, I always say." Gregor released a rumbling chuckle at his brother's scowl.

"Gregor. You forget yourself. There are ladies present," his mother scolded.

Isobel giggled, but Seonaid's soft voice cut short her sister's musical tinkle.

"The outcome will be most interesting, I've no doubt." Seonaid glanced between Yancy and her sister. "No, no doubt at all."

Her family's startled gazes flew to her.

Lady Ferguson met her husband's eyes, concern flitting across her lovely face, and several of the assembled threw speculative glances Yancy's way.

Her keen gaze alert, Seonaid simply inclined her head at him and forked a bit of stovie into her mouth.

What the devil?

He swore the younger sister knew something she kept to herself. Something she found entertaining from the glint in her eye and the impish tilt of her lips.

Isobel's expression transformed from amused to perplexed and, lastly, wary.

"You see, they are quite anticipating the entertainment as much as I am." Yancy rubbed his throbbing hand.

Harcourt flashed his white teeth. "You cannot disappoint us, Miss Ferguson."

With a barely audible sigh, Isobel bowed her head in acquiescence. "As you wish, Your Grace."

Yancy eyed her.

Her response lacked enthusiasm. Why the reluctance to have an audience? Mayhap she'd overstated her skill and regretted challenging him, fearing he would shame her in front of her family. She did have a rather low opinion of him, didn't she?

Matters had gotten devilishly complex, but he could not let her win. Given the sightings of the Claustons, trotting around unguarded outside the keep was unthinkable. He held every confidence the Blackhalls and MacGraths skulked about as well.

The three clans were reminiscent of the uncivilized and barbaric Celtic tribes once populating Scotland. However, if he wasn't gallant and allowed Isobel to save her pride, he would further damage his chances to win her.

Yancy fingered his wineglass, suddenly coming upon a magnanimous solution. He'd let Isobel triumph in the first game, and then he'd be the victor in the second. He would proclaim a truce, and she'd be keen to agree, not recognizing his chivalry as a ruse. A touch of masculine valor might prove most advantageous in warming her regard for him.

"I give you my word I shan't make a May game of you, Miss Ferguson." Yancy kept his voice quiet.

"Indeed?" Her fine eyebrows soared skyward, her gaze lingering on his lips for a moment before focusing on his cravat. "I make no such promise, my lord. I intend to have great sport with you."

She directed her attention back to Harcourt's nattering.

Spirited, wasn't she? Visions of exactly what kind of sport he would like to engage her in sprang to mind. Something else leaped as well. He adjusted his position on his chair, grateful for the tablecloth.

Yancy cast Isobel a sidelong glance. The sun, pouring in from the mullioned windows, ringed her head, creating a golden aura. She radiated innocence, but was she truly virtuous?

Matilda's young features crept into the recesses of his mind—proof that an angelic façade could conceal a siren's wanton soul.

Isobel had her head turned away from Yancy, her entire focus upon Harcourt.

The slim arch of her neck begged for Yancy's kiss. He itched to run his fingers over the silky flesh, right below the pink bow secured at her nape. Did she ignore him intentionally? Or was she succumbing to Harcourt's attempts to charm her with his rakish appeal?

"So, Miss Ferguson, I understand there is quite an interesting conglomeration of kin residing within the keep." Harcourt munched a pickle, his mirth-filled eyes meeting Yancy's over the crown of her head.

Shifting to face the table once more, she nodded and patted her mouth with her linen napkin before responding.

"Yes, Ewan's father died when he was a toddler, and our mother married my father a couple of years later."

Harcourt's dark gaze wandered the length of the table, resting on the attractive middle-aged couple. "I met Lady Ferguson and Sir Hugh at the Clarendon's Yuletide ball, but missed introductions today when we arrived."

"The large, dark-haired man at the other end who looks a great deal like Ewan is his paternal uncle, Duncan." She angled her head toward a handsome blond woman. "His wife, Kitta, is sitting between their sons, Gregor and Alasdair."

The duke blew out an exaggerated breath. "Egads, they're enormous chaps, aren't they?"

Yancy's reaction had been much the same the first time he'd met the entourage of gargantuan Scots.

Isobel chuckled, a husky sound that tickled along his nerves. How could a laugh sound so innocent and yet wholly erotic at the same time?

"They are indeed. Kitta is Norse, a direct descendent from Sigurðr the Powerful, one of the first earls of the Orkney Isles. She stands over six feet tall." Isobel nibbled a fat strawberry, the juice leaving a faint red stain upon her lips.

Yancy forced his gaze away from the display, barely stifling a groan. *Bugger it*. Must he find everything Isobel did so sensual? Needing a distraction, he absently cut a piece of cold meat while observing Ross.

Why had he accompanied his niece to Craiglocky, anyway? Wouldn't he better serve Laird Farnsworth by staying at Tornbury Fortress? Tornbury boasted some of the most premier grazing and farming lands in all the Highlands.

That was the first order of business, a meeting with Miss Farnsworth's father. Then Yancy would confer with the other clans' leaders and negotiate a compromise. Lydia, and that boor, Ross, would toddle back to Tornbury, and in less than a fortnight, things would be set right once more.

MacHardy, however, was a whole other issue. He wouldn't rest until he'd stirred dangerous contention within the clans. If not now, then most assuredly later, and if not with the Blackhalls or MacGraths, then another discontented tribe. A few Highland clans still held a great deal of resentment toward England.

Unfortunately, the baron's actions weren't treasonous, or Yancy would have hauled him before the House of Lords weeks ago.

His focus yet on Ross, Yancy stuffed a forkful of meat into his mouth, almost gagging on tongue. Had he been so bemused he served himself *tongue*? He loathed the stuff. With supreme effort, he swallowed, then shuddered.

God Almighty.

Seizing his wineglass, he gulped the contents. The foul meat's taste lingered. A mouthful of tangy dark bread swiftly followed. Then another.

What he wouldn't give for a tankard of ale at the moment. He chewed the bread and examined the table. No ale, just wine.

His gaze snapped to Ross, whose attention was riveted on Isobel. The gleam in the eye of the Friday-faced man set Yancy's teeth on edge.

Unadulterated lust.

Hadn't anyone else noticed the cur's leering?

Yes, from the stern glowers the giant blond brothers and Dugall sent Ross, they knew full well what musings the churl entertained in his dark head. Rash man, to antagonize that brawny trio.

Harcourt waved his hand in Dugall's direction. "The young man talking with Duncan McTavish, he's your brother I take it?"

A wicked grin on his lips, the duke's gaze dipped to the slab of tongue on Yancy's plate. His Grace's lips twitched. "He bears a great resemblance to Sethwick."

Yancy clenched his jaw.

Damn him.

Harcourt, the bounder, had slipped the tongue onto Yancy's plate when he stood to assist Isobel. He knew Yancy couldn't abide animal organs. The vile taste succeeded in putting Yancy off the rest of his food.

Setting her fork on her plate, she nodded, looking at the handsome brute. "That would be Dugall, my rapscallion brother. He's always into some mischief. Seonaid, wearing the yellow gown and seated beside Mr. Ross, is my younger sister by one year."

Isobel selected a grape. "Of course, you already know Lydia and her uncle. I shan't bore you with the names of the clansmen."

She popped the fruit into her mouth, her lips pursing around the orb. To have those lips on his . . .

Her marine eyes sparkling, she chuckled. "You'll only get confused. Their names are so similar, Your Grace."

Yancy suppressed a grin, recalling the names of the tartan-clad Scots who'd joined the family for their meal. "True, every one of their names began with Mac or Mc—something or other."

"Tell me, Miss Ferguson, if you will, why you speak with scarcely a trace of Scot's brogue?" Harcourt dipped his spoon into his pudding.

Isobel's gaze roamed the table. "With the exception of Ewan—and that's likely because he spends so much time in London— the men prefer speaking Scot's to the King's English. My sisters and I are accustomed to speaking otherwise."

She chuckled and fiddled with her knife. "More, I think, as a result of an overzealous governess who was determined to turn us into proper *English l*adies. It frustrated her no end that she wasn't entirely successful in ridding us of our brogues."

Harcourt relaxed in his chair, surveying the group. He turned and winked at Yancy. “Can *you* imagine marrying into *this*?”

He wiggled his fingers at the animated throng lining both sides of the table.

The emphasis on the two words wasn’t lost on Yancy.

“Harcourt,” he warned, fully aware Isobel angled her head to stare at him.

Her gaze held wounded accusation.

“No, I suppose not.” Harcourt toyed with his napkin. “You’ve always said you won’t ever marry.”

Chapter 8

Isobel choked on a suppressed gasp. *Never marry*? Lord Ramsbury was all but betrothed. Matilda Darby had made that clear as polished glass at Adaira and Roark's ball last December. Why would he keep such important news from his closest friends?

After her one and only dance with his lordship, Isobel had sought the ladies' retiring room. The girl, for Miss Darby was scarcely more than a child, had followed Isobel into the chamber.

Miss Darby shouldn't have been present at all, as neither she nor her aunt, Cecily Yancy, had received an invitation. However, as houseguests of the Oldershaws—close neighbors of Adaira and Roark—little could be done when the two women had attached themselves to the Oldershaws' coat sleeves.

Or so Adaira had muttered upon spying the interlopers entering the ballroom.

A feline smile on her painted lips, Miss Darby cornered Isobel by blocking the doorway to the ladies' retiring room.

"I think it only kind to tell you, a union has been arranged between Lord Ramsbury and me as soon as I reach my eighteenth birthday. We are . . ." Miss Darby coyly lowered her lashes, feigning diffidence. "We are on *very* intimate terms, if you understand my meaning. Goodness, we've resided under the same roof since I was five, practically my entire life, and it has always been understood we would marry."

That someone so young was versed in the ways of the

flesh, and Isobel had yet to be kissed, was somewhat—no, wholly—disconcerting. More than disconcerting. Appalling. Particularly, his lordship's taking advantage of someone so young, and a ward underneath his roof, to boot.

Now, months later, a wave of angry humiliation engulfed her. Miss Darby had experienced his lordship's kisses, something Isobel would never do. Heat scorched her, and she curled her toes in her soft slippers.

I am not jealous.

None of that mattered. The earl had compromised the girl. Though Isobel admitted she still found him sinfully attractive. Nevertheless, nothing could come of it.

For pity's sake, he'd bedded a near child.

It wasn't altogether uncommon. Girls married in Scotland as young as twelve. But he hadn't married Matilda yet he had enjoyed her favors. Another blot against his already-dark character.

"Shall we make our way to the salon?" Yvette scooted her chair back, indicating an end to the meal. She beamed as Ewan took her hand, and they both stood.

Ridiculously in love, those two, and most of the time, Isobel admired their relationship. Today, however, it served as a painful reminder of her limited prospects and made her restless and discontented.

If only her parents would allow her a Season.

It didn't have to be in London. She'd quite happily settle for Edinburgh's smaller Season. At least she'd have a chance to see the historic city, take in the famous sites, and perhaps, meet someone an iota less rustic than the Highlanders frequenting their table on a regular basis.

When their aunt had taken ill and needed a companion for several months, Seonaid had been allowed an extended visit to France, and to escape imprisonment, Adaira had fled to Gretna Green with Roark. Why couldn't Isobel have her own adventure? Just one tiny exploit to sustain her for a lifetime?

You'll not be content with one.

No, but one was better than none.

Isobel glanced round the table before her attention sank to her plate. She stared at the congealed blobs of food. She could stall, object she hadn't finished eating, except her appetite had dwindled to nothing. Better to get the blasted chess game behind her.

"I don't believe Miss Ferguson has quite finished her meal."

Isobel flung a startled peek at Lord Ramsbury. He'd noticed her nearly full plate when no one else had.

"No, I'm satisfied, thank you." The food had stuck in her throat like cold, lumpy porridge, and she couldn't gag down another bite.

Lord Ramsbury needed this comeuppance. He truly had no idea what he'd gotten himself into.

She examined the mantle clock. Half past one.

If she concluded the chess game in thirty minutes, she would have time to work on Yvette's gift and catalog the relics from today's digging before preparing for dinner.

She wasn't being arrogant or a braggart about her chess-playing skills. The movements on the checkered board played out in her head, much like a theatrical performance on stage. She simply selected the most advantageous plays.

Could she extend the game to make it last thirty minutes? She might have to sacrifice a knight. She could nick the earl's isolated pawns to compensate. A slight thrill swept her. Lord Ramsbury might very well prove to be a worthy opponent.

She couldn't wait to see his face when she captured his queen. Eagerness tingled along her nerves in anticipation of discovering precisely how clever Lord Ramsbury might be. Let the others gawk all they wanted. The earl had brought this on himself.

"Let's be about it, shall we?" Isobel laid her napkin on the table before smoothing her skirt.

In an instant, the duke stood and extended his hand. "Please permit me the honor of escorting you to the salon."

Isobel rose. "Thank you, Your Gra—"

"I think it most ungentlemanly of ye to demand an audience and humiliate Miss Ferguson." Mr. Ross rose with the others. He stood angry and rigid, his hands fisted at his sides, glowering at Lord Ramsbury.

Isobel gaped before snapping her mouth shut. Should she be grateful or angry? His defense, although unexpected and heroic, bordered on insulting. "I assure you, I shan't be humiliated, Mr. Ross, but I thank you for your concern."

"I admire yer courage, Miss Ferguson, but yer a woman. He's England's War Secretary." Mr. Ross shot a contemptuous glare Lord Ramsbury's direction. "Ye *dinnae* stand a chance, lass."

She set her teeth against the retort that thrummed against her lips. Lord, she wished she possessed Adaira's daring. Isobel would tell Mr. Ross to go bugger himself. Instead, she hid her true feelings, and inclined her head, forcing a gracious smile.

On his way to the door, Dugall whacked Mr. Ross between the shoulders. Dishes and silverware rattled and clanked when Mr. Ross snatched at the table's edge.

Dugall did that on purpose, bless his wayward heart. She met his eyes, biting the inside of her cheek to keep from grinning.

"You haven't seen me sister play chess. She be fine. The earl, on the other hand . . ." Dugall raised two fingers to his brow in a mock salute before swaggering from the hall.

Isobel placed her fingertips on His Grace's extended arm.

Hmm, no odd tremors tingled anywhere at the contact, and the Duke of Harcourt exemplified handsomeness. She pressed the solid, muscular forearm beneath her fingers.

Not a single quiver.

Upon entering the salon, she immediately swept to the

pedestal table nestled in a nook before a bay window. After flinging her shawl over the back of her chair, she sank into her seat.

The others settled themselves around the room; everyone except Duncan and the clan members engaged in training practice in the bailey. The duke and Mr. Ross commandeered the two armchairs nearest the chess table.

Of course, they would.

She braced for Lord Harcourt's pithy remarks and Mr. Ross's dark glowers throughout the contest.

Fabulous.

Harcourt crossed his legs and relaxed into the Pomona green and Apollo gold chair. He apparently intended a lengthy stay.

She would see about that. A swift appraisal of the longcase clock revealed another ten minutes had passed since the meal ended. *Bah.*

Looking wholly out of place perched on the dainty carved piece, Lord Ramsbury took the seat opposite her. He shifted to get more comfortable, but the parlor chair groaned in protest. Carefully, he eased his long legs under the table. The chair complained again, and he stilled.

Lips quivering, Isobel arranged the ivory playing pieces. She caught Father's eye as he joined Mother on the settee before the fireplace. "Father, might I trouble you to bring his lordship a sturdier chair?"

After exchanging chairs, his lordship dropped into the stronger piece of furniture. "Much better."

"Yes, I was afraid, given your size, the other wouldn't bear up well." Isobel turned her attention to the black figures.

"*Dinnae ken* why these fragile things be in here," Father muttered. "There be not a man within the keep who can sit comfortably in one."

He sank onto the brocade settee beside Mother. She'd

taken up her sewing and busily stitched, no doubt making another garment for Adaira's babe.

"Are you implying I'm stout?" Humor laced Lord Ramsbury's voice.

Surprised, Isobel raised her eyes to his. "Nothing of the sort, my lord. You simply have a well-muscled, manly form."

Inwardly, she groaned.

Do shut up, Isobel.

"'Well-muscled form?'" Lord Ramsbury's eyes twinkled, although something more powerful glittered in their depths.

"Indeed, a *well*-muscled, *manly* form," came His Grace's droll affirmation.

Shut up!

Sensations of the earl's firm body mashed to hers on the stable floor bounded forth. Her nipples prickled, giving her a severe start. She almost dropped the chess piece. Grasping it tightly, she lifted the bishop, avoiding his lordship's eyes.

"Light or dark?"

Isobel slanted a glance to the reed thin figure of Mr. Ross. She doubted he weighed as much as she, despite the fact her head didn't quite reach his shoulder.

"I shall take the black." Lord Ramsbury rotated the board until the ebony pieces lay before him.

Isobel gave him a wry smile. "I assure you, I don't need first-move advantage."

He tapped his manicured fingers on the edge of the board. "Didn't entertain the notion for a moment. I believe the light pieces more representative of the fair maiden who challenged me."

Isobel gaped at him. Did he wax poetic?

The Duke of Harcourt chuckled heartily as the ladies tittered in approval.

Male cries of, "Hear, Hear," almost drowned out Mr. Ross's disapproving grunt.

"Well said, my lord." Yvette beamed her approval.

Ye gods, Lord Ramsbury had them all bamboozled. His handsome face and pretty manners might hide his deceptive, blackguard's heart from them, but Isobel remained impervious to his wiles and schemes.

Keep telling yourself that and maybe you'll come to believe it.

With a final glance about the room, she set her attention to the board. He would soon regret his magnanimous gesture, for she had every intention of laying him low.

As she trotted Emira from the keep's outer gates tomorrow, she'd give him a victorious wave.

Well, I'll be damned.

Yancy fingered the purplish raised mark on the back of his hand. Isobel's fingernails had left a nasty welt.

When the first game ended in a draw, he would have sworn on his dead mother's grave, Isobel was as surprised as he at the stalemate. Now, an hour later, their audience having dwindled to Miss Seonaid, Miss Farnsworth, Ross, Harcourt, and Alasdair, he wasn't convinced she hadn't deliberately sacrificed her pieces the first go round.

Such a brilliant strategist would have made one superior general.

He'd long since put aside his valiant notions of permitting her an easy victory. The game they were immersed in was a test of skill and strategy, and he feared Isobel would whip him soundly.

Skimming the board, he relaxed against his chair while she nibbled her lower lip and scrunched her nose in concentration.

Adorable.

Running her fingers, over and over, across the glistening

pearls at her neck, she stared at the board. All at once, her face lit up. Her gorgeous eyes dancing jubilantly, Isobel made her move.

"Checkmate, my lord."

She'd done it.

Beaten *him*, the master player.

He, the Regent's choice for War Office Secretary, had been bested by a slip of a girl.

Grinning, she leaned back into her chair, radiating satisfaction.

Now what?

"Isobel, you won." Miss Farnsworth jumped from her seat, dropping her embroidery on a nearby table before rushing to give Isobel a hug. "I'm sorry, my lord, I mean no offense, but I thought you being the War Secretary, and Isobel . . ."

"No offense taken, Miss Farnsworth."

Yancy stood, and then bowed deeply. "Congratulations, Miss Ferguson. You were a most worthy opponent. Never in all my years of playing the game, have I encountered such acumen or supreme strategy."

He didn't exaggerate.

Astonishment registered on her face and her cheeks pinkened to match the ribbon across her crown. She fiddled with a bishop. "Thank you, my lord."

Isobel rose. "If you'll excuse me, I've some matters I need to attend to before dinner. Thank you for the matches, my lord." She dipped into a quick curtsy, and then, accompanied by Miss Farnsworth, left the salon.

Ross trailed behind them, trying to get Isobel's attention. She strode from the room so quickly, the fellow practically ran on his spindly legs to keep up.

"Now she gets to leave the keep unattended." Harcourt offered the obvious with a victorious show of his teeth.

Hands linked behind his neck, Yancy stretched his legs before him. He met his friend's gloating expression.

"No, she doesn't. She wagered that if she won, she wouldn't have to leave the keep with *two* escorts."

Chapter 9

The clock had yet to chime a quarter past seven when Isobel, humming a Scottish ballad, made her way to the informal dining room the next morning.

With its creamy yellow walls and cerise wainscoting, the dining room nearer the kitchen possessed a much cozier atmosphere. She didn't particularly enjoy eating surrounded by the hunting trophies and weaponry displayed on the hall's stone walls.

A foot into the cheerful chamber, she paused. She'd expected the room to be vacant. A pair of red starts on a bird cherry tree outside the beveled window chirped happily. Bright morning sunlight dappled the oblong table and the men seated there.

Lord Ramsbury and Alasdair already enjoyed heaping plates of food. Beside his lordship's dish lay the papers, no doubt last week's *The London Gazette*, since it took seven days for the mail coach to deliver the newspaper.

The men rose upon her entrance.

Attired in a nutmeg-brown hunting jacket and buff buckskins tucked into glossy Hessians, the earl appeared absurdly attractive. Then again, when had she seen the man when he didn't?

"Good morning, my lord, Alasdair."

The men sat, and Alasdair dove into his meal once more.

She sniffed in appreciation. *Cinnamon rolls.* A favorite of hers.

"Good morning, cousin." Alasdair winked before shoving a sticky piece of a sweet roll into his mouth. He closed his eyes, exhaling an exaggerated sigh. "Yer lucky I left ye any of Sorcha's cinnamon buns."

Though they weren't cousins by blood, they'd been raised as such. She adored the giant man and his equally gargantuan brother. Except when they teased her, which, given they had no sisters, they were wont to do on a regular basis.

"What a pleasure to see such loveliness this early in the day." Lord Ramsbury's gaze skimmed her simple ivory and peach morning dress.

Doing it up a bit brown, wasn't he?

After his pretty compliment, he folded the paper into a tidy pile. "Are you always such an early riser?"

Isobel nodded. "Yes, I enjoy mornings. They are my favorite time of day, though sometimes I take a tray in my room and read before venturing forth."

Especially when *he* visited.

She also frequently enjoyed a stroll around the loch or brisk ride before breaking her fast, but he needn't know that.

She made her way to the sideboard. "Good morning, Fairchild. Yvette mentioned we'll have the pleasure of your sons' company for her birthday celebration."

The majordomo dipped his silvery head.

"Indeed. Isaiah and Josiah's ship should arrive in London next week." He picked up a silver-rimmed plate. "What do you prefer to break your fast, Miss Isobel?"

"Just a cinnamon roll and a piece of ham for me, please." She eyed the cocoa pot. "I believe I shall have hot chocolate rather than tea this morning."

As a child, she'd been quite addicted to the sweet concoction, which helped contribute to her well-rounded cheeks and plumpness in other places until five years ago. She particularly liked the drink topped with Devonshire cream.

In an effort to keep her curves manageable, she discontinued that practice. *More's the pity.* She rarely indulged in Sorcha's pasties either.

Mother and Seonaid were fuller-figured than Adaira, but beside Isobel, they appeared svelte. She wished she had Adaira's slight build.

Isobel's arms and legs were trim enough, and a man's hands could span her waist—granted they had to be large hands—but she possessed a generous bosom and wide hips. To her immense consternation, males seemed captivated by both.

The number of times she'd caught one ogling her upper and lower regions was past counting. She'd rather have Mr. Ross's knobby frame than be endowed as the Good Lord had designed her. Only her family, Lord Ramsbury, and the Duke of Harcourt didn't make her self-conscious about her lavish curves.

Accepting her plate from Fairchild, she turned to the table. She hesitated for a fraction then opted to sit beside Alasdair rather than the earl.

When near his lordship, her pulse did all manner of peculiar things, and she could never quite think straight. Catching whiffs of his subtle cologne, listening to the low timbre of his voice, observing his long fingers with their light smattering of blackish hair across the knuckles all muddled her.

No, she deemed sitting across the table much wiser.

The birds, startled by her passing beside the window, released frightened chirrups and took to wing.

Isobel twisted her mouth into a wry smile. Rather how she behaved with the earl nearby.

Fairchild placed a tall, royal-blue chintz patterned cocoa cup before her. "Use caution, Miss Isobel. The chocolate is quite hot. I would let it cool slightly before taking a drink. Did you want clotted cream?"

“Thank you, Fairchild, but I’ll pass on the cream.” She unfolded her napkin.

Lord Ramsbury’s lips curled into a mysterious smile when she’d sank into the chair opposite him, almost as if he had read her mind.

To hide the blush heating her cheeks, Isobel promptly raised the rich cocoa to her mouth, and burned her tongue.

Confounded earl.

She pressed the singed organ against the back of her teeth to stifle the oath that threatened and to numb the sharp pain pulsing on the tip.

Clamping her lips, she drew in a calming breath. Virtuous women didn’t curse in public. Only the earl tempted her to cast off propriety and ring him an unladylike peal.

Expecting the chamber to be empty, she intended to grab a bite to eat and pilfer enough food that she might enjoy her midday meal amongst the fossils and caves. Eager to explore the formations she’d found yesterday, she hadn’t waited for Maura to bring up the customary tray.

Besides, Isobel’s giddiness from drubbing his lordship at chess had kept her restless all night.

What other reason could there be for his face to keep appearing in her mind? Or the odd unsettled sensations that had her heaving sighs and flopping from her front to her back most of the night?

Dawn had scarcely whisked her colorful palette across the horizon before Isobel swept aside the counterpane atop her bed. Standing before her favorite window, she enjoyed a few moments admiring the pastel hues dusting the sky.

Tendrils of silvery smoke spiraled skyward beyond the meadow.

The travellers.

A visit to their encampment was in order. A variety of baskets, intricately detailed shawls, and other fascinating whatnots could always be found there—not to mention the most delectable tarts.

She would have to wait until Mother organized an outing, however. Isobel wasn't so bold as to venture to the tinker's encampment alone.

The women of Craiglocky would delay that outing until Vangie arrived. Part Roma, actually a gypsy princess, Lady Warrick spoke Romany but not the Gaelic cant of Scottish Highland travellers.

Nevertheless, many of the words were similar, and most travellers spoke English too. Some of these local gypsies claimed a familial relation to the countess, albeit quite distant.

Isobel had hastily gone about her morning ablutions, eager to get an early start. Now, hope of gathering food for later was dashed. She blew on the hot chocolate. Perhaps after she changed into her old gown, she would stop by the kitchen and ask Sorcha to put a something together for her and Tira to eat.

Cheese, rolls, an apple or two, and stovies would suffice.

Lord Ramsbury took a bite of an oatcake. "Might I persuade you to go riding this morning? Miss Farnsworth and Ross, as well as McTavish here, have agreed to an outing at half past eight."

Wary, Isobel raised her eyes to the earl. "Unfortunately, my lord, I have other plans. I thank you for the invitation, but I found some fossils yesterday I want to examine."

She bit into the light sweetness of the cinnamon roll.

A ride with Mr. Ross and Lord Ramsbury was not her idea of a pleasurable start to the day. The former she could not abide, and the latter she tried hard to remain impervious to.

Easier to do if spared his company.

Otherwise, he ambushed her emotions, and she was wont to gawk like a green schoolgirl. How could her heart be so warped? She knew Lord Ramsbury for a charlatan, and yet she remained irresistibly drawn to him.

Rather like a moth to a flame, certain to get singed or worse, but unable to fight the powerful allure.

A shadow flitted across his lordship's face, immediately replaced by a cool mask of politeness.

An alarm chirped in the back of her mind. Taking a tentative sip of chocolate, Isobel considered him. She'd beaten him fairly yesterday. He couldn't order her to take attendants with her.

Let's just test the waters, shall we?

"I'm sure being an honorable man, my lord, you fully intend to keep your word about the escorts."

Alasdair made a choking noise that sounded suspiciously like a cross between a laugh and a snort.

Her attention hurtled to him.

Turning from her scrutiny, he coughed into his hand.

If he really choked, she'd eat her slippers.

Her unease escalated. Did he know something she did not? She stared at him hard, silently challenging him to say what he knew.

He gave her a sheepish look and promptly stuffed his mouth full of ham. Most likely so she couldn't question him.

Coward.

She angled her head and raised an eyebrow. "Lord Ramsbury, am I to assume you intend to renege on your word?"

"Yes, well as to that . . ." Lord Ramsbury scratched his brow, and then had the audacity to give her a saucy grin. "I wouldn't call it reneging, precisely."

Isobel stiffened, clenching her fingers about the cup's fragile handle. She feared she'd snap the bit of porcelain right off or hurl the cup at his handsome head if he dared voice what she suspected he was about to.

Only years of rehearsed behavior enabled her to respond calmly. "And what *precisely* would you call it? I specifically said if I won, I wouldn't be taking escorts when I left the keep."

Lord Ramsbury relaxed against the chair, his fingers entwined across his flat abdomen. The signet ring on the little finger of his left hand glinted against the black and taupe of his waistcoat.

"Actually, you said if you won the game, you wouldn't be taking *two* escorts with you. Our party will number six, unless your sister and Gregor decide to accompany us. Naturally, the men will be armed."

Lord Ramsbury delivered the news with such self-assured confidence that had her parasol been handy she would have thumped him on his noggin. Soundly. She'd half a mind to retrieve her sabre and pin him to the chair like a beetle on exhibit.

The earl had neatly outmaneuvered her. Or so he believed. He thought to play another type of game, did he? The deceptive, green-eyed toad.

Isobel curled her toes in her slippers until she feared the appendages would snap. She fought to control the outrage thrumming through her and demanding to spew from her burned tongue. Eyes cast downward, she took a controlled sip of the cocoa.

Too hot, still.

An image of the chessboard and pieces flashed across her mind, immediately followed by Lord Ramsbury's face right before she declared checkmate.

Had he let her win?

No, he hadn't, she was certain. But he'd seen his imminent loss, and the cretin had determined another nefarious way to waylay her.

She sniffed the cocoa, cautiously dipping her tongue into the tasty brew to test its heat.

The earl thought himself a brilliant strategist, did he?

We shall see.

She gave him her most beguiling smile.

Surprise flitted across his features, and he blinked twice as if momentarily dazed. A maelstrom of emotion entered his eyes, swiftly replacing his stunned mien.

Isobel knew full well how her smile affected men. "Well then, I suppose I have no choice. I so wanted to examine the fossils I came across yesterday."

His lordship flashed a rakish grin, his teeth white against his tanned face. "I would quite like to see them myself. My maternal grandfather was a collector of unusual artifacts."

Alasdair groaned and rolled his eyes toward the ceiling. "Ye might regret that, yer lordship. Isobel can natter on for hours about those dusty bits of . . ."

His voice tapered off at the impatient look she fired at him.

Was it any wonder she wished to go off by herself?

Who was he to speak of nattering? She'd listened to more boasting and drivel about weapons, hunting, fishing, wrestling, and sparring than anyone, especially a female, should ever have to in a lifetime.

She fingered her cup's handle. "Fairchild, might I have more chocolate?"

Raising her cup, she swiveled toward him. Her grip on the handle slipped, and before she could utter a squeak, the cup tilted. Hot, sticky chocolate splattered across the tablecloth and streamed onto her lap as brown droplets littered the red and champagne-colored carpet underneath the table.

"Ouch!" Shaking her gown, she jumped to her feet. "I'm sorry, Fairchild. How utterly clumsy of me."

The butler rushed to the table bearing extra napkins.

She dabbed at the splotches on her gown.

"I must remove my gown at once and give it to Maura to launder or else it's sure to be ruined." Isobel held the damp cloth away from her legs. "I fear it may be too late already. Please excuse me."

She pivoted toward the door, but turned back partway. "You said half past eight, my lord?"

"Yes." The earl nodded, his attention fixated on the dark stain marring her gown. Worry creased his brow. "Did you get burned?"

Genuine concern laced his voice.

Her thighs stung where the hot chocolate seeped through her gown and chemise. "Nothing serious. The cocoa had partially cooled."

She rushed from the dining room without a backward glance, lest his lordship see the victory that surely must be evident in her eyes.

Chapter 10

Isobel suspected she might have a welt or two but no severe burns from the mishap. The spill hadn't been an accident. A few hours of discomfort was well worth the time she'd gained with her theatrics.

Her performance had been believable, if she didn't say so herself. Lord Ramsbury suspected nothing amiss.

Ten minutes later, the stained morning dress stuffed beneath her bed, Isobel crept from her bedchamber. She wore an older gown, but not the Kersey she favored for digging. Either Maura hadn't laundered the garment or she'd sent it to the rubbish bin. The later seemed more probable as she'd tried to throw the gown out for years.

Simple and serviceable, yet of unquestionably high quality, this charcoal and black wool gown was more appropriate for a woman of gentle breeding. No one would mistake her for a village lass or servant.

That should make Lord Ramsbury happy.

Confound his lordship, the sneaky twiddlepoop. Who did he think he was, manipulating her?

Isobel peeked around the corner of the seldom-used servants' stairwell.

Empty.

Clutching her bag, she hurried on tiptoe along the passage to the kitchen. See what he'd driven her to? Skulking about in her own home, afraid of encountering someone and having to explain why she sneaked below stairs.

Irritation and her silent footsteps thrummed in unison. If he thought she would wait patiently, like a tethered horse, until the duke, Lydia, and Mr. Ross made their way below stairs to break their fast, the earl didn't know her at all.

Isobel had sent word to the stables before eating to have Emira saddled and waiting. Now, she had only to escape the keep undetected.

Sorcha and the other cooking staff would know she'd left. But Isobel frequently used the scullery courtyard exit. They'd think nothing of it.

Painting a smile on her face, she strode into the spotlessly clean, comfortable kitchen. Drying herbs hung from the overhead rafters, lending a pleasant aroma to the already-fragrant room. The staff scurried about, some loading trays to take above stairs, and others beginning preparations for the midday and evening meals.

"Good morning, Sorcha." Isobel scooped two apples from a bowl atop a wooden counter worn smooth from decades of constant use. She dropped them into her bag. "Might I have a couple of cinnamon buns to take with me?"

Wiping her floury hands on her apron, Sorcha nodded. "*Aye*, Miss Isobel. Ye be wantin' a boiled egg or two, pickles, and a bite of cheese as well? And I suppose ye need shortbread biscuits for the hound."

Dash it all.

Most likely, Tira was in the great hall snoring away with her brother and sister. Best not to let Sorcha know.

"Yes, please, and stovies. A flask of water, too."

Isobel would have to explore the cliffs alone today. Moses himself could not get her to venture from the kitchen, not even to get her faithful dog. She hoped the boarhound wandered the bailey and would hear her when she whistled.

She slid a covert glance to the kitchen's main entrance, half-expecting Lord Ramsbury to appear, a smug grin on his perfect mouth. She wandered to the door exiting onto the courtyard. From there, she could hide in the keep's shadows and make her way to the stable.

Chewing her lower lip, she scanned the kitchen entrance again.

Hurry, Sorcha.

Though slightly longer, the forest path to the caves afforded more cover. She would take that route today. She scanned the small clock atop a shelf filled with spices. Not yet eight o'clock. She'd have a good head start on the others.

Even if they visited the fossils and caves on their excursion, and she suspected the earl would insist they do so, she would still have a little time to herself.

He would have to find her first. She wouldn't make locating her easy. Mayhap she'd further explore the caves today. She had two tapers stowed in her bag, enough to provide several hours' worth of light.

Obstinate man.

Why couldn't he mind his own affairs? And why did he insist on seeking her out when his attentions could lead to nothing honorable? She would be no man's mistress, the only feasible reason she could conceive of why Lord Ramsbury persisted.

Ewan would call him out if his lordship so much as hinted at such a liaison.

Sorcha handed her a cloth-wrapped bundle and a leather flask. "Here ye be. Will ye be back fer luncheon?"

"Thank you." Accepting the food and water, Isobel shook her head. "I don't think so. I fear the weather will turn for the worse again, and I really want to investigate the caves on the far side of the crags."

"*Humph.* I *dinna* like ye wanderin' the tors right now." Sorcha shuffled to the stove, where she took up a large paddle-like wooden spoon and set to stirring whatever bubbled in the pot atop the cast iron monstrosity.

"You sound like Maura." Isobel tucked the bundle and flask into her bag.

"Don't worry. I shan't be alone the whole while. Lord

Ramsbury and several others are riding this morning too. Besides, only a dullard or a reckless fool would dare venture onto Craiglocky's lands without Ewan or Duncan's consent. You know my brother has men monitoring the borders."

She opened the door. "Even the black tinkers ask permission, and they've camped along River Falkirk every spring and fall for as long as I can remember."

"*Aye*, that be true." The cook's full face folded into deep wrinkles as she smiled. "I feel better knowin' ye'll have company."

A twinge of guilt speared Isobel. She wasn't one to twist facts to deceive others. "The earl expressed an interest in seeing the fossils."

No lie there. What kind of relics had his lordship's grandfather collected?

With a wave and smile, she slipped out the arched opening. She'd nearly pulled the door shut when Alasdair's jovial voice echoed in the kitchen.

Isobel peeked through the crack.

"Sorcha, can ye pack a picnic lunch for five or six? Miss Farnsworth and her cantankerous uncle be ridin' with me and a few others." Without waiting for her reply, he snatched a cinnamon bun and sprinted from the kitchen, calling, "Be back in thirty minutes to pick up the food."

Sorcha waved her spoon at his retreating form. "Yer a thief, Alasdair McTavish."

"*Aye*." His boisterous laughter echoed in the hallway.

Isobel lifted her skirts and tore to the stables.

Chapter 11

"Fairchild said you wished to see me, Sethwick?"

Advancing into the castle's study, Yancy flexed his left hand and finished tugging on his riding glove. He'd never liked this room. Even with several candles lit, the stone-walled chamber resembled a bloody medieval tomb. "You just caught me. A small riding party is off for a morning jaunt across the moors."

Seated behind his hulking desk, Sethwick, a quill in his hand, scratched away on foolscap. He didn't look up.

"Yes, Yancy. Give me one moment, if you will."

"Certainly." Yancy tossed his hat onto one of the worn deep back leather chairs before the desk.

Sethwick affixed his signature, and after setting the feather aside, sprinkled sand atop the wet ink. With a satisfied sigh, he relaxed against the high-back chair. "That's done. I don't know about you, but I find corresponding with my solicitor about as exciting as licking hot coals."

Wandering to inspect a display of pole weapons, Yancy chuckled. "That bad?"

"Well, perhaps that is doing it up a bit brown. Nonetheless, it's not my favorite task." Sethwick scratched his nose and edged his lips upward a fraction. "Alasdair mentioned you planned an outing, which is why I summoned you."

Yancy cast him a cursory glance over his shoulder then selected a Lochaber axe sporting an ugly eighteen-inch blade. Holding the weapon parallel to the floor, he lunged.

And almost fell over.

One eyebrow elevated, Sethwick leaned forward and

rested his elbows atop his desk, his fingers interlaced. "Yesterday, I mentioned I had information that I thought would be of particular interest to you."

Yancy swung the Lochaber in a small arc. He stumbled a pair of steps to the right. The axe was heavy and damn awkward to wield.

"Ramsbury, will you stop playing with that blasted thing and listen?"

Frustration edged Sethwick's tone, giving Yancy pause. He laid the weapon aside.

"Forgive me. I assume your news is troublesome?" Arms and ankles crossed, he rested his hip against an elongated table and gave Sethwick his full attention.

"That's what I don't know. Something's off, to be sure. As I'm certain you've learned by now, Blackhall, McGrath, and Clauston clansmen have been lurking about. Some of them have been seen in Craigcutty conspiring with the Scottish tinkers, and my border patrols have found evidence of unauthorized camping on my lands."

Instantly alert, Yancy uncrossed his ankles. "I assume these vagrants are not the Highland travellers?"

"Extremely improbable. The gypsies know they've an open invitation, and they make their encampment near the river. Their involvement with those clans is most irregular. I'm not sure what to make of it."

That piece of information also perplexed Yancy. There had to be a connection neither he nor Sethwick were aware of.

Shaking the sand from the letter, Sethwick folded the paper then sealed it with wax. Setting the missive aside, he stood. A massive boarhound appeared from behind the desk as well. "My informants tell me MacHardy may be attempting to incite the discontented clans to rebellion."

Yancy stiffened and leveled Sethwick an intent stare. Even MacHardy wasn't that rash. Such an act would be suicide. "Pure foolhardiness if that's his intent. Prinny will squash him, and any who attempt a revolt, as easily as an ant beneath his royal heel."

"Of that, I have no doubt." Sethwick came round his desk, his expression somber.

The dog trailed him, and eager for a pet, pushed his huge head into his master's palm. Sethwick complied and scratched the hound's head.

"Don't know why you bother with horses when you've those beasts galloping here and there." Yancy flipped his fingers at the dog then surveyed the mantel clock. Twenty past eight. Time to be on his way.

He quite anticipated spending the morning with Isobel. She was the most stunning and intelligent woman he'd ever encountered, and he found himself in a constant state of arousal—mentally and physically—in her presence. As if to confirm his thought, his male member pulsed.

"The Highland clans have suffered a great deal."

Sethwick's comment doused Yancy's amorous contemplations.

"First"—Sethwick continued to pet the dog—"they were forcibly recruited to fight in the war, and then they endured the crop failures of a couple of years ago."

"And now, they're unhappy with the price of wool and weavers' wages." Yancy pulled on his earlobe, grinning as a bit of dog drool plopped onto one of Sethwick's Hessians.

Sethwick straightened his waistcoat and gave a curt nod. He pointed to the floor. "Lie down, Arig."

The hound dropped to the floor, head between his paws, his brown-eyed gaze affixed adoringly on his master.

Damn, the clans' situation became more complex by the minute. "MacHardy mightn't have to work very hard to agitate the disgruntled Scots."

"*Aye*, that's what has me worried."

Cocking his head, Yancy noted the lines of uneasiness sharpening the angles of Sethwick's face. "And, I'm to soothe these malcontents. Your confidence is most flattering. Who do you think I am, Tranquillitas?"

Releasing a short bark of laughter, Sethwick slapped Yancy on the shoulder.

"A Roman Goddess you are not, my friend, but I've every confidence in your diplomacy skills. For now, I think it best everyone stay near the keep and only leave in armed groups. I shall inform the staff immediately. The others riding with you today are armed as well?"

He perused Yancy's sword.

Yancy patted the blade at his side. "Naturally."

"Excellent." Sethwick returned to his desk, and after retrieving the letter, tucked the missive into an inside coat pocket. "I am of a mind to keep our activities as normal as possible, although I'll be leery and on guard. Venture no farther than the loch or the forest's border. No sign of intruders have been found that close to the keep."

He gestured to the mullioned windows. "I've assigned another score of men to scout my lands and to keep their ears open in the village. They're to report anything they see or hear."

"Most wise." Yancy eyed the dog, now noisily grooming himself, slobber flying every-which-way in the process. "I hope to meet with the troublesome clan leaders by the end of the week. I sent messengers requesting an audience yesterday. I suppose a great deal depends on MacHardy."

Yancy didn't doubt the belligerent churl would resist an attempt to assemble a council of chieftains and lairds. For two decades he'd been a pebble in England's shoe——no, more like a festering barb in the arse.

"Isobel rides this morning?"

The question caught Yancy off guard. "Yes, although, I suspect you knew that already."

He searched Sethwick's face, only detecting innocent regard registered there. Yet, Yancy swore something more ominous lay buried in his friend's gaze. Ah, this was about yesterday's mishap in the stable.

Unfamiliar warmth stole up Yancy's neck.

Hell, now he colored like a schoolgirl caught with a lad's hand up her skirts. A choking urge to tug at his neckcloth overwhelmed him.

"My sister is not one of your London light-skirts." Sethwick fingered the inkwell's carved-glass stopper. "Isobel is naïve and rather green when it comes to men, despite her intellectual brilliance."

He met Yancy's unflinching gaze. "Don't trifle with her affections."

"You think so little of me, you warn me off your sister?" Ire and betrayal battled for supremacy. "By God, do you know how ruddy insulting that is?"

Yancy snatched his hat from the chair before marching to the door. His hand on the handle, he turned to Sethwick. "My intentions toward your sister have always been, and will continue to be, wholly honorable."

"That may well be, but Isobel's enamored with you, although I suspect she's not delighted with her feckless emotions—if she's aware of her feelings." A sarcastic smirk twisted Sethwick's mouth. "You do rather confuse the ladies."

Enamored?

Yancy hid a delighted grin, more determined to redouble his efforts to win Isobel's approval and her hand.

His features less severe, Sethwick joined him at the door. "You've never shown the slightest interest in marriage, Yancy. All I'm asking is that you not encourage Isobel. You'll break her heart if you do."

Yancy had no one but himself to blame for Sethwick's estimation of him. He hadn't directed so much as a sniff in an honorable woman's direction before. His friend's concerns were well-founded, except Sethwick didn't know about Yancy's change of plans.

A hint might prove helpful to gauge his reaction.

Yancy fingered the brim of his hat. "Tell me, old friend, which is your greater concern? That your sister might harbor sincere regard for me, or that I might have a genuine, enduring interest in her?"

With that pithy remark, he turned his back, biting his tongue to keep from laughing at Sethwick's sagging jaw and the dumbfounded expression on his face.

Yancy's grin widened.

He'd flummoxed Craiglocky's laird, no easy feat.

Several moments later, he stood atop the gatehouse stairs. He checked his watch for the third time in the past five minutes. Eight forty-five.

Where was Isobel?

Snapping the watch closed, he returned the timepiece to his waistcoat. Impatient to ride, he whacked his hat against his thigh.

The rest of their party, except for Harcourt, already sat mounted, every man armed with short swords and dirks. A bow and quiver lay strapped to Miss Farnsworth's back, and a dagger nestled in one of her half-boots.

Trained in weaponry, she expressed a desire to target practice on their excursion today. More complex and capable than Yancy had first imagined, Miss Farnsworth might very well be the key to settling this whole clan unrest.

Harcourt, lounging at the base of the stairs, yawned widely then blinked as if to focus his sleepy gaze.

"Not used to being separated from your mattress and pillow this early in the day, Harcourt?" Yancy couldn't refrain from needling him. He'd seen the pert upstairs maid slip from the duke's chamber early this morning.

Harcourt stopped fussing with his coat sleeves.

"I'm following your advice, old chap." A sly smile quirked his lips before he emitted another yawn. "I've found the locals most obliging when it comes to offering unfettered . . . er, distractions."

Yancy made an impolite noise. "You'd best not let Sethwick hear of it. He doesn't approve of dalliances with the staff under his roof."

Walking their horses about the bailey, the others murmured quietly amongst themselves. Gregor had accepted the invitation to ride too.

Miss Farnsworth had returned to the bailey, having rushed to her room to change after finding a split seam in the skirt of the gray and black riding habit she had been wearing.

Now, attired in Pomona green trimmed in black velvet, her hair tucked into a hat tilted at a jaunty angle upon her head, and a panel of plaid wrapped from her shoulders to waist, she epitomized the gently-bred Scotswoman.

A green feather stood at attention on the right side band, and a finely meshed veil covered her face. She sat regally upon her mount, patiently waiting for Isobel and chatting with Alasdair.

In all the years Yancy had been a guest at Craiglocky, he'd never seen Isobel in a riding habit; had never seen her ride, for that matter.

By God, did she ride astride?

Countesses did not ride astride.

Ross kept sending hopeful glances in the entry's direction. Too bad the gloomy sod hadn't declined Yancy's forced invitation. The Scot probably hoped to woo Isobel today. He would find himself hard-pressed to get anywhere near her if Yancy had his way.

A basket had been tied to Alasdair's saddle and balanced behind him. He'd seen to a picnic lunch for their outing.

Yancy hadn't planned on being gone that long, but he didn't object. A picnic gave him more time with Isobel.

Showing an interest in her hobby might garner him a jot of favor. Truth to tell, her discoveries genuinely interested him.

One of his prized possessions included his grandfather's collection of odd artifacts from sojourns to exotic places. Grandfather Whatleypoot had been a peculiar old buzzard. He'd traveled extensively and had enjoyed life to the fullest up until the day he died after tumbling off a camel.

Yancy retraced his steps.

Fairchild met him at Craiglocky's entrance. "May I be of assistance?"

"Would you please send a footman to Miss Isobel's bedchamber and inquire how much longer she might be?" Yancy glanced over his shoulder.

Harcourt had mounted his horse and joined the others.

Yancy returned his attention to the butler. "Please tell her everyone is waiting."

"At once, sir." Fairchild reentered the castle.

A niggling suspicion pricked Yancy's mind.

She wouldn't dare.

Adaira, Lady Clarendon—the incorrigible sister—would have. But Isobel was the demure Ferguson daughter, the one who knew how to behave with decorum and sophistication matching her beauty. The sister who would grace the London assemblies and upper salons with the perfected poise expected of his countess.

By Hades, she wouldn't openly defy him or her brother.

Would she?

Curse it, the Isobel of the past twenty-four hours would, especially if intent on a secret meeting with a lover.

He'd underestimated her. Foolish of him, given her keen mind. A muscle ticked below his right eye, and he slapped his hat atop his head, swiveling on his heel.

She had upped the stakes.

He ran down the steps. Without sparing a word to the other riders, he vaulted onto Skye. Trotting the blue roan gelding the short distance to the stables, Yancy fabricated multiple ways he would chastise Isobel if she'd disregarded him.

"M'lord, can I help ye?" The bandy-legged stable master approached, rubbing his hands on a soiled cloth.

Yancy perused the stalls, searching for a nameless horse, or rather its taffy-haired owner. Impatient to be off, he swung his attention to the groom. "It's Jocky, isn't it?"

"*Aye*, sir. Ye be needin' somethin'?" Jocky stuffed the tattered rag into his waistband.

Shifting in his saddle, Yancy wedged his hat firmer onto his head. "Did Miss Isobel leave already?"

She had better hope the crusty old groom said no.

Jocky released a grave chuckle, his eyes crinkling into a dozen weathered folds at the corners. "*Aye*. The young miss be eager to find more arrowheads and dead rock things."

"Fossils?"

"*Aye*. She be headed to the caves today, she said."

"Alone?"

The servant gave a cautious nod, his gap-toothed smile fading. Apprehension replaced the merry twinkle in his faded eyes. "Be there a problem, m'lord? Miss Isobel said ye'd be followin' in a wee bit."

His throat worked nervously as he peered up at Yancy.

This wasn't the groom's fault. Yancy ought to have asked Sethwick to speak to the staff sooner.

"Jocky, until further notice, no one is to leave the keep unescorted, most especially not the women."

"Yes, sir." Jocky's gaze sank to the straw-littered floor. "I be sorry, yer lordship. I *dinna ken*."

Yancy offered a conciliatory smile. "It's not your fault. I should have sent word yesterday."

He clenched Skye's reins so tightly, his leather gloves pinched his fingers. Isobel had no idea the danger she'd put herself in.

Sensing his master's agitation, the roan sidestepped and snorted.

"Shh, we'll be away soon, my friend." Yancy bent and rubbed the gelding's neck. With a final pat, he straightened. "How long ago did she leave?"

His wrinkled face creased with worry, Jocky lifted a scrawny shoulder. "An hour. Maybe less."

Reining Skye around, Yancy clamped his jaw until his back teeth ached. Isobel had lied to him, and there would be consequences. He cantered to the others, and as he drew near, they looked up expectantly.

Other than raising an eyebrow questioningly, Harcourt, for once, had the good sense to remain silent.

"*Nae* lass?" Gregor peered behind Yancy then twisted in his saddle to inspect the castle entry. His gaze swung to his twin, and he rubbed his chin, a pensive gleam in his eyes. "*Och*, I guess she's flown."

"*Aye*." Alasdair's gaze focused on the dense crop of trees standing at attention well beyond the drawbridge. "I kent she might. She be prickly as thistle of late."

"You might have warned me, McTavish. Where are these fossils of hers?" Clicking his tongue, Yancy kneed Skye's sides and called over his shoulder. "We need to find her before she encounters the trespassers Sethwick said are lurking about."

Chapter 12

Isobel picked her way across a mound of slate-colored rocks littering a portion of the cave's entrance. Huge lichen and liverwort-covered boulders blocked the other, which made seeing inside and accessing the cavern difficult.

Mountain aven, their smooth white blossom and jonquil yellow centers long since spent, huddled between the stones and atop the yawning opening. Their verdant leaves contrasted with the dull gray world surrounding the intrepid evergreen, and proved slippery as ice when stepped upon.

The cave, partially hidden below a craggy overhang, appeared deceptively easy to access until she neared the entrance. Uncertainty nudged her. She hadn't attempted to enter this cavern before. What if some wild animal had made the hollow its den?

She perused the entrance and listened for movement within. Other than Scottish wild cats and red foxes, nothing of substantial size roamed these hills and moors.

Her bum pressed against a rock twice her size, Isobel gingerly edged onward. She bent and peered into the cave's dark recesses several feet way.

Complete darkness stared back at her.

"It's black as the Earl of Hell's waistcoat in there."

Shading her eyes, she sent a glance skyward and frowned. The clear azure sky she'd rode out under a jot more than an hour ago, now hung heavy with gun-metal gray clouds. This morning's comfortable breeze had stiffened into a biting wind.

Unwanted company would soon be upon her, for she had no doubt Lord Ramsbury thundered to the cliffs like a rutting buck after a doe, determined to disturb her treasure seeking.

Her lips twitched into a gratified smile. Oh, to have been there and seen his arrogant face when he realized she'd disregarded his directive, the deceiving snake.

Who did he think he was, manipulating her like that?

She was not such a slowtop as to put herself in danger. Surely, if a real need for concern was present, Ewan or her parents would have explained the circumstances. These mysterious secrets and Drury Lane theatrics were entirely unnecessary, and this whole clan feuding business appeared nothing more than a few covetous, power-hungry men stirring up discontent.

Lydia had resided at Craiglocky for months because some troublesome baron was determined to marry her in an attempt to acquire her father's lands. Now, other clans had become embroiled in the chaos.

Greed and power—two of the devil's most destructive weapons.

Emira's low nicker carried to Isobel on the soft, heather-scented breeze. She'd left the mare ground-tied in a copse of Scots pine a few hundred yards away. The horse had been trained to remain where Isobel left her, and Emira wouldn't leave unless Isobel whistled.

Scooting her bottom along the rock, Isobel advanced further until a rough edge snagged her skirt. She gave a firm yank, and tore a three-inch rip in the material.

A short chuckle escaped her.

Lord Ramsbury wouldn't approve.

He'd loathed the Kersey gown she'd worn yesterday. His displeasure had been etched all over his noble face. Admittedly, she did resemble a humble, village lass when wearing the drab garment. She fingered the wool of her current dress. He would be hard-pressed to find fault with this gown, even though it had seen three winters.

Her humor evaporated the next instant. *Hmph.* His approval meant nothing.

Creeping another couple of inches across the rock, she released a defeated sigh. Why did men dictate everything women could do and what they should think? If God hadn't wanted women to use their own minds, then why had He given them a brain?

Years of suppressing knowledge and opinions behind decorous behavior had reached a pinnacle, and Isobel wasn't certain she would ever be able to return to that docile and demure young lady. Truth be told, she didn't want to. She could no more pretend to be an empty-headed ninny than The Prince Regent could turn somersaults.

Even now, she must rush to explore caves a man had dictated she couldn't.

She squinted into the horizon. Yes, there in the distance, riders approached, moving fast from the looks of them.

God's toenails. I haven't made the cave yet.

Emira whinnied. The other horses' scents likely carried to the mare on the wind.

This would be Isobel's last solo outing. Of that she had no doubt. His lordship would see she didn't sneeze without his permission. In the future, her shadow would be allowed more freedom than she would.

How her fickle heart could yearn for such a man boggled her mind. Yet there remained an unexplainable, wholly illogical attraction—no, more of an uncontrollable draw—to him.

Och, such absurdity made no sense.

Placing one hand on a boulder for balance, she deliberately kicked some loose stones. That should alert anything residing in the cave and encourage the creature to make a hasty exit.

Trepidation quickening her pulse, Isobel gathered a few pebbles. She tossed them at the cavern's mouth, and several rolled inside. Ducking behind a boulder, she waited, her lips compressed and her breath suspended.

Nothing.

Only the screeching cry of a golden eagle overhead disturbed the quiet.

Stop being such a dunderhead.

As she maneuvered around an odd-shaped rock, she slipped and scraped her elbow.

"Ouch."

Clutching her arm, she waited for the sharp sting to pass.

She pushed her cloak from her shoulder and inspected the injury. Droplets of blood dotted her shredded sleeve. Wincing, she straightened her arm and grabbed a final handhold. With a gusty sigh, she jumped to the ground and left the last of the cumbersome rocks behind her.

Tiptoeing the remaining few feet to the cave's opening, she cautiously stepped inside and peered around. She sprang backward and tripped in her haste, landing hard on her bottom. Paralyzing fear seized her for a heart-stopping moment.

Hell, Hades, and Purgatory too.

She'd experienced the bloody fright of her life.

Isobel had heard tales of people fainting or wetting themselves from fear but dismissed the stories as nonsensical balderdash. She'd be rethinking that notion since she about did both.

Alarm and pain urged her to rise.

She'd counted five bedrolls inside. Someone had been using the cave as a shelter. In addition to the bedding, cookware, discarded bones, and an extinguished fire further testified to that fact.

Emira neighed again, followed by the undeniable sound of men's voices and horses' hoofbeats. Not Lord Ramsbury and the others. Even riding neck or nothing, they couldn't have reached the bluffs that swiftly.

Dread rendered Isobel immobile. Dear God, what if the intruders were armed?

Of course they are, featherbrain.

Their reasons for being here couldn't be legitimate, or else why use the cave?

Danger threatened those riding her way, and she blamed her damnable pigheadedness. Why had she been so self-centered and impetuous? Lord Ramsbury and the others would be armed, but unless she warned them, they might be ambushed.

Closing her eyes, she drew a calming breath and forced her panic aside.

The men's voices drew nearer.

Isobel opened her eyes and sought a hiding place or a means of escape. There, on the far side of the cave, almost hidden by heather, was that a path?

What a pity she'd scaled the outcrop when a trail led to the cave. How long had these men been using the cavern anyway? The weightier question was why?

She worried her lip. God's teeth, Lord Ramsbury had been right. Unless she hid amongst the boulders, she'd be found. She swiftly examined the outcrop. Above her, rocks projected creating a shadowy shelf. Her cloak should blend with the stones.

Shoving the straps of her bag up her arm, Isobel charged to the boulders. Her hem crammed in her belt, she scrambled over stones. She tried to listen while moving silently and succeeded in doing both poorly. Gloves protected her hands, but her worn half-boots slipped and slid, causing her knees to bang painfully against the rocks several times.

Teeth clamped, she cursed beneath her breath like a Highland whore. Mother would have apoplexy if she suspected Isobel possessed such an extensive vocabulary of profanity.

Her injured elbow protested, and rocks bit into her forearms and calves. Sweating and panting, she scooted below a crevice offering protection from above and most of the way around her.

After yanking her hood over her head, she wiped the beads of moisture from her upper lip and forehead. Her gaze fixed on the exposed side, she removed her dagger. She set the bag beside her before crouching into a ball.

The wind whistled amongst the rocks, and she shivered.

"He *canna* be far away. He left his beasty untethered." The voice came from a few feet away.

Isobel flinched, her heart nearly leaping from her chest. Pray God, they hadn't heard her clambering across the rocks. Ever-so-slowly, she inched her head to the right. A crack between the boulders afforded her a partial view.

Four hulking men wearing unfamiliar plaids stood clustered a mere twenty feet away.

She'd never seen such shaggy, unkempt Scots before, not even amongst the rattiest Highlanders.

Wild, tangled hair hung to their shoulders, and each sported a bushy chest-length beard and hair-matted torsos. Except for one, none wore shirts, but rather a leather vest, belted at the waist. More wooly hair covered their cudgel-like forearms and massive legs exposed by their soiled kilts.

Isobel swallowed her revulsion and concentrated on the men.

The Scot wearing a shirt scratched his chest, his keen gaze roving the area. "Must be a laddie. The saddle be too small for a man."

Heavily armed, the men resembled the barbaric Highlanders of Grandma Ferguson's legends of old. One held Emira's reins.

No, devil it.

Fighting tears, Isobel leaned her forehead against a stone and prayed.

What was she to do?

The shirted man seemed to be their leader. He motioned at Emira. "Baines, ye and Kilgore take the beastie and tie it yonder, by the cave, then git yerselves into hidin' with the others. Take yer horses. Riders approach, and Dunbar said the Farnsworth lass be with them."

Isobel tightened her grip on the dagger.

"*Aye*, Angus."

"*Och*, be about it then. We needs be hidden to grab the *hoor*. Dunbar and the others already be in the pines."

Her pulse stuttering in alarm, an icy chill wracked her. She dipped to her knees, daring to peek above one of the sheltering stones. Those from the castle must be warned. She turned to scurry to the ground, but froze as the man called Angus spoke, his words drifting to her on the increasingly brisk wind.

"Kill the men. Hide their bodies in a cave. The Farnsworth wench comes to no harm, ye ken?"

Chapter 13

Hugging Skye's back, Yancy threw a glance to the riders following behind. The others, including Miss Farnsworth, charged after him. Worry, *and jealousy*, if he were honest with himself, prompted him to ride hard in pursuit of Isobel, the foolish chit.

"There be the outcrops Isobel usually ventures to." Voice raised to be heard above the wind, Alasdair pointed to a rugged pile of rocks about a half mile away.

As he spoke, a few random droplets of rain splattered to the earth. A tempest approached by the looks of the ever-increasing clouds on the horizon. Movement atop the stone snared Yancy's attention. He squinted against the brisk air scratching his face.

Damn inhospitable Highlands.

He couldn't leave for England soon enough to suit him.

An odd-shaped bush swayed, its tormented branches flailing. He peered closer. The wind flattened billowing cloth against a frantically waving figure.

A woman.

Not just any woman.

Isobel.

He raised his hand. "Halt."

The riders rumbled to a stop.

"Why we be stoppin'?" Gregor sidled his horse next to Yancy's.

The others drew close, and Yancy pointed.

"Isobel's waving her arms, there atop that tor." Fiend seize it. Yancy had used her first name without thinking.

Only Harcourt noticed and responded with a sardonic twitch of his mouth.

Damnation, Harcourt knew him too well.

How the devil had she managed to climb to the peak of the outcrop? Bloody dangerous, that. No other woman of Yancy's acquaintance would attempt to do so, let alone succeed.

Ross edged his mount ahead, an idiotic grin on his face. "I do believe the lass be waving at me."

He lifted his arms and flapped them in imitation of her, rather like a giant crow in the throes of death.

Gregor leaned near his brother and muttered out the side of his mouth, "And the mighty Robert the Bruce wore a corset and a lace bonnet into battle."

Alasdair chuckled. "And lip rouge, too."

Waving excitedly, Ross hurled them a frosty glare.

"Cease, you dolt." Yancy pinned Ross with a glare.

A headless chicken possessed more wits than the Scot.

Harcourt stared at Ross as if he possessed three heads. "Please tell me why you presume she's waving a greeting and not a warning?"

A mutinous frown twisting his mouth, Ross's arms fell to his sides.

Miss Farnsworth's mare pranced in a nervous circle. "Where's Isobel? I don't see her."

Yancy wrenched his attention to the horizon once more.

Isobel had disappeared.

Senses honed, his spine tingled in alarm. "I don't like this. Something's afoot."

An eagle screeched high amongst the clouds, the cry an ominous warning confirming his premonition.

He covertly scanned the dark stand of pine trees to the left of the rock run. A glint amongst the trunks caught his eye.

Blade? Gun?

"*Aye*, me hackles be raised." Gregor, his expression taut, scrutinized the area.

Alasdair gripped his sword's hilt. He canted his head. "Someone lays in wait in yonder woodlands."

Yancy fingered his dirk. "Why, and is he alone?"

More importantly, what danger did the bugger present to Isobel?

"I would wager my new barouche, that's no solitary gent lurking amongst the greenery." Harcourt flicked a manicured forefinger in the direction of the mysterious gleam.

Yancy snorted and removed his gloves. "They're idiots to attack English and Scottish citizens under the protection of the crown—and on Sethwick's lands, to boot. He'll see them imprisoned."

"MacHardy's promised them something that makes the risk worthwhile, I would guess." Harcourt followed suit and removed his gloves. He patted his stomach. "I would have eaten something more substantial this morning had I known I'd be required to exert myself this early in the day."

At Harcourt's sarcasm, Yancy elevated a brow. "I shall do my best to assure you return to Craiglocky in time for luncheon."

In his rush to pursue Isobel, had he led them into a trap?

He didn't question the McTavish brothers' ability to fight. After all, their father was Craiglocky's war chief. Hell, he might have to call upon Duncan McTavish and his men to assist with this feuding clan business.

Harcourt's skill with a blade was second only to Sethwick's, but what of Ross?

Yancy eyed the lanky fellow and tried to imagine him swinging a Lochaber axe. Hardly more than a bag of bones, a strong gust of wind could knock the sot on his skinny arse.

The weapons Miss Farnsworth carried would be of little use against gunfire. Besides, their small group might be outnumbered, likely was.

He didn't hold to striking women, but when he got his hands on Isobel, her deliciously rounded bottom would suffer a pinkening. If not by his hand then her father or brother's.

He took a measure of relief in knowing she possessed a shrewd mind.

Blast, he needed Harcourt, Gregor, and Alasdair with him. They knew these lands and were experienced in fighters. Ross was the sort to get lost while using the privy.

Something besides the Scot's fixation with Isobel set Yancy's teeth on edge. For all of Ross's bumbling ineptitude, Yancy sensed there was more to the man, and his instinct shouted caution.

He swung his gaze in Craiglocky's direction and drummed his fingers on his thigh. An experienced rider could make the castle in ten, maybe twelve, minutes of hard riding and be back with reinforcements in fewer than thirty.

Thirty minutes seemed a lifetime when the woman you cared for faced unknown danger.

Yancy maneuvered Skye to face the others. "If we try to reach Miss Ferguson across this meadow, we're easy targets and can be picked off like pheasants on snow."

The remains of his morning meal churned in his stomach. Every minute they delayed, the peril to Isobel increased.

He forced his emotions aside and concentrated on strategy.

The sky had darkened to the same shade of slate as the boulder-strewn ground behind them. The rain fell harder, great, fat, splattering drops, which saturated his coat in minutes. The pungent odors of heather and damp earth wafted by on the wind.

"Is there another way to that outcrop?" Yancy slanted his head without turning around.

"*Aye*, but the paths be through the forest or clear around the loch." Alasdair turned to Miss Farnsworth. "The weather be turnin' ugly. Ye should return to the keep."

She jutted her dainty chin out. "Thank you for your concern, Mr. McTavish. Nonetheless, I shall wait to hear what Lord Ramsbury suggests."

Her pert response earned her a frown from Alasdair, a grin from Harcourt, and a rude snort from Ross.

"I be responsible for me niece, McTavish. If anyone be tellin' her what to do, it be me."

"You'll do no such thing, Uncle." Annoyance flashed in her eyes. "You would do well to remember, you are not my guardian."

Fury contorted Ross's features. "Ye'll do as I say, or—"

"Stubble it, Ross." Harcourt edged his mount beside the Scot, pinning the man's leg between the two horses. "Before I forget I am a gentleman and that my cousin is present."

Antagonism glittered in Ross's eyes.

Yancy gripped Skye's reins against the urge to plant the man a facer, niceties be damned.

"Listen, and listen well, Ross. I'm in charge here until Sethwick says otherwise. You and your niece will do exactly as I say." Yancy pointed at Miss Farnsworth. "She's at the root of the reason I am here in the first place, and though it may have escaped your attention, she could, even now, be in danger."

Miss Farnsworth's eyes widened, and her face drained of color, though to her credit, she steadily returned his gaze.

He set his hat firmer atop his head and gave Ross a dismissive stare. "I don't have the time or patience for prideful posturing. Do you understand?"

Ross's face reddened, and he opened his mouth to retort, but a quelling glare from Miss Farnsworth had him snapping it shut.

Yancy would wager the cur bit his tongue or gnashed his teeth in fury.

Miss Farnsworth shifted slightly in her saddle. The once-perky feather on her hat drooped over the rim like a dead lizard. “Forgive us. Isobel is in danger. What must we do?”

Yancy offered her a reassuring smile. “I don’t believe they discovered Miss McTavish is here—”

“Unless that idiot”—Gregor jabbed his large hand toward Ross—“wavin’ his arm like an oversized, pished crow alerted them.” Palpable contempt radiated from him as he glowered at Ross.

Yancy firmed his lips. “Yes, there is that possibility, but we don’t dare separate. We’ll all ride in the loch’s direction. Once out of sight, Harcourt, you head for the keep, hell bent for help, and alert Sethwick.”

At one time a member of England’s Diplomatic Corps, the monarchy possessed no better tracker than Sethwick.

The grass dipped and swayed with the wind’s renewed onslaught, and the rain dripped steadily from the sky, soaking the ground and making it easier for tracking if the need arose.

“Ross, take your niece and return to the castle as rapidly as possible,” Yancy ordered. “And stay there.”

Miss Farnsworth angled her head. “I shall make straight for the chapel to pray for Isobel’s safe return.”

“Ah, that means we have the privilege of sneakin’ his lordship to yonder pile of pebbles.” Alasdair grinned and winked at his twin.

Shouts, followed by a terrified scream, sailed across the howling wind. A riderless horse charged from the forest.

Chapter 14

After Lord Ramsbury's party halted on the opposite side of the moor, Isobel breathed the minutest iota easier. Thank God, he'd seen her waving from atop the outcrop.

No one could call him a dullard. A lesser man might not have pondered her actions. But Lord Ramsbury wasn't an ordinary man, and the Regent hadn't appointed him War Secretary for nothing.

Then that slowtop, Mr. Ross, had flailed his arms and alerted anyone watching the riders to her presence. Oh, to be able to thwack him, stupid, stupid man. He possessed the common sense of a turnip.

No help for it. She must dash to freedom and warn Lord Ramsbury of the murderers' intent. If her parents had a single notion she had been scaling outcrops and avoiding renegades, they would forbid her to venture beyond the bailey from now until hell sprung wildflowers.

It made no difference. Ramsbury would see that she never ventured out alone again.

Isobel feared certain discovery when the Scot called Baines tethered the mare to a branch a few feet from the cave. Emira had smelled her and wrenched her head in Isobel's direction, but the surly intruder had been in a hurry and hadn't noticed.

Emira raised her head, her eyes rounded and alarmed.

"Shh, girl. It's me," Isobel whispered. The mare mustn't give her away.

Scrambling and sliding her way to the rock base once more, Isobel abandoned her bag of supplies. They would slow her. Her dagger nestled in her half-boot, she managed to mount the horse. Tension churning her stomach, she cautiously guided Emira along the path. Every step the horse took resounded as deafening as a peal of thunder.

Her ears flicking back and forth, the mare lifted her head and bunched her muscles, as if she, too, sensed danger.

Isobel's means of escape lay along a path leading through the woodlands harboring the rogue Scots. By the grace of God, maybe they wouldn't notice her straightway. She would be much closer to the rock run than the opening where she had left the mare tethered when she'd arrived.

Rivulets of rain bathed her face. Her hair had come loose and drooped in a tangled half-knot at her nape. The wind wrapped sopped strands around her neck, and several tendrils stuck to her face.

She shoved them behind her ears and peered into the trees.

A rabbit streaked across the trail.

Emira's ears stiffened, and she jerked her head, stepping backward a few feet.

Isobel's unsteady pulse ran amuck as she soothed the mare.

The meadow paralleled these woods. The intruders, intent on intercepting Lord Ramsbury, would have their backs to her. A couple of minutes would see her past the danger and give her a head start if the clansmen gave chase.

They would.

These blackguards meant to kill her loved ones and to abduct Lydia.

Guilt, sharp and piercing, clawed her belly. She'd put those from the keep in danger. Except, if she hadn't ridden ahead, she wouldn't have stumbled upon them. Perhaps her obstinacy might prove beneficial, after all.

Wiping the rain from her eyes, Isobel's terror and racing pulse reduced her breathing to short puffs.

She would give up her desire to travel if she knew where the intruders had tethered their horses. The two or three minutes it took for them to race to their mounts might give her the time she needed to escape.

Though she risked capture, she must warn Lord Ramsbury. Mouth dry as the Sahara in the summer, Isobel strained her ears and eyes while gently urging the skittish mare onward.

She traveled no more than a few cautious yards into the trees before two bellowing Scots dropped to the ground from overhead. The hulks lunged for her.

Shrieking, she kicked one man in the chest, knocking him on his bum.

The other lurched toward her horse. Several more swung to the earth—giant hairy baboons, every one.

Yanking Emira's reins, Isobel strained to urge her past the shouting throng.

Men grabbed at the terrified horse, and the mare struck with her front leg. Eyes rolling, Emira reared.

Isobel clutched the horse's mane as the panicked beast bucked. Wrenched from the mare's back, Isobel flew through the air. She landed with a strangled screech atop one of the heathens.

The air knocked from her, she lay stunned. The scunner beneath her clamped his arms around her waist. She couldn't breathe. He reeked to high heaven, and she gagged.

With a furious squeal and kick of her powerful rear legs, Emira stampeded from the thicket. Pine needles and dirt churned in her wake.

Isobel's mind raced as she kicked and twisted. She screamed, and then screamed again. Surely, her shrieks and the mare charging from the woods would alert Lord Ramsbury. Emira would run to the keep, and an alarm would be raised when she arrived riderless.

Isobel clawed at the trunk-like arms encircling her. Like a creature possessed, she flailed her fists, connecting with her captor's chin and face as her elbows damaged his ribs and stomach.

He grunted and cursed, yet his hold merely tightened.

She gasped against the pain. Her ribs would sport bruises if they didn't crack from the pressure. Rearing up, she slammed her elbow into his ballocks.

"Gawd dammit, ye bitch." He tossed her aside, and moaning, clutched his groin.

Hearty guffaws and gleeful hoots echoed round the thicket from the ten fierce men facing her.

Isobel scrambled backward until a tree's solid trunk halted her. She tried to gather her wits, to commit as much to memory as she could.

Two swarthy Highland travellers stood beyond the Scotsmen. Expressions somber, their dark gazes swept her. A shimmer of kindness, or perhaps remorse, glinted in their eyes.

The tinkers *had* collaborated with the rebels.

She frowned. For certain, she'd seen these men before. Did they recognize her?

"Get the horses. Now." The man named Angus plowed toward Isobel, sword in hand.

Two men scurried to do his bidding.

I'm going to die.

Petrified, Isobel swallowed convulsively.

Contorted in rage and marred by a ragged scar from his reddish-brown beard to the corner of his left eye, the man named Angus's countenance rivaled that of demons she'd seen depicted in religious books.

Surely, she faced the devil himself.

His emotionless ebony gaze bore into her. Grabbing her hair, he hauled her to her feet.

Excruciating pain lanced her scalp, and Isobel cried out. She clutched at the large hand meshed in her hair.

"Shut up." He gave her a violent shake and slapped her across the mouth.

Her head spun dizzily. Black spots danced before her eyes. Coppery bitterness met her tongue, even as a trail of blood trickled over her chin. She fought to stay conscious.

His hand fisted in her locks, the leader swung his baleful glare to the men. "Dunbar, be she the Farnsworth lass?"

Isobel bit her tongue to stifle her gasp, but a small sound escaped.

Oh, my God.

The leader threw her a piercing scowl.

She and Lydia vaguely resembled each other. Yet, anyone acquainted with either of them wouldn't mistake one for the other. Isobel averted her face. If the travellers recognized her and gave her away, she was as good as dead.

"Dunbar, git yer arse up." Angus pointed his sword at Isobel. "Be she the right wench?"

The man she'd landed upon struggled to stand. Hunkered over and holding his crotch, he glared at her. He shuffled to her and leisurely took her measure from boots to hair.

"*Aye*, Angus. She be the right size, and she be a *verra* bonnie lass." He licked his lips, a lascivious glow in his pale-green eyes.

Isobel darted a glance at the others from the side of her eye.

To a man, they ogled her, lust engraved on their coarse features.

Trembling, she dropped her gaze.

Dunbar dared to grab a handful of hair and run his fingers through the strands. "She has dark hair too."

She snatched her head away and glowered at him.

Wet, her hair appeared darker, but Lydia possessed rich sable hair.

"What of the woman out there?" Angus pointed his short sword in the moor's direction.

Dunbar met Angus's stare and shrugged.

"I *dinnae ken*. Maybe she be one of the Fergusons? Craiglocky be full of young, bonnie women." His lecherous gaze raked over Isobel once more. "We could take the other wench too. We'd have a *hoor* 'til we reach Dounnich."

Base desire tinged his words.

Angus thrust his sword threateningly, the point resting on Dunbar's Adam's apple. "We be takin' one woman only. And she better be the lass MacHardy paid for. Ye *ken* what's at stake."

Dunbar motioned to Isobel. "This one. She be wearin' black like I be told she would."

A traitor at Craiglocky? Her gaze clashed with Dunbar's. "Who told you there—?"

"I told ye to shut up." Angus swung his beefy fist.

Chapter 15

Isobel.

Yancy swung Skye toward the scream, intent on charging straight into the woods, caution be hanged. Moments later, eight roaring Scotsmen erupted from the trees.

Their plaids identified them as Blackhalls and MacGraths.

He threw off his hat. “Draw your weapons.”

Unbuttoning his coat with one hand, he quickly freed his sword with the other. Seconds later, one shaggy cur toppled from his saddle, an arrow deep in his chest.

Mouth gaping, Yancy speared his attention to Miss Farnsworth. *I’ll be damned.*

Stern concentration written on her face, she let fly with another arrow. Her nostrils flared as she hit her mark square on, and a man toppled to the ground.

Swords drawn, Alasdair and Ross flanked her while Gregor and Harcourt took positions beside Yancy. The men awaited his orders.

“Ross, Harcourt, get her out of here.” Yancy jabbed his sword at Miss Farnsworth. “Miss Farnsworth, go. Now. We’ll hold them off.”

“I can help.” She took aim once more, and with remarkable precision, sent a third Scot to hell.

“Dammit, woman, do as I say.” Yancy was having none of it. He already had one defiant woman to rescue. He didn’t need another.

Alasdair laid a hand on her arm. “Go, lass. I *canna* fight if I *ken* ye are in danger.”

Biting her lip, she gave a sharp nod.

"God keep you safe." Her gaze swept everyone. "All of you."

Harcourt grinned crookedly at Yancy. "I'm not leaving."

The Scots bore down upon them.

Ross grabbed Miss Farnsworth's reins and handed them to her. "Lydia, get movin'."

With a final glance at the men charging across the moor, Miss Farnsworth and Ross spun their mounts about and thundered away.

Hunched low in her saddle, she glanced back at them. "We'll send—"

The raging wind stole the rest of her words.

Sword raised, Yancy tore his attention from the oncoming menace and met Harcourt's calm gaze. "I don't trust Ross. Do you?"

Harcourt's brows shot to a vee, and he twisted in his saddle to stare at his cousin's retreating form.

"Blister it, I don't either." Sheathing his sword, he gave a sharp salute. "Try not to get yourself killed, Yancy."

"Five to three. Seems unfair to me, brother." Gregor waved his blade at the approaching men.

Not the best odds, nevertheless Yancy had wagered and won against far worse.

"*Aye*, but *dinnae* be mad at the lass for dispatchin' three of the bloody scunners." Alasdair winked at his twin. "She be tryin' to help, not ruin our fun."

Emitting battle cries wild enough to cause the hair on the back of Yancy's neck to stand straight up, the McTavish brothers surged forward.

In the following frenzy, Yancy came to appreciate Sethwick's kinsman all that much more. While he fought with a monstrous brute, they each cut down a bull of a man.

"Come on, *Sassenach*," the Scot Yancy battled taunted. "Ye be *nae* match fer a Blackhall."

"Perhaps, not in brute size." Yancy nicked the behemoth's forearm. "But since one of my ballocks is larger than your brain, the outcome is certain."

The Scotsman growled and swung his weapon wildly.

Yancy's slighter build enabled him to maneuver much quicker, and though repelling each of the Scot's mighty blows threatened to dislocate Yancy's shoulder, he waited for the opportune moment.

Sword raised high, a smug sneer splitting his broad face, the Scot lunged. "Say a prayer before I send ye to hell."

"Better that you say one." Yancy swiveled and sliced his blade neatly between the man's ribs.

Astonishment swept the Blackhall's face before his eyes glazed over. He crashed to the sodden earth, sending muddy spray in every direction.

Yancy spun to assist the McTavishs.

Both now battled on foot, their opponents every bit as huge as the enormous, grinning twins.

Dismounting, Yancy snatched his dirk and prepared to enter the fray should Alasdair or Gregor need help. He needn't have bothered.

Less than a minute later, the remaining assailants lay staring into the tumultuous sky, rain pouring into their sightless eyes.

Dripping wet and spattered with blood and grime, the brothers laughed and embraced. With a final pat to the others back, they trudged to their horses.

Yancy scraped his sopping hair from his forehead and turned to do the same. They had been lucky. The Blackhalls and MacGraths had earned their reputations as merciless fighters.

A coarse shout sounded.

He spun around. A wounded Scot pointed a pistol at Gregor's back.

"Gregor!" Yancy bolted toward the MacGrath.

Gregor whirled to face Yancy then dove to his left. The ball slammed into his side. He convulsed and collapsed.

With a flick of his wrist, Yancy sent his blade sailing into the renegade's bullish neck.

Burn in hell.

Before the dead man plunged, face first, to the dirt, Yancy sprinted to Gregor.

Anguish chiseled on his face, Alasdair crouched above his brother, pressing his hands to Gregor's crimson side.

Gregor lay ashen and unconscious. The nasty gash paralleling his hairline oozed blood. He'd collided with a rock when he fell.

Yancy dropped to his knees. "Is he . . .?"

Alasdair shook his head. Voice unsteady, he managed to mutter, "*Nae*, but I need to get him to the keep."

Yancy yanked off his coat then his waistcoat. He unwrapped his cravat. "Here, we can use the waistcoat as a bandage and tie the neckcloth around his ribs."

Once they'd secured the makeshift dressing, Yancy removed the blanket and basket from Alasdair's saddle. He helped hoist Gregor onto the horse's back.

Yancy retrieved Gregor's mount. "Will he follow you, or do I need to tie him to the halter?"

"He'll follow." Arms wrapped around his brother, Alasdair frowned. "Yer not returnin' to the castle?"

"No. Isobel's out there, alone and no doubt terrified." Yancy secured the basket and blanket to the rear of Skye's saddle before swinging into the seat. He patted Alasdair's shoulder. "Get your brother home, and ask Sethwick to send a search party."

Yancy pointed Skye to the forest. "I'm going after her."

Chapter 16

Isobel forced her leaden eyes open, regretting doing so instantly. Crushing agony hammered her skull and sent a wave of nausea scraping at her throat. She tried to swallow the burning bile, but a filthy cloth crammed into her mouth and tied behind her head made the task difficult.

Her face and lower lip ached. Memories hurtled to the forefront of her mind. She had been planted a facer by that fiend of a man. He'd yanked her hair, too, which explained the tenderness behind her head.

What had become of Yancy and the others? Were they dead?

A wave of guilt impaled her. The blame for endangering them rested upon her. Stinging tears leaked from the corners of her eyes as wrenching pain seared her chest with such brutal intensity, she feared she suffered a seizure.

She should have heeded him.

He hadn't been trying to control her, but had been intent on keeping her safe. If only he and Ewan hadn't been so protective and had told her their worries, she wouldn't have been so stubborn.

Please, God, let them be safe. And, please, send someone to help me.

The renegades had dared to trespass onto Ewan's lands, their intent murderous. Something powerful drove them to take such a monumental risk.

Oh God, they think I'm Lydia.

What would her abductors do when they discovered they had the wrong woman?

Isobel tried to swallow again, gagging on the rag. She had never been so thirsty in her life. Terror dried her parched mouth further. She tried touching her throbbing face and found her hands tied behind her.

Trussed up tighter than a Christmas goose.

She shook her fingers and wrists, gasping as shards of pain streaked to her elbows.

A dank, earthy smell permeated the air. A gust of cold air speared her, and she shivered. She must be outdoors, and from the clammy material clinging to her, she would guess wet as fresh-washed fleece.

From the raucous chorus of frogs ebbing and flowing, a pond must be nearby. Another torrent of gut-wrenching fear slammed into her.

Did her abductors mean to defile her? She'd seen the hunger in Dunbar and the other Scots' lascivious gazes. If they discovered she wasn't Lydia, they would ravish her in less time than it took to butter bread.

Terror squeezed her ribs, and she couldn't inhale.

No, she wouldn't panic. Calmness and reason must be her weapons. If only she'd been conscious while they traveled, she would have an idea of her location and possible escape routes.

Forcing her body to relax, Isobel drew in a bracing breath and counted to ten, then exhaled bit by bit. She must keep her wits about her. She'd gotten into this mess; she may very well have to get out of it alone.

First, where was she?

Cracking an eyelid open, she surveyed her surroundings. She lay in a smallish cave—not much more than a hollow in the hillside—barely large enough to stretch full length in.

She carefully turned her head in the direction of the raspy murmur of male voices.

A few feet beyond the cavern's entrance, her abductors sat before a fire eating what appeared to be roasted rabbit. A pair of drowsy horses stood tethered to a pine tree beside a trickling stream.

Where had the gypsies got to? And the other Scots?

Judging from the few stars visible between the pewter clouds and scraggy tree tops, night had long since fallen. The storm had passed while she'd been unconscious.

How far had they travelled? Avoiding the main roads and in foul weather, carrying an insensate woman, they couldn't have covered more than ten miles.

One of her captors lifted a flask to his lips and took a long pull. He belched and passed wind.

Angus.

The other guffawed before tipping his flask and greedily gulping the contents.

Dunbar.

Stifling a groan, Isobel managed to roll onto her side. The tight cords binding her arms and legs tore the tender flesh. The renegades weren't taking a chance that she would escape. She would have marks for days, perhaps even permanent scars.

Something tickled her palm. She released a weak screech and struggled to her knees. Brushing her hands together, she tried to dislodge the creature, doubtless a hairy spider or other repulsive, crawling pest the likes of which she didn't want to imagine.

Angus swung his attention her way, his expression unreadable. After tearing a leg from the animal he'd been eating, he rose and withdrew a dirk from his belt.

Dunbar gave her a leering look and grabbed his crotch, bucking into his hand. He laughed and took a swig from his flask while stroking himself.

Drunken sod.

Palpable loathing and fear sluiced Isobel. She sat on her heels and winced as her numb legs protested the added weight.

Angus trudged up the gentle slope to the cave, rabbit leg in one hand, ugly blade in the other. Did he mean to dine while disposing of her?

He bent to enter the hollow, his large frame filling the space. The fetid odor of his grimy plaid, combined with body sweat and the rancid grease in his beard, sent her stomach reeling.

He smiled as if reading her thoughts and tossed the charred rabbit leg into her lap. "Turn around. I'll cut yer hands loose."

Isobel shuffled on her knees and presented her back.

The cold blade sliced through the rope binding her wrist. She cried out as feeling returned to her numb hands. A thousand hot, needle-fine, coals pricked her fingers.

"Eat. We ride in ten minutes." Angus returned to the fire.

Plopping onto her bum, she rubbed her wrists until the most extreme pain receded. She untied the gag and flinched. The cloth tore at the dried blood caked at the corner of her mouth.

She ran her tongue along her teeth. All there and none seemed loose. Tentatively touching the tip to the sore area on her mouth, she encountered the split lip she'd expected.

Grimacing against her protesting muscles, she leaned forward and worked the knot securing her ankles free while covertly eyeing the two men.

They meant to ride at night.

Those tracking her would find trailing them more difficult, and she wouldn't be able to commit the route they traveled to memory as easily.

An owl hooted, the echoes haunting and lonely.

She didn't much care for owls. Not that she believed that nonsense about the birds being harbingers of death or that seeing one in daylight brought about bad luck.

Using the cavern wall for support, Isobel stood. Her

ankle twinged after the violent connection with the brick-like chest of the Scot she'd kicked in the woods.

The forgotten rabbit leg rolled to the ground. Just as well. She doubted her rebelling stomach would retain anything solid.

Legs trembling, she swayed as lightheadedness engulfed her. Closing her eyes, she raised a shaky hand to her forehead. Female weakness be hanged. Gently probing her swollen cheek, she felt for broken bones.

God's blood, her face and head hurt.

Had she suffered a concussion? If so, riding so soon was pure foolishness, but what choice had she?

She dared a tiny snort. These devils weren't going to delay their journey because she ailed. Angus, no doubt, would flop her, belly down, behind one of the saddles and bind her hands and feet.

Imagine what that would do to her already-throbbing head and roiling stomach?

Gritty determination compelled her to the cave's entrance.

The men paused and looked at her.

"Might I get a drink from the stream?" Afraid she would topple over, she didn't dare point. "And I also need a moment of privacy."

Mortification suffused her. Discussing something so intimate with complete strangers, especially men of their ilk, galled.

Dunbar released a lewd chuckle. "I'll take ye into the bushes, lassie."

Isobel dredged up a dark scowl. The man was a veritable pig, and she would like nothing better than to see him run through. Or mayhap, given the opportunity, she'd do it herself. Her ability to wield a blade brought her no shame.

My dagger.

Had the blade gone undetected, and remained snug in her boot? She wriggled her ankle the merest bit.

Yes.

Wisdom weighed against the urge to draw the weapon at once.

Wait. You'll not get two chances, and you cannot take on both of these barbarians at once.

"Those will suffice." She inclined her head the tiniest bit in the direction of some shoulder-high shrubberies across the narrow creek.

"*Shite*, now I be playin' lady's maid." Angus rose once more. Grumbling, he strode to the horses where he retrieved a length of rope.

Feeling slightly stronger, Isobel wobbled a few steps beyond the cave. The night air, though brisk, did much to revive her. As did the knowledge her dagger lay within her boot.

The owl hooted again, its eerie call sending a shiver skittering across her shoulders.

She clasped her hands to her middle. "Where are you taking me?"

Ripping a piece of meat with his teeth, Dunbar jerked his hand to the north. "Home, for now."

Angus returned, uncoiling the rope. "Lift yer arms."

She reluctantly raised them. "What do you intend to do?"

"This." He looped the line about her waist.

Rigid as Mrs. Bracegirdle's back during Sunday sermons, Isobel flattened her lips and stared past his shoulder as his chest pressed into hers—deliberately, she would vow.

After giving a final tug, he pulled several arms' length of rope free of the coil.

"Go on with ye."

Isobel fingered the rough restraint, anger and disbelief

tempering her speech. "You actually mean to tether me while I get a drink and relieve myself?"

"*Aye*, if ye want privacy. Or else I be lettin' Dunbar escort ye." A vile chuckle rumbled from him.

Cretin.

Squaring her shoulders, she lifted her chin and proceeded to pick her way behind some low-lying shrubs bordering the pathetic excuse of a stream. Nothing like exposing her bum for the world to see.

Once she'd taken care of her personal business—almost toppling onto her face twice from dizziness—she crouched before the brook and scooped water into her mouth. The cold liquid tasted wonderful, and she drank her fill.

Dampening her cloak's edge, she attempted to gingerly wash her face. Without a looking glass, she couldn't be certain she'd cleansed away the blood, but the cool water should help reduce the swelling.

Gently patting her cut lip, she glanced to the fire.

The men, absorbed in an intense, whispered conversation—or perhaps an argument—gestured toward her every now and again.

Angling her back, she tore a strip from her chemise. She hung the shred on a branch out of their sight then quickly arranged a few hand-sized rocks into an arrow pointing north.

"Aren't ye done yet, fer God's sake?" Angus tugged the rope, his harsh voice cutting through the night.

Holding the last stone, Isobel froze. "Yes, I'm coming."

She took a couple of steps, shaking out her skirt and cloak to distract them.

A few moments later, after dousing the fire, Angus mounted his horse.

Dunbar reached for her. "Up ye go, lass."

Isobel swatted his hands away.

"I'm not riding with you. I shall walk." She gathered her wrap closer and marched past him only to jolt to a stop when the rope cut into her stomach.

Angus dangled his end, a cruel grin curving his mouth. "*Nae*, ye *wilna* walk. Ye look like ye'll topple if ye sneeze. It be nigh on fifty miles to Dounnich, and we be in a hurry."

He'd revealed their destination.

So typical of men, underestimating a woman. She might not have traveled much, but she'd studied maps aplenty. A few more clues and she would determine her exact location.

He leaned frontward and rested his forearm on his saddle. "Either ye let him lift ye before me lass, or ye ride with him. It be yer choice."

Hands fisted and teeth clamped, Isobel stamped to Angus. She had no choice. Riding with Dunbar put her virtue at serious risk, even atop a horse. He would molest her the entire journey.

Dunbar shambled forward. Scooping her into his arms as if she weighed no more than a bairn, he seized the opportunity to paw her breast and thigh. Fondling her bottom, he planted her sideways on Angus's horse.

"Get your filthy hands off me." Isobel swung her legs at his chest.

He leaped away, a lecherous promise in his disturbing gaze.

Both men guffawed.

"I can mount a horse myself, gentlemen." Shoulders stiffened in rage, she wished them a speedy journey to the lowest level of hell.

"We be no gentlemen, lass, and I *winna* deny Dunbar his bit o' fun. Or me either." Angus buried his face in her hair. He snuffled loudly and groped her breasts. "Ye smell like spring and flowers."

You smell like something died and took up residence in your ratty beard.

Her skin crawled from his stench and their lecherous handling. She feared for her virtue. There wasn't an iota of decency or valor in either man.

"I *dinnae* recall a lass who smelled so *guid*." Like an ill-mannered hound, he sniffed her again.

"I assure you, the same cannot be said for you or your friend." Isobel shoved his hand away and wrinkled her nose, choking back a gag.

Another shout of laughter erupted from Angus. "Damn me, if I hadn't promised I would deliver ye to MacHardy, I'd keep ye for meself."

That was twice he'd mentioned MacHardy, the wretch behind the turmoil with Lydia. The baron would be furious when he found they'd abducted the wrong woman. Given his reputation, Isobel had better escape before then.

"Why *dinnae* ye marry the wench yerself? Ye may not be the Laird, but ye be the war chief, and ye have more say than the laird does with the clan." Dunbar wiped his nose on his arm before mounting his horse.

He slanted Isobel a calculating gaze. "*Canna* the same thing be accomplished if'n *ye* marry the lass?"

She clenched her teeth to stifle her squeak of horror.

Angus stared at Dunbar for an extensive, disquieting moment.

The frogs had become eerily silent as well.

The damnable owl hooted again, and she started. Her nerves were tauter than Artemis's bowstring.

Angus's gaze dipped to her face, and for the first time, she saw something flicker in the depths of his wintry eyes.

He's truly considering it?

She'd rather die.

"Aren't you going to remove this?" Isobel plucked at the rope.

Leaping from the horse and charging through the forest held real appeal at the moment, the consequences be damned.

"*Aye*, if ye promise not to try to run." Angus steered the horse between two trees. "I would have to knock ye out again."

She twisted to gape at him.

His eyes, once again as emotionless as a dead person's, calmly returned her gaze.

He *would* hit her again, without a qualm. And likely enjoy it too. She'd heard about men such as he; men who enjoyed beating women.

Angus wasn't a man to underestimate. His vileness penetrated to his soul. If he hadn't already sold it to the devil.

"Mister . . ."

"Just Angus will do ye."

"Angus, I'm a gently-bred woman. You don't really think I would go pelting off alone into these woods?" She shuddered delicately and clutched her throat, widening her eyes in a manner she hoped made her appear vulnerable.

"There are all manner of wild beasts out there." She made her voice quiver and choked on a fake sob as she fluttered a hand toward the trees. "If I were that foolish, how would I ever find my way home? I would need a man's guidance, for sure."

About as much as she needed a man to help her don her stockings or win a game of chess.

Lord Ramsbury's green eyes, shining with amusement during their chess game, interrupted her playacting.

Real, remorse-induced tears misted her eyes.

He cannot be dead. Even if he was a cad and a scoundrel. *And my fickle heart is set on him.*

Angus grunted and shrugged, the movement releasing a fresh waft of fetidness and forcing her wayward reveries back to the present.

She batted her eyelashes and formed her mouth into a *moue*. "I would be an imbecile to attempt escape."

A Drury Lane actor performed no better.

"*Aye*, that be true." Angus clawed at his face, scratching his beard with dirt-encrusted fingernails.

She narrowed her eyes trying to see amongst the bristly hairs. Did the unruly bush harbor louse? She eased away as another shudder scuttled across her flesh.

Devil a bit, he'd touched her hair.

Now, she would be scratching her head, envisioning the horde of tiny bugs scampering to live there. What she wouldn't give for a bath and a way to wash her hair.

Angus's huge hand settled on one breast, pinching the nipple. She shoved it away amid his laughter. Whether his beard harbored a whole slew of vermin was the least of her worries.

Isobel's captors rode hard, barely stopping long enough for the horses to rest. Desperation, bleak and daunting, plagued her as they plodded onward. Mile after mile she journeyed farther from Craiglocky, and she didn't detect a single sign anyone followed them.

No horses whickering in the distance; no smoky tendrils spiraling heavenward; no unexplained sudden hushing of birdsong, or outraged red squirrels' chatter.

Dunbar let slip his clan's name less than twenty-four hours into their journey. Dense as wormy cabbage, the dolt boasted of MacHardy's promise to give the Blackhalls a portion of Farnsworth's lands for delivering Lydia safely to the baron.

Isobel continued to tear strips from her chemise to leave as markers, and whenever she had the opportunity, used sticks, rocks, even bones from their meals, to form crude arrows or words.

Would anybody see her clues? None had been in the open, lest Angus or Dunbar catch her.

After stopping to relieve themselves late last night, Isobel had dared to creep a few extra feet from Angus.

"Stop right there." His face a mask of fury, he stomped to her. He circled her throat with his mammoth hand and tightened his fingers until tears smarted in her eyes. "Be warned, wench. If ye try to run, I'll break yer legs."

Struggling to breathe, she gasped and tore at his fingers.

Chuckling evilly, he released her. "The baron only cares about marryin' and beddin' ye. Ye *dinnae* need to be able to walk."

Chapter 17

Saddle sore after two days of rigorous riding, Yancy drew Skye to a halt before a ramshackle crofter's cottage. Bone weary, he dismounted and patted the gelding's neck.

"Well done, old friend."

The horse blew out a gusty breath, no doubt every bit as exhausted as his master. Probably as hungry, too.

Yancy's heart demanded he press onward until he could no longer see, but wisdom and fear for Skye's safety insisted he stop for the night.

He had found Isobel's bag of supplies and added them to the picnic stash. He'd also found the Scot's hideaway in the cave and helped himself to cooking utensils, the least-soiled blanket, what little food they had stored, and, saints be praised, two bottles of whisky.

Why the hell had they been holed up in a cavern for days, maybe weeks? Instinct told him someone at the castle, or perhaps with access to Craiglocky, was involved.

Yancy swallowed a frustrated growl and raked his hand through his hair. Not as equipped as he would like—no balm for is aching arse—at least he possessed some stores, and they would suffice for a few days.

The Scots were four, maybe five hours ahead of him. He'd lost their trail yesterday and had to circle back—twice—losing precious time.

Damn, he needed Sethwick here. *Now.*

Isobel's outings had no more been a clandestine lovers' tryst than him stumbling upon Matilda in the conservatory had been. He'd allowed jealousy to fuel his suspicions, something that chagrined and confused him.

The unfamiliar emotion warped his reasoning and distorted his focus.

"Sorry about the poor accommodations. I shall let you eat your fill of grass in the morning, and I promise a thorough grooming and extra oats when this business is over." After unsaddling Skye, Yancy hobbled the gelding underneath a semblance of a lean-to.

He ran his hand over the gelding's shoulder. "This is better than last night, don't you think?"

Yancy had spent the first night under the trees and woke up to an irate squirrel pelting him with early acorns and scolding worse than a fishwife in her cups.

Skye nudged Yancy in the chest, and he obligingly rubbed the horse's forehead. "Sorry, no treats just now."

Stretching, the muscles in his buttocks and lower back protesting, he faced north and heaved a sigh.

Isobel.

How fared she? Had the sods harmed her? Where did they take her? For what purpose?

Not knowing ate at his normally stoic emotions.

So help him God, they would pay. Every inclination told him MacHardy had initiated the attack and abduction, albeit indirectly.

Why take Isobel? Convenience?

It didn't make sense.

To Yancy's knowledge MacHardy held no grievance against Craiglocky's laird. Sethwick had a legendary temper, although not often roused. He would wreak vengeance on everyone involved, no matter their excuses.

Isobel's reputation lay in complete tatters, even in the less pompous and pious Highlands. A young woman held captive by a band of renegade Scots for hours, let alone days, was compromised beyond redemption, no matter her social standing or familial connections.

His gut clenched as if a jagged blade twisted his innards.

God, what Isobel might be enduring.

Vengeance demanded he harshly punish those responsible for ruining her and wounding Gregor.

How did the giant Scot fare?

Recovering, Yancy prayed. Few men could boast the inherent decency the McTavish twins possessed.

Collecting the pilfered goods, he entered the hut and set about lighting one of Isobel's tapers. He rummaged and found a tin plate to use for a candleholder atop a lopsided table surrounded by four uneven chairs.

Dust covered every surface, but the place wasn't too shabby, better than the outdoors with half-crazed squirrels lurking about. Most likely, the remote building served as a hunting cottage.

The door seemed sturdy and so did the two square, shuttered windows in the main room. An intact soot-stained, stone fireplace commandeered most of one wall, and a side chamber boasted a bed, complete with a straw tick and bedding, the cleanliness of which he couldn't determine in the dim light.

A quick inspection of the shelving revealed a mismatched set of dishes, a tin containing more candles, soap, a candlestick, cooking utensils, a worn towel, and a few raggedy cloths. A good-sized kettle hung from an iron hook above a dry sink, and no vermin or other pests called the hut home.

Outside, a sizable stack of firewood stood beside a washtub and bucket. He would indulge and build a fire to take the edge from the night's chill and to dry his clothes.

An hour later, he sat before a roaring fire, having eaten a portion of his store of food. He'd taken an apple to Skye and received a nicker in appreciation.

Yancy had tugged off his thoroughly ruined Wellingtons, standing them upon the hearth to one side of the fire. His drying stockings and coat hung from the wobbly backs of the spare chairs.

He rasped a hand over his bristly jaw. A wash and a shave would be welcome. However, he hadn't a razor.

If this humble abode boasted a well, he hadn't seen it. Perhaps a stream or creek meandered nearby. He would have to find water for Skye tomorrow, in any event.

Legs stretched before him, he stared into the mesmerizing flames. He could almost see Isobel's beautiful face, her mouth curved in welcome and a challenge in the depths of her blue-green eyes. Her sweet voice raised in laughter echoed in the recesses of his mind.

Yancy shut his eyes against the pain of remembrance. When had she come to mean so much to him? Despite his determination to avoid that deuced emotion, he loved her.

God knew he hadn't wanted to love any woman, had strived to avoid such a problematic entanglement, but the sentiment penetrated his soul despite his best efforts to remain impervious. He could no more deny the truth of his affection for Isobel than he could wipe the sparkling stars from the sky or touch a rainbow's colors.

He loved her.

Wholly and absolutely with such intensity, he wouldn't have believed such emotion possible had he not experienced the euphoria for himself.

He better understood the captivation Sethwick and the others had willingly succumbed to—why they sacrificed their oaths of bachelorhood.

The realization that he loved Isobel elicited no negative reaction, no jump in Yancy's pulse or oaths of incredulity. No, rather the knowledge surrounded him in contentment and peace.

A sense of coming home, at last.

"I'll find you, Isobel, I promise."

And when he did, they would be wed by the first Scot handy.

Dounnich House
The Blackhall Stronghold

Isobel paced back and forth in the stark chamber she'd been thrust into yesterday. No simple manor, Dounnich House was a rustic, medieval castle, older than Craiglocky Keep.

From what she'd observed as a brute hustled her to this chamber, the keep was in sad repair, in need of a good clean, and rodents obviously had free run of the place.

Drafty and reeking of God knew what, she shouldn't have been at all surprised if a goodly number of spirits, evil no doubt, roamed the corridors at night, moaning.

Pushing her hair behind her ears, she curved her mouth, forming more of a rueful grimace than a true smile. Being held prisoner wasn't at all the sort of adventure she'd desperately yearned for. A damp whoosh of air billowed through the window, and she clasped the cloak more snugly around her neck.

Surely, Ewan had assembled a contingent of clansmen to pursue her. How long had it taken them to discover her absence and that of the others? Had anyone survived and made their way back to the keep?

Bitter tears stung behind her eyelids, and her throat convulsed against the dread that seemed permanently lodged there.

By day, her hope rested in the knowledge the motley Scots that attacked her in Craiglocky's woodlands hadn't made an appearance. She prayed, almost hourly, they'd been defeated and Yancy and her cousins had been spared.

Nights proved the worst, however.

Isobel's imagination ran rampant, and she pictured Yancy impaled by a sword, his spectacular green eyes staring sightlessly heavenward. She cried herself to sleep every night, smothering her self-recriminating sobs within her cloak.

She tried to keep warm by walking about the dismal chamber wearing her filthy cape and hugging herself. The movement helped ease the hollow ache of an empty belly as well. She'd eaten scant little over the past days.

Last night, a frightened maid, scarcely more than a child, had crept into Isobel's chamber. Eyes downcast and without uttering a single word, the girl shoved a bowl of flavorless broth and a piece of dark, dry bread, along with a tankard of ale into Isobel's hands.

Two burly clansmen stood outside the entrance, relocking the heavy door the instant the maid departed.

Isobel had yet to break her fast today, although the time must be well past noon. Her stomach's rumbling resonated to her backbone.

"Is starvation part of their blasted plan?" She pressed her hands to her protesting middle and perused the meager chamber.

Absent of all but basic necessities—a thin pallet, a rough blanket, and a chipped chamber pot—the stone room boasted the same hospitality as a dungeon cell.

She wasn't permitted a fire, and the single candle she possessed would last but a few hours more.

An arched window opened onto a narrow ledge three stories above the ground. Once more, as she'd done at least a score of times already, Isobel fully opened the shutter and peered through the narrow slit.

Her room faced a lush meadow where several head of shaggy Highland cattle milled about. A narrow track led into the dense forest she'd passed through on their last leg to the keep.

No battlement surrounded the rear of the castle, the singular thing in her favor. Well, that and the apparent lack of patrols or lookouts at the keep's rear. A lumpy band of crumbled stones, partially covered by earth and grass, revealed a wall had been present at one time.

Unless a person had the ability to climb like a spider or fly, this side of the keep appeared impenetrable. No windows graced the lower levels, and only a child or smallish woman could pass through the narrow, rectangular openings serving that purpose on this floor.

She slapped the casement in frustration then winced as stinging pain lanced to her shoulder. Not a tree or lattice to aid with escaping. The lone blanket tied to her cloak wasn't long enough to hang from the window and use as a makeshift rope, and had it been, the chamber contained nothing to use as an anchor.

Other than climbing onto the ledge and creeping to the oriel's tiny balcony, at least four windows away, fleeing proved impossible.

She closed her eyes and leaned against the cold wall. Heights terrified her. God's bones, the very notion of slinking along the thin ribbon and climbing over the balustrade in long skirts made her lightheaded. If her stomach weren't as empty as Hannah's womb, she would cast up her accounts.

Besides, that chamber, and the others between her and her only hope of salvation, could be occupied and someone might sound the alarm as she skulked by.

One arm braced against the sash, she hung over the wide sill. Too bad she couldn't change her hair into wings like the mythical Persinette and fly from this jail.

Think, Isobel.

She still possessed her dagger since no opportunity to escape had presented itself on the journey.

Angus had left the dratted rope secured to her middle the entire time. He'd tied her hands to the cord at night and slept with the other end circling his bullish arm.

A shadow fell across the ledge from the room beside hers.

Isobel dove back inside. Peering between the shutter and the rough wall, she held her breath as a raven-haired child climbed onto the windowsill.

Dear God, he could fall.

"*Keck,* no, György. You are too *tikni* to be near the window." A beautiful young woman, her hair and waist tied with colorful scarves, appeared above him. "Remember I told you. You mustn't climb on the sill. You might fall."

Isobel mashed her face closer to the gap, staring in disbelief.

Highland travellers? *Here*?

"I want to go *keré,* Tasara." Looking up at her, György's lower lip trembled. "I miss *Dya* and *Dat*."

She kissed the top of his head. "I know. I miss Mother and Father too." Tasara stared into the distance, her expression troubled. She gave him a quick hug. "We'll go home soon."

Picking him up, she cast a woeful look to the trees and then withdrew from the window.

"You promised *Dat* and Keir and Jamie and . . . and the clan would come for us." The boy's voice quaked.

"They will, *bad inderi*. They will." Doubt and despair shadowed her words.

The unmistakable sound of sobbing and murmured words of comfort carried through the open portal.

A commotion in the corridor had her hastily shutting the shutter. She flew on silent feet to the pallet and had no sooner sat than the key scraped in the lock. Folding her hands in her lap, she willed her heart to return to a steady cadence.

A parade of people, all laden with goods, marched into the chamber. One Scotsman bore a chair, another an armful of wood, and two others dragged in a copper hip bath followed by footmen toting pails of water. The servant with the wood immediately set about lighting a fire.

One maid held toiletries, another towels, and a third stockings, stays, and a chemise, and the fourth, an exquisite periwinkle gown and slippers.

"Come, lass." A thin-faced maid darted a nervous peek at the men loitering in the room. "We needs to see ye bathed and yer hair washed. Yer weddin' be this evenin'."

Chapter 18

Isobel's heart seized for a moment as the breath hissed from between her stiff lips.

Hell, Hades, and Purgatory.

She stood, and the room spun. She'd risen too quickly.

"I'm not taking a bath, and I most certainly am not getting married." Drawing on every ounce of courage she possessed, she raised her chin. "I have been abducted and am held prisoner. When my family—"

Angus sauntered into the overfull chamber. His coffee-brown gaze slithered over her. "Either ye let the lasses help ye undress and bathe, or Dunbar and these laddies be havin' the pleasure."

The knaves undressing her with their eyes elbowed one another and whispered amongst themselves.

Tears of frustration welled. They would find her dagger, sure as spittle flew in the wind.

She twisted her hands in her cloak.

"I'm not accustomed to so many eyes upon me during my toilette, especially strangers." She sucked in a trembling breath, aware he preferred cowering, defeated females. Making her voice quiver, she asked, "Might I be permitted to disrobe and bathe myself?"

Begging this despicable oaf galled. "Please?"

He tilted his head and stared at her a lengthy moment.

Surely, he would deny her request.

"*Aye*. Two lassies will stay and help ye wash yer hair and get ye dressed." He dug at his beard then gave his chest a vigorous scratch. "Me men be outside should ye try anythin'."

He ought to consider a good scrub and a shave himself.

Isobel released her breath and unfastened her cloak. She might yet be able to keep her dagger concealed. "That's acceptable, thank you."

It wasn't acceptable, but what choice had she? No one except Maura had seen her naked since she wore diapers, and Isobel had known the nursemaid her entire life.

More tears threatened. Isobel blinked the weakness away and dropped her cloak onto the pallet. She swayed slightly as another wave of dizziness engulfed her. Her head still hurt from Angus's blow, and that, combined with lack of food, caused her lightheadedness.

"Ye two stay." He pointed to the skinny girl and the servant holding the gown.

Everyone else obediently turned to file from the room, Angus at the rear. He took her measure, his keen gaze lingering far too long on her bosom. "Have ye eaten?"

Surprised he would concern himself with something so mundane, Isobel returned his appraisal and resisted the urge to cover her breasts. "No, not today. I had some broth and bread last night."

"That be all?" He pivoted toward the guards waiting in the entrance, bitter lines carved into his scarred face. Dead calm, he stared pointedly at the messy contents of trays strewn outside the door. "Ye ate her food?"

His tone chilled her to her toes and raised the hair on her arms.

The sentries exchanged anxious glances.

A second later, Angus plowed his fists into their faces, one right after the other.

They slumped to the floor. Blood dripped from one man's gashed cheek and oozed from the clearly broken nose of the other.

Trepidation glinting in their eyes, the rest of the terrified servants stood stock-still.

They reminded Isobel of a family of mice cornered by a ravenous fox, not daring to flee, yet certain if they remained, they would be the beast's next victim.

His knuckles bloodied, Angus pointed to the youngest Scotswoman. "Fetch a generous tray for the lass, includin' ale, and if ye dare to eat a crumb, I be guttin' ye."

He jammed his thumb in the door's direction. "Git. Send Dunbar to stand guard, and take these worthless pieces of *shite* with ye."

Angus kicked the nearest guard in the ribs.

The servants scampered to do his bidding, except the women he'd told to remain.

If the situation weren't dire, Isobel might have appreciated the ridiculousness of the oversized men cowering before Angus. What kind of man inspired such intimidation?

She didn't really want to know. What she'd experienced at his hands explained much about the man. What humanity he had once possessed had long since departed.

He turned his peculiar, dispassionate gaze on her. He had rendered two giants unconscious, and not a whit of emotion lingered on his bland countenance.

Despite the fire burning brightly, she shivered but refused to avert her eyes.

His full lips edged upward a fraction. "Eat first, and then bathe. I *canna* have ye swoonin' durin' the ceremony."

MacHardy's here? *Already*?

She'd missed his arrival. No surprise there. The gatehouse entrance graced the opposite side of the keep. The urge to tear to the window and screech for help until she was hoarse choked Isobel.

Assuredly, Ewan tracked her, but she couldn't wait for her brother. She must escape before MacHardy saw her and revealed she wasn't Lydia. Isobel's very life depended on it.

Angus strode to the door as the women hustled about, preparing her bath and repeatedly sent him apprehensive glances beneath their lashes.

"When . . ." Isobel licked her chapped lips, forcing her panic aside. How much time did she have to escape? "When does the ceremony take place?"

He turned halfway back to her. "As soon as the rector arrives. Should be sometime before the evenin' meal."

Angus smiled then, a humorless bending of his wide mouth. "It's meant to be our weddin' feast."

Yancy loosely tied Skye's reins to a branch before squatting and inspecting the tracks pressed into the drying ground. They'd been made by a horse carrying two riders, and not more than a few hours old, if he had to guess.

A few hours.

How many? Four? Eight? More?

Still crouching, he exhaled a long breath. Where the hell was Sethwick? This was his area of expertise. He should have overtaken Yancy yesterday. Unless Sethwick chose to take a different route or something at Craiglocky had delayed his departure.

Damn, had Gregor died?

Sethwick's delay became increasingly worrisome by the hour. Yancy frowned and rubbed the back of his neck. His studied the rugged track ahead. Not the most travel-friendly course he'd ever taken, to be sure. Truth be known, he preferred a comfortable carriage for extensive journeys.

Unaccustomed to such long hours in the saddle, his legs and arse ached. He wrinkled his nose. And he stank, almost as foully as MacHardy.

The Scots had headed straightaway for Blackhall lands, which meshed with Tornbury Fortress's borders for a good seventy miles. To his knowledge, the Blackhalls had no grievance against the Farnsworths. What exactly were the scunners about, then?

Isobel was of no use to them.

He'd thought long and hard on that particular, and the conclusion he'd arrived at sent dread snaking along his spine.

The bastards had snatched the wrong woman.

He clenched a fist and pounded his thigh. Miss Farnsworth had been the intended victim. He didn't want to contemplate what they would do to Isobel when they discovered their error.

Yancy fully expected a hostile reception at Dounnich, and there wasn't a by-blows' chance of inheriting a dukedom he would get farther than the outer gate without a plan and massive reinforcements.

How had it come to this? He'd journeyed to Scotland to restore order amongst the clans, and instead found himself on the receiving end of a sword's tip, the woman he adored in jeopardy.

The knowledge sent another wave of ire boiling through him, especially since his chance of rescuing her was slim to none without a vicious fight. Good men might die—would surely die—in the skirmish.

Perhaps Sethwick had concluded the same and sent word to the nearby clans. Waiting for the recruits to arrive would have delayed him.

In the meanwhile, Isobel remained at the mercy of fiends.

"Bleeding hell." Yancy heaved a stone at a nearby tree. He smiled in grim satisfaction as bark splinters exploded every which way.

Exactly what he yearned to do to the faces of the bastards who'd taken her.

He traced the hoof's indentation.

The Scots didn't appear to attempt to hide their trail after the first day and a half. They hadn't expected anyone to tail them so speedily. Bold as ballocks they'd been, waging an attack on Craiglocky lands, no doubt certain of a victory.

Arrogance and stupidity on their part. They'd started a conflict they were destined to lose. Not only was Sethwick a powerful chieftain, but Prinny favored him, and as War Secretary, Yancy had authorization to use British troops at will.

He would pulverize the MacGraths and Blackhalls into dust and pave the streets with their crushed bones if they'd harmed Isobel in any way.

Skye snorted and pawed the ground, and Yancy twisted to gaze at the horse. "I know, I'm frustrated, too."

Something white beyond the gelding caught Yancy's attention.

Another sign from Isobel.

Straightening, he hurried to the spot and collected the soiled strip. He pressed the scant cloth to his nose. Her subtle, mellifluous scent lingered on the scrap.

What other woman would dare, or have the faculties, to leave bits of fabric and makeshift arrows or partial words scraped into the ground to guide her rescuers? Each time he found one, his heart lifted the merest bit.

It meant she was well; at least as well as she could be given her perilous circumstances. He folded the scrap before adding it to the others nestled in his pocket.

Skye nudged his shoulder then nibbled his coat.

Yancy chuckled. "No, you cannot eat it. It belongs to your future mistress." He swung into the saddle. "We've a damsel to rescue, old chap. Both our sweet tooths will have to wait to be satisfied."

Several hours later, he skirted a pitiable village, nothing like Craigcutty, the thriving hamlet on Sethwick's lands. Wisdom dictated Yancy keep his presence a secret. Likely the villagers had orders to inform the keep the moment anyone noticed a stranger in their midst.

Though a road split the forest as neatly as parted hair, he kept to the shadows and outer woodland border as he advanced toward the castle.

Dismounting, he surveyed the sky. Charcoal-colored clouds promised more rain and darkened the dismal afternoon, much like a fine mist blanketed his depressing thoughts.

He led the horse around another downed tree and after tethering Skye to a lengthy branch poking upright from the center, inspected the area. Well away from the road, yet far enough inside the woodlands to be invisible from the meadow, Skye should remain undetected.

The castle, a bleak, rectangular, stone monstrosity, interrupted the otherwise pleasant horizon. A high curtain wall with strategically placed turrets wrapped the front portion of the keep. The drawbridge lay open, as if the castle residents expected welcome guests rather than an army of enraged Scotsmen.

Had the Blackhalls thought their actions through at all? This was not the fifteenth century, for God's sake. Surely, they had to be aware there would be consequences for their rashness.

Perhaps they intended to start a war with England and the clans who'd pledged their fealty to the crown decades before. He didn't doubt that two hundred years from now, some Scots would still strive to regain independence from England.

Blister and rot, nothing good could come of this nonsense.

Giving Skye a final pat on the shoulder, Yancy left the gelding. Mindful to keep hidden from the lookouts posted, he crept from trunk to trunk. Slim chance existed that he'd be spied him amongst the pines. However, he deemed caution prudent. A wounded or dead man couldn't rescue anyone.

Subtle movement to his left caught his attention. He silently withdrew his dirk and turned, ever-so-slowly.

A traveller crouched behind a fallen tree, staring at the castle. If the gypsies collaborated with the Blackhalls, why did this man hide in the forest?

Suddenly, the man straightened and shaded his eyes.

Yancy followed his gaze.

A third story window framed a black-haired woman.

"Tasara." The man's agonized whisper floated through the trees.

Another woman appeared in the next window.

"Isobel." This time Yancy's murmur penetrated the forest's half-light.

His gaze flashed to the traveller. He had moved forward, his hands on his hips.

A twig snapping under Yancy's boot gave him away.

Blade drawn, the gypsy spun in his direction. Fury darkened his already-swarthy skin. "Who are ye?"

Yancy didn't doubt the man's ability to use the weapon he wielded.

"I might ask you the same question." Yancy lowered his blade marginally. "I mean you no harm."

Never taking his gaze off the gypsy, he inclined his head in the keep's direction. "Someone dear to me is being held there."

"Me *chi* and *chavvis*, son and daughters, be as well." The man's harsh features eased, although misery immediately replaced the tension.

"Bartholomew, Earl of Ramsbury." Yancy sheathed his dirk and approached the man, his hand outstretched.

The tinker returned his evil-looking knife to his waistband, before shaking Yancy's hand. "Balcomb Faas, yer lordship. Ye be English?"

"Yes, brought to Scotland on His Majesty's business."

Balcomb bowed his ebony head nobly. "I be a member of the Scottish Highland travellers. Someone from that castle"—he pointed without looking behind him—"took me children captive almost three weeks ago."

Yancy's gaze drifted to the keep.

He blinked, shook his head, and then blinked again.

"Holy, bloody hell."

Chapter 19

A shudder of revulsion skittered down Isobel's back.

Our wedding feast.

Angus's words echoed over and over in her head. He intended to marry her himself.

Over my dead body.

Mind churning, she fingered the lavender-blue satin at her waist. Though a trifle too short and low-cut—her breasts threatened to spill from the bodice if she took a deep breath—the gown would do nicely.

If her circumstances weren't so dire, she would be agog over the confection. How had such an exquisite gown come to be here? Perhaps the dress belonged to the lady of the castle or the laird's daughter.

An insidious notion slithered into her mind.

Or, had the gown been ordered for the wedding? Come to think of it, the garment did seem perfect for someone Lydia's size. That meant the abduction had been planned for some time.

By whom? MacHardy? Laird Blackhall?

Isobel frowned, her fingers stilling. She hadn't met the laird, or anyone else for that matter, with the exception of Dunbar, Angus, and those petrified servants earlier.

Wouldn't the clan's leader want to meet his prisoner?

When she'd been ushered into the keep, she had caught a glimpse of a disheveled, gray-haired man seated at a table on the great hall's dais. He and several others had been hunkered over tankards, but no one had turned to see who'd entered the fortress.

They had appeared deep in their cups, at midday, too.

Ewan wouldn't tolerate such drunken slothfulness.

Dunbar said Angus was the Blackhall war chief. Was he related to the laird then? Precisely who governed here?

Somewhat revived and blessedly clean, although scared witless, she'd eaten a bowl of surprisingly tasty mutton stew. She would need her strength if an opportunity to flee presented itself.

The women, occupied with preparing her bath, had taken no notice of her. The sheathed knife now lay secured to her thigh with another strip from her chemise. If ever a garment were worthy of reward, that decimated scrap of fabric had earned a place of honor.

Worry gnawed, its hundreds of razor sharp teeth nibbling at her stomach. She had expected to be escorted below promptly upon completing her toilette. Pray God something had delayed the cleric, although in Scotland one needn't be present for a couple to wed.

Anyone could officiate, as long as the bride and groom agreed to the union. A reverend did bind things up a mite tighter should anyone contest the joining later, but since the Scottish kirk permitted divorces, even church marriages could be dissolved.

If she didn't agree to wed him, Angus would kill her, and if she did, he'd kill her when he discovered she wasn't Lydia.

Opening the shutter, Isobel searched the landscape. A disheartened sigh escaped.

They won't get here in time.

"Hello?"

Isobel whipped round.

The young woman from earlier stared at her from the adjacent window. A puzzled expression furrowed her forehead and worry shone in her heather-colored eyes. "I thought I heard someone over there today. I am Tasara Faas. Are you held captive too?"

Should Isobel reveal her real identity?

Everyone would know soon enough.

She moved as close as the window would allow. Brushing her hair behind her back, she whispered, "I am Isobel Ferguson, and yes, I was abducted. They intend to force me to marry the war chief this evening. Although, they believe I'm someone else, and I fear for my life when they learn the truth."

She patted the windowsill. "If I had a rope, I would use it in a blink. What of you? Why are you here? I saw a young boy earlier. Your brother?"

Tasara sent a swift glance behind her. "Yes, he and my sister are sleeping."

"You have a sister with you as well?"

An entire family? The Blackhalls had much to account for.

"Lala's four. We were seized many days ago—almost three weeks, now—when I took the children to collect the stray goats."

She glanced inside her room again. "I don't dare try to escape with the little ones, and I cannot leave them behind. I think we are being used as blackmail."

Fear shadowed the delicate lines of Tasara's bruised face. She'd suffered at the hands of those brutes too. She toyed with the fringed end of the scarf tied around her head. "I overheard one of the Scots mention something about forcing my tribe to help them."

Isobel frowned. What in God's precious name were the Blackhalls about? Abducting gypsies and noblewomen? Coercing the travellers? Did they want to start a war, for heaven's sake?

"Help them? With what?"

"I *dinnae ken*. I haven't seen this Scottish clan before." Tasara's lovely face brightened. "I shall help you escape. Then you can send others to rescue us."

She tore the scarf off her head. A cascade of ebony tresses billowed about her shoulders. Pushing her hair over a shoulder, Tasara turned her attention to untying the scarves at her waist.

She held them up. "With these and lengths of blanket, we can make you a line to escape. I have a knife."

Isobel shook her head. "I don't have anything with which to tie a rope in my chamber."

Uncertainty swept across Tasara's features. Her gaze fell to the ground before meeting Isobel's again. "Can you walk along the edge to my room? There is a heavy bed in here."

Licking Angus's filth-covered boots held more appeal, but providence had handed Isobel a means of escape, and she wasn't going to let a phobia ruin her one chance.

"Yes." She forced air into her constricted lungs and offered Tasara smile that probably wobbled.

"I have a knife too. Start cutting the blanket and tie the ends together. I'll do the same over here."

Tasara nodded before disappearing into her room.

Dashing to the chair, Isobel wedged its back below the handle. It wasn't large or sturdy enough to keep anyone out for long, but it might buy her a jot of time. She didn't dare waste a second. Angus might send for her at any moment.

After untying the dagger from her thigh, she snatched up her blanket. Why hadn't she thought of cutting it into strips?

Terror, hunger, and a concussion might have a whit to do with the oversight.

Isobel's heart whooshed in her ears, and her fingers seemed thick as sausages as she worked. Dear God, she must hurry, or else . . .

Once she'd tied the pieces together, she stood on one end and yanked each knot to tighten it. A gnat's antenna couldn't pass between them now, and the ties would provide handholds as she descended.

Flying back to the window with the blanket's remnants, Isobel cast a hurried glance to the sky. Clouds pregnant with moisture drooped low. Her escape would be that much more difficult, trying to hide her trail on the sodden ground.

"Tasara, I'm done."

Tasara immediately poked her head out her casement.

"I've tied mine off to the bed." She flung her rope over the sill. "See, almost halfway."

Reeling the material up, she formed the length into a ball.

"Catch." She lobbed the makeshift rope at Isobel. The wad fell short.

Isobel smothered a groan as she speared an anxious glance to her chamber door.

More time wasted.

Determination carved on her face, Tasara compressed her lips and removed her bracelets. After looping a scarf through the clinking metal, she knotted the ends and heaved the line again.

Bracing her legs against the wall and gripping the casement, Isobel leaned out as far as she dared and snatched the rope with her free hand as it unfurled.

Grinning, Tasara gave a little triumphant clap.

Isobel removed the bracelets then secured the two lines together. Taking a deep breath, she lowered the rope. At least ten feet remained between the end and the ground. However, once she hung directly below Tasara's window, there would be a few more feet hanging horizontally.

Not too bad. She stood over five feet, making the drop nearly insignificant.

As long as I manage without falling.

She pulled the cord into her window, daring to entertain a glimmer of hope.

"I'm going to change shoes. What should I do with your bracelets?" Isobel held up the trinkets.

"Throw them out the window. They aren't valuable, and if you leave them in your room, the Blackhalls will know for sure that I helped you." Tasara inspected the ground and pointed. "Maybe over there, in that tall grass."

Once she'd kicked off the embroidered silk slippers, Isobel stuffed her feet into her half-boots. Worrying her lower lip, she laced them with trembling fingers.

Heights so frightened her that as a child she hadn't climbed trees. But she had scaled the rocks and that hadn't bothered her. Climbing out a window and poking along a narrow ledge wasn't so very different.

Balderdash.

Pressing her hands to her cavorting middle, Isobel sucked in a bracing breath. She had to do this. Angus would kill her if he discovered she wasn't Lydia.

After sliding her dagger into her boot, she glanced around the room. A leftover piece of cheese and hunk of bread sat on the plate. She wrapped them in her cloak before hurrying to the window and dropping the bundle to the ground. The lump landed soundlessly.

"Isobel, wrap the rope around your back and underneath your arms and tie it in front." Tasara demonstrated what she wanted Isobel to do. "You will be more secure, and the line should be long enough."

Should be?

Isobel swiftly secured the cord as Tasara had suggested. She did feel somewhat safer, though fear of slamming into the stones continued to plague her.

She pressed her lips together. There was nothing for it. Risk her life escaping or risk Angus forcing her to marry him and then discovering her true identity. At least the former offered her a slim chance at life.

The latter, none at all.

She tossed the extra line over her shoulder then clutched the sill with one hand. She shoved her gown above her knees before gingerly climbing onto the opening.

Oh, my God!

Turning sideways, she eased through the crevice. The fit proved snug. The stones snagged her gown and scraped her skin, forcing her to wriggle to free herself.

Damned wide hips.

Terrified, she clutched the casement. One slip, and . . .

Biting her lip, she cautiously wiped her damp palms on the dress, one at a time. A cold sweat dampened her upper lip and forehead.

"You can do it, Isobel," Tasara assured encouragingly.

Surely Isobel's thundering heart had alerted all within five miles of her intent. The Blackhalls undoubtedly streaked to the back of the keep at this very moment.

Grasping the knot below her breasts with one hand, she groped the craggy exterior with the other and inched along the strip, determined not to look down.

Step by petrifying step, she crept along, the minutes dragging as if the hands of time had slowed.

"A few more steps and you will be directly in front of my window," Tasara promised. An eternity later, she touched Isobel's ankle. "I'll help you inside. How does that sound?"

Positively horrid.

"Fine." The strangled croak Isobel forced past her stiff lips clearly indicated otherwise. After this, she wouldn't set foot anywhere taller than herself again.

Ever.

A minute later, she stood quaking inside Tasara's chamber.

The gypsy's gorgeous eyes swam with tears, and she embraced Isobel. "I don't know another woman as brave-hearted."

"Bravery had nothing to do with it. Desperation did." Isobel wiped the sweat from her face. "That is the most God-awful thing I have ever had to do."

The children slept on, their cherub mouths partly open, oblivious to the drama playing out beside them.

At least descending the rope, she would face the stones and couldn't see how blasted far the drop was. "Let's be about it. I want to be well and gone before my disappearance is discovered. What about you? They will know you helped me when they see the rope."

Tasara sent an anxious glance to her brother and sister. "I can untie the rope and then drop it outside. If you hide the line, they will have no proof."

Isobel had no idea where she would stuff the crude rope, but Tasara had risked much to help her. "Yes, that will do. I shall hide it in the woods somewhere."

Tasara's hand on her arm stayed Isobel.

"I know my father or others of my clan are near. Find them in the forest, and they will help you to your people." A tear crept from the edge of her eye.

She brushed the droplet away. "Our troop is not large enough, nor do we have the weapons to fight these . . . these *vafedi mush*, evil men. Perhaps you know someone who can help us?"

Isobel nodded. "My brother is Ewan McTavish, laird of—"

"Craiglocky." Hope glimmered in Tasara's eyes. "All the brethren know of Laird McTavish."

The children started to stir from their naps, and Isobel hugged Tasara again. "Ewan will help, and one of his greatest friends is England's War Secretary. Lord Ramsbury won't hesitate to assist my brother in any manner he is able."

If Yancy is alive.

Now wasn't the time to think of that. More than her life hung in the balance. She must make good her escape for the Faas's sake too.

Once more, she clambered onto a window ledge. "Are you sure you are strong enough to lower me? I could try to slide down the rope."

Tasara already busied herself wrapping the crude rope around a bedpost. "I'll use the post for leverage."

Isobel gave one sharp nod, not trusting herself to speak.

God, if you let me survive this, I shall never seek an adventure again.

Chapter 20

God's bones!

Yancy gaped, unable to believe Isobel dangled outside the castle from a . . . He squinted. He had no idea what the mismatched glomeration she hung from consisted of.

Isobel would get herself killed.

Silly, brave fool.

His heart kicked viciously behind his ribs, threatening to crack them, one by one, as every ounce of blood he possessed pooled in his boots. Did all the Ferguson sisters wish to send the men who loved them to an early grave?

Leaning from her window, the gypsy helped Isobel. She slowly eased the pathetic excuse for a rope encircling Isobel along the keep's side.

Yancy spun to the traveller. "Balcomb, do you have a horse? Do you know where the village is?"

Eyes wide and worried, his gaze fixed on Isobel, the gypsy swallowed and jerked his head up and down.

"Look for Viscount Sethwick. Tell him what's happened. He's a friend." He yanked his signet ring from his finger. "Give him this."

Yancy sprinted to Skye.

And please, God, let Sethwick be there.

Yancy leapt into the saddle, his focus trained on the blue form inching down the castle on the improvised rope. "So help me God, Isobel, I shall spank that luscious bum of yours myself."

Yancy kicked Skye's sides, and they burst, *ventre a terre*, belly to ground, from the woods. His pulse beating every bit as loudly as the horse's hooves pounding beneath him, he mouthed a silent prayer. With every heartbeat, he expected Isobel to plummet to the ground. And he wouldn't be there to catch her.

Anyone could see him tearing like a man possessed across the moor. It mattered not. Isobel's life literally hung in balance. Jaw clenched so tight his back teeth ached, he thundered toward her.

He must reach her in time.

She used her feet to keep from knocking into the rugged exterior while holding on to the rope. Every now and again, she would look upward as if speaking to the gypsy. As she neared the first floor level, the cloth under her arms gave way.

Her terrified shriek raked across his heart.

I'm not going to make it.

Yancy gnashed the inside of his cheek until he tasted blood to check the cry that surged to his lips. If he startled Isobel, she might let go.

Kicking her legs, she clutched the swinging rope with one hand. She swung precariously and slammed into the keep's stones. Somehow, she managed to grasp the cord with her other hand.

The air surged from Yancy's lungs. By God, if she survived this, he would shake her until her perfect teeth rattled. And afterward, he would hug her until she squealed, and then kiss her breathless.

She wouldn't leave his sight again, and once they had married, he vowed she would curtail this rebellious bent. She would be too exhausted from his constant bedding to entertain risky ideas of any sort.

Practically lying in the saddle, Yancy urged the gelding, "Come on, Skye. Faster."

As if sensing his master's alarm, the horse lengthened his strides, flying across the heath.

Almost there.

All at once, dread frozen on her face, Isobel peered over her shoulder. Her eyes grew round as twin moons. A large purplish-blue bruise covered most of one cheek and dried blood congealed on her split and swollen lower lip.

So great was Yancy's urge to kill, his gut knotted tighter than a hangman's noose, and a red haze blinded him.

"Yancy." Isobel smiled, that dazzling, mind-numbing curving of bow-shaped lips that rendered a man incapable of coherent thought.

Arms outstretched, he rode underneath her. "Let go. I'll catch you."

"No, I am too heavy." She shook her head, eyes now squeezed tight as a pickpocket's fist. "I'm not a small woman, and I'll hurt you."

"Damn it, Isobel. Let go! We've got mere minutes to flee." He softened his voice. "I promise, darling, you're not large at all, and I'll not let you fall."

Her pink mouth formed an '*O*' of surprise. She released the rope and plopped in an ungraceful tangle of skirts into his lap.

Yancy seized her in his arms and planted a fierce, possessive kiss on her unbruised cheek. Cupping her face, he rested his forehead against hers.

"So help me God, Isobel, I lost twenty years from my life in the past few days, and ten of those in the last couple of minutes alone."

"You are alive." Bursting into tears, she twined her arms around his neck and buried her face in his throat. "You are really alive."

He folded her into his embrace, breathing her in.

Violent sobs wracked her as her tears soaked his neckcloth. "I thought you had been killed."

He kissed her hair, savoring the gift of holding her in his arms. Wonder rendered him mute. Had she grieved for him?

The rope thumped Yancy atop the head, and he craned his neck upward.

"As joyous as your reunion is, you must go." Balcomb's daughter peered over the ledge. "Someone could come at any moment. Please hide the rope."

She pointed behind Skye. "Isobel's cloak is just there."

With a quick kiss to her nose, Yancy shifted Isobel off his lap. He turned her face to his and stared into her glistening eyes. "Stay on the horse, but scoot back and sit astride."

She gave a tiny nod and managed a wan smile.

He dismounted and after gathering the rope, ran to Isobel's wrap. In less than a minute, he returned and shoved everything into her arms. He vaulted into the saddle then peered upward once more.

"Miss Faas, your father has gone for help. Isobel's brother is coming." Yancy swung Skye away from the castle. "We cannot wait for him. It's too dangerous."

A child's cry echoed within the chamber.

"God go with you." With a wave, she disappeared inside.

"Isobel, hold on tight. We ride hard. We'll rid ourselves of the rope, and you can put your cloak on once we've put some distance behind us."

She obediently clasped her arms around his waist. Her breasts, pressing into his back, created a lovely, but unwanted, distraction.

With a click of his tongue and a kick of his heels to Skye's sides, they plunged toward the forest. Any second, he expected to hear a cry of alarm or feel a lead ball pierce his flesh. Fear of discovery looming mile after frantic mile, Yancy pushed Skye to the end of the faithful horse's endurance.

The heavens opened up. Though the shower was short-lived, the torrential rains soaked them through. As if contrite for their poor behavior earlier, the clouds then drifted apart and allowed the moon and stars to emerge.

The meager light they provided permitted him to travel far into the night. Hours later, utterly exhausted, Yancy searched for a place to stop to rest.

No warning had sounded as they raced from Blackhall lands, and as near as he could tell, no one trailed them. Hopefully, that meant Sethwick had stormed the stronghold and killed the bastards who'd abducted Isobel.

Still, wisdom decreed caution. Sethwick mightn't have arrived, in which case, until Yancy had Isobel nestled safely at Craiglocky again, he feared for their lives. The greater distance he put between Dounnich House and them, the better.

Snuggled against his back, Isobel shivered.

They had discarded the rope over a cliff and eaten the bread and cheese while moving. Hunger gnawed, but he refrained from breaking into the last of his stores.

"They thought I was Lydia." Isobel shifted and pressed closer. "Somebody at Craiglocky helped them."

She had to be freezing. He certainly was. Then her words registered. "At Craiglocky? Do you have any idea who?"

"No, but there were two travellers with the men who captured me. Somehow, all this ties in with Tasara, the gypsy girl." She sneezed then sneezed again. "Excuse me."

"Bless you." Had Isobel caught a chill?

"MacHardy's behind my abduction." Shaking, she snuggled closer. "He intended to force Lydia into marrying him for Tornbury's lands."

Yancy stiffened, ire heating his blood, but he forced a calm response. "I deduced as much."

"But Angus—I don't know his surname—he betrayed MacHardy and decided to marry me—that is—Lydia himself. He'd arranged for the ceremony to take place tonight."

Yancy choked back a foul oath. "God's blood, if I had been any later."

"But you weren't. You saved me." She tightened her embrace. "I wouldn't have gotten far on foot and when Angus learned who I was—"

An incoherent sound, part oath, part snarl escaped Yancy.

Isobel burrowed tighter to his back, trembling harder. "He's evil, Yancy. He would have killed me and not blinked twice."

Such dread choked her voice, he almost missed her calling him by his given name. Aching to hold her in his arms and erase her fear, he brought Skye to a halt. Had they traveled far enough? Did they dare stop for a few hours' rest?

Skye groaned.

They must. The horse could carry them no farther. Yancy loved the beast too much to risk killing him in their flight. "I had hoped to find some sort of shelter, but my horse is done in. We'll have to make do under the trees. I have blankets and the rain has ceased."

For now. One could acquire a fortune wagering on rainfall in Scotland as autumn approached. "I should warn you. The squirrels in these parts are crotchety little buggers."

Isobel giggled and leaned away. The sudden wave of coolness assaulting his spine left him feeling oddly bereft. "We came this way. Around the next bend, although it's obscured from the path, I am certain I saw a thatched roof. We passed through at night, but there are farms and hunting cottages, even an inn or two, scattered throughout this area."

Weariness laced her words, yet not a word of complaint had escaped her lips.

"I stayed in a hunting cottage one night. The place proved quite quaint." Yancy clucked his tongue and gently kneed Skye's sides.

Head low, the horse shambled onward.

"That's a faithful chap." Yancy patted the gelding's shoulder. "Not much farther, boy."

Isobel continued to amaze him with her fortitude and gumption, and yes, vex the hell out of him at times too.

He would have thought she would be too traumatized to take note of their whereabouts. He had gotten turned about more than once. Truth be known, poking about in the woods wasn't his strong suit. He wound up chasing his own tail half the time; a mite humiliating for a man in his position.

"Isobel, how is it you are able to remember the path your abductors took?"

She chuckled, the sultry sound winding round his senses in a pleasant, although distracting manner. "I remember practically every detail I see and can conjure an almost exact image in my mind."

"Indeed?" She was quite the most fascinating female of his acquaintance.

"Uh-hum." Mumbling sleepily, she hunched into his spine. "Yancy, what happened to the others? Why are you alone?"

More than cold shook her voice.

Yancy hesitated to tell her of Gregor since he didn't know her cousin's condition or if he survived. "Everyone returned to the castle to alert Sethwick."

Not precisely the truth but Isobel didn't need more to worry about. Their circumstances were precarious at best.

"And you set out after me alone?" She flattened her hands against his ribs.

The heat of her palms wreaked havoc with his already-overstimulated desire. His muscles jumped, and his manhood flexed against the saddle.

"I couldn't chance losing the Scots' trail." What he wanted to say was, *I couldn't chance losing you*, but feared her reaction.

"That was most valiant of you." Her soft response revealed little.

After a few more minutes of riding in silence, Isobel pointed over his shoulder. "Just there, to the right beyond that outcrop of trees."

Yancy laughed aloud at the welcome sight. The same humble hut he'd made use of loomed before them. "My lady, Bronwedon Towers never held as much appeal."

"Bronwedon Towers?" She yawned and perched her chin on his shoulder.

"My principle estate in Suffolk. My stepmother and her niece are in residence there at the moment." Did he imagine it, or did Isobel stiffen and pull away?

After they dismounted, he untied the bundle behind the saddle. Taking Isobel's elbow, he guided her to the entrance. "Wait here while I light a candle, in case some creature has decided to make this home since I was last here."

"Of course." Teeth chattering, Isobel tugged her wrap tighter and stared into the darkness.

Skye heaved a gusty breath, no doubt eager to be rid of the saddle.

Moments later, Yancy had a crooked taper glowing. He lit another before placing the first on a flat, wax-covered rock protruding from the chimney specifically for that purpose.

Clutching her cloak closed, Isobel hurried into the cottage and glanced around curiously. Face drawn and lips firmed together, her shoulders slumped with fatigue. She resembled a sodden kitten with her scraggly hair and woebegone eyes.

Her poor, beautiful face, all puffy and discolored. What kind of a bastard struck a woman, especially in the face? The cawker might have broken her jaw or cheekbone.

She swayed slightly. How she remained standing was beyond him, for he could scarcely find the energy to attend to Skye.

"I shall get a fire started as soon as I see to my horse." He pointed to the shelves. "Linens are stacked there. Get that wet cloak off and dry your hair."

Quaking head to foot, she fumbled to unfasten her cloak.

"Here, let me do it." Yancy nudged her stiff fingers aside.

The corners of her mouth tilted upward the merest bit, but misery shadowed her face. She quivered so hard, he feared she had already caught a chill.

Pushing damp tendrils off her cheek, he inclined his head. "There's a bedchamber through that door. Get your wet clothes off. All of them."

Chapter 21

"*All* of them?" Gaping, Isobel choked on an outraged squeak. Yancy could not be serious.

Eyes narrowed, she angled her chin. "And what, pray tell, shall I put on, my lord? I assure you, I'm not parading about naked for your enjoyment."

A rather erotic image flitted through her mind. One in which she didn't mind standing nude before him in the least.

She'd come across a book or two *or three* in the library she was confident neither her parents nor Ewan had the slightest notion existed as part of the immense collection. Books that had provided quite an *unusual* education.

Even weary-eyed with rough stubble covering his jaw, Yancy looked too tempting by far. A burst of warmth swelled from her pelvis to her breasts.

Blast the unfairness.

Tousled and disheveled, he roused enticing images of dashing pirates and gallant knights while she resembled a washerwoman scrambling from beneath a pile of soiled laundry.

His lips quirked into a crooked smile, and his heavy-lidded gaze dropped to her bosom.

Another flicker of awareness caused Isobel's nipples to firm into hard pebbles. She trembled and crossed her arms. Her chilled state was to blame for her perky breasts, not his scorching gaze.

Fustian rot and rubbish.

"As much as I would enjoy the enchanting spectacle of seeing you nude, you are cold to the marrow. I don't want you catching lung fever." He strode to the table and after loosening the string, yanked a rough blanket free of the mound dumped atop the scarred surface.

"Here." Extending the woolen cloth, a challenge glinted in his eyes.

Did he think she would refuse to comply? Saturated to the skin as she had been these past several hours, a tangible risk of fever existed. She wouldn't jeopardize her health out of some misplaced sense of propriety or stubbornness. Besides, warmth and dryness were temptations not easily ignored.

Yancy gathered the cloths from the shelf, as well as one of the candles, and pressed the items into her numb hands. Placing his palms on her shoulders, he turned her in the direction of the bedchamber and gave a minute shove. "Go. I promise not to peek. *Much.*"

She spun to face him, prepared to give him a proper setdown.

Already at the door, he laughed, a rich, rumbling baritone, and hurried into the night.

Confounded man.

He had her in a dither, and he well knew it.

Isobel stomped into the bedchamber. Only one window, and the shutters dangled askew. The room smelled musty, as if it hadn't been aired in some time.

Candle held high, she approached the narrow bed, wary of what might be crawling within. A relieved sigh escaped her. The bedding appeared reasonably clean. She bent and drew back the blankets, revealing coarse sheets that looked surprisingly fresh.

She spied a whisky-colored strand of hair on the pillow, and a hint of sandalwood wafted upward. Yancy had slept here.

After tugging the bedding back into place, she tossed

the blanket and towels on the hand-stitched quilt. She set the candle on a triangular table beside the bed and shivered.

Scarcely bigger than Emira's stall, chilly, outside air drifted into the tiny room through gaps between the stones. Isobel hastily undressed, leaving her sopped garments in a heap on the floor. Goose pimples puckered atop her clammy skin.

She rubbed a cloth over herself before wrapping the scratchy blanket around her back then securely tucking the edge underneath one arm.

Sitting on the bed, she briskly toweled her hair. Smoothing the tangles by running her fingers through the strands proved impossible. Perhaps Yancy had a comb or brush with him.

Shaking, she fashioned another blanket into a shawl. Holding it shut, she gathered her wet garments and boots. Cold spiraled up her calves from the frigid floor, and she wiggled her icy toes.

Would she ever be warm again? Other than those couple of hours at Dounnich after her bath, she had been colder than a witch's heart for days.

Egypt is warm. So are Spain and the Caribbean and Greece.

No!

No more daydreaming and fantasizing about adventures—far past time she married and started a family. She'd made God a promise and fully intended to keep her word.

If anyone would have her now.

Men had been eager to court her and take her to wife before this. However, the tiniest hint of moral scandal was enough to send them sniffing about someone else's skirts and shun her.

Or else offer her a less than honorable proposition as a kept woman, complete with a written agreement detailing exactly what she could expect from her protector. Never mind that not a one of them could claim virginity, and yet her virtue remained intact.

Hypocrites.

With a firm shake of her head, Isobel clutched the blanket tighter. There was naught to be done about her reputation now. She couldn't change her circumstance any more than a molting chicken could shove a fallen feather back on its bald bum.

Why had Yancy come after her alone? Most foolish, though she would be a cretin to be ungrateful.

Isobel touched her uninjured cheek. He'd kissed her.

Momentarily overcome at finding her safe, or did the kiss mean something more? Now who was foolish? A kiss on the cheek hardly bespoke intense passion.

If Yancy weren't already affianced, she might dare to follow her smitten heart.

Ifs and ands were pots and pans, there would be no need for tinkers.

"Yes I know, Grandmother," Isobel muttered crossly.

Noises in the outer room announced Yancy's return to the cottage.

Emerging from the bedchamber, she hesitated in the doorway.

He crouched before the roaring flames, prodding a log with the poker. He had removed his boots, coat and stockings. The latter two he'd draped across a chair to the side of the fireplace. Steam rose from his hunting jacket.

His wet shirt clung to the hard lines of his sculpted torso. The muscles flexed and bunched as he urged the fire hotter. The male perfection hunkered a few feet away lured her as much as the comforting crackle of the fire and the pleasant aroma of wood burning.

Glancing up at her entrance, his mouth curved into a roguish smile. He leisurely inspected her from her pink toes peeking from beneath the blanket, to her hair tumbling about her shoulders to her waist.

At the glint in his eyes, she almost turned tail and fled into the bedchamber. She might as well be standing naked as a robin, so ravenous was his expression.

His hot gaze didn't veer for an instant as he stood upright. "I've managed to make some tea, and there's an apple, two oat rolls, and a wedge of cheese left."

Their fare sat atop the table, now placed nearer the hearth. He'd also lit two additional candles.

Yancy approached her. The expanse of dark, curling hair exposed by his parted shirt sent a ripple tingling along her spine.

Isobel forced her feet to remain planted, though every instinct screamed for her to flee. He was as dangerous to her untried senses as her abductors had been to her physical body. More so, since she seemed unable of summoning a whit of resistance to him, his ridiculous malachite eyes, or his superbly molded mouth. *Or deliciously sculpted chest muscles.*

Stop staring and say something, Isobel.

"Your horse is well?" *Bleeding brilliant.* But the poor beast likely hadn't been properly groomed or fed since this whole disaster started.

Yancy grinned as if he knew full well the tumultuous thoughts warring in her head.

"Yes, Skye's none too happy with me at present. The old chap quite enjoys his oats." He plucked the wet clothes from her arms, his long fingers brushing her bare skin.

Those bothersome sensations started up again, skipping across her nerves. The feeling quite muddled her mind and did the most erratic things to her breathing.

"Have a seat at the table while I lay these out to dry." He lifted her garments and shoes.

Sinking onto a hard chair, discomfit heated her face as he padded around arranging her stockings, stays, and chemise about the pleasantly warm room as naturally as a husband would.

In the act of draping the last stocking across a chair, he stilled, his attention fixated on her calf.

Glancing downward, mortification seized Isobel. The blanket gapped open, revealing her leg from ankle to above her knee.

She tugged the ends together.

Yancy brought his gaze up to hers, and their eyes locked, their souls fusing.

She was no more capable of looking away than she could cease breathing.

Hunger tinged with something nameless shone in his cat-like eyes. His gaze caressed her across the distance as surely as if his fingers trailed her flesh.

The air left her lungs, and her limbs turned to jelly. Desire flooded her.

I'm in serious trouble.

Alone, stark naked beneath a scanty blanket, and reluctantly in love with a man whose mere glance had her willing to fling propriety aside and beg him to make her a woman—yes, she was in deep, *deep*, ruinous trouble.

"*Ma heid's* mince," Isobel muttered under her breath. She simply couldn't think straight at the moment. Truth be known, the phenomenon occurred with annoying regularity in Yancy's presence.

Desperate for something to do to distract her treacherous musings, her hands unsteady, she poured tea into the two chipped cups.

"I'm sorry. There's no milk or sugar." Yancy's palms cupped her shoulders, his fingertips gently pressing into the flesh.

Isobel jumped, one knee hitting the table and jarring their scanty meal.

His bare feet silent on the worn floor, he'd crept up behind her.

She took a hasty sip of tea and burned her tongue. Rather than spew the hot liquid into the cup, she swallowed, singeing her throat.

Hell, Hades, and Purgatory.

Must she always act a complete goose in his company?

Gathering her tangled mane, he smoothed the strands down her back. "I found a comb. Sit sideway in the chair, and I'll untangle your hair."

Anticipation rendered her mute, but she obediently shifted her position.

"Go ahead and eat. I've had my fill." Yancy pulled the other chair behind her then drew the comb through her tresses, the movements slow and hypnotic.

She took another tentative sip of tea, practically sighing in appreciation. The man brewed a superb cup. Had he really eaten or had he left the meager meal for her?

Taking a bite of cheese, she tried to ignore the wonderful sensations his gentle ministrations caused. She turned her mind to home. She couldn't wait to reach Craiglocky and see her family, to assure them she hadn't been compromised.

"Isobel?" Yancy's voice grew hoarse. "Did they *harm* you?"

Did they despoil me, you mean?

She picked at an oat roll, certain her cheeks flamed. "No. I count myself rather fortunate in that regard."

His breath warmed the top of her head as he released a heavy sigh. "I was so afraid for you, that they'd force you."

"The real danger lay in them discovering I wasn't Lydia."

He stopped combing her hair and drew his hand through the tendrils. "You have beautiful hair."

He traced small circles below her ear with his fingers.

Every bone in her body must have gone soft because she couldn't move. Not even when he replaced his fingers with firm lips, and his beard gently rasped across her skin.

Had anything ever felt so glorious? Wisdom shrieking in protest, Isobel bent her neck, offering him easier access.

Yancy eased the shawl from her shoulders and smoothed his palms across the bare flesh as he feathered kisses across her nape, drifting lower to her shoulder. "Isobel?"

She turned her head and met his eyes, dark with desire.

Did hers shimmer with the same intense yearning?

She traced his mouth with her fingertips. She wanted to kiss him, just one time to experience a kiss from the man she'd secretly loved for years. She was ruined already. What difference did it make if she created a memory to treasure throughout her life?

He sucked one finger into his mouth.

She gasped as sensation surged between her legs and the tips of her breasts. How could something so simple cause her core to contract? If this was passion, she had waited far too long to experience it. No, far too long to experience it with *him*.

Yancy drew her to her feet. The blanket covering her shoulders slithered to the floor and pooled there.

Holding the back of her head with his large palm, he drew her nearer, until her breasts above the blanket's fabric met his hair-matted chest.

Isobel stood on her tiptoes and twined her arms about his neck, desperate to feel the friction of his crisp hair against her. Sweet euphoria sang through her veins.

This, now, with Yancy was all that mattered. Later, on her lonely mattress, she would examine her impetuousness and chastise herself to China and back.

As if sensing her desperation, he stepped from her embrace and tore off his shirt. His sculpted muscles bunched and flexed when he threw it carelessly on the floor.

In the few moments it took for him to remove the garment, she felt bereft. She required his touch just as the earth needed the sun's caressing rays.

Winding an arm across her back, he urged her closer, while tilting his hips and pressing the solid bulge in his trousers into her soft belly.

Yancy brushed his lips against her hurt cheek, the barest whisper of a kiss. "My darling, I'm so sorry."

He rained tender, reverent kisses over her injuries as if he sought to erase the pain.

She touched his mouth with hers, a butterfly's stroke. "Kiss me, Yancy."

"I don't want to hurt your mouth."

"You won't."

And he wouldn't, not this gentle, considerate man.

At last his mouth took hers in a tentative kiss. A torrent of longing burst upon Isobel, as fierce and intense as the rainstorm that drenched them earlier today.

He probed her lips with his tongue, urging her to open for him.

Ravenous for everything he had to teach her, she eagerly complied. She moaned against his mouth and clutched his back, the wide planes smooth and warm.

Framing her face with his hands, Yancy kissed her, almost as an act of worship. He found his way inside her blanket and fondled her breasts.

Isobel sighed, arching into his caress.

He eased back, and her remaining blanket glided to the floor.

Chapter 22

Yancy hadn't ever been this overcome with longing. He'd been a man about town, and a woman's form held no secrets. But Isobel—God in heaven—she was beyond any of his erotic fantasies. And he'd had plenty of them.

Magnificent breasts—almost too big for her frame, the nipples large and coppery-tinted—taunted him unmercifully. He ached to feel their generous weight in his hands, to bury his face in their creamy softness, and suckle those glorious tips. His palms could scarce contain the ripe bounty of her full breasts.

They rose and fell in cadence with her rapid breathing.

A vision of her astride him, her breasts jiggling as she rode him to completion, left his mouth chalk dry and his penis straining against his pantaloons.

Her slender waist tapered in to wide, perfectly plump hips. Centered between her ivory thighs, a nest of almond-colored curls beckoned, as mesmerizing as Venus and as addictive as opium.

Imagining his groin settled against that soft treasure, gripping the luscious mounds of her derriere as he thrust into her, had Yancy on the verge of spilling his seed where he stood.

He hadn't been this moon-eyed and out of control since Julia Cambrill sank her talons into him.

Bereft of covering, Isobel's mouth dropped open in surprise and uncertainty danced across her beautiful features. She bent to retrieve the blanket, presenting him with her tantalizing buttocks.

Groaning, he snared her around the waist, yanking her to his aching shaft. One hand cradling a breast, the other her pelvis, he ground his hips into her bottom. “See what you do to me, Isobel?”

She trembled. “Yancy. I’m not . . .”

He trailed his tongue to her shoulder and bit gently.

A throaty moan left her in a rush of air, and she sagged against him. She smelled sweet and womanly.

Burying his face in Isobel’s hair, he sucked in a great, gulping breath. They would be married as soon as he spoke to her father and the contract was signed. “I promise, I shall make all the settlement arrangements—”

Isobel stiffened, remaining rigid and immobile for an instant, before wresting from his arms.

“Darling, what’s wrong?” He tried to embrace her once more, but she shied away and snatched the other blanket from the floor.

Swiftly wrapping it about herself, she hid her woman’s bounty from him. Eyes averted, she gestured between them. “I blame myself for this.”

Hands on his hips, he studied her. Why the barriers now?

Her lower lip quivering, she blinked several times and swallowed. Her gaze kept skipping to his bare chest. She wasn’t any more capable of resisting him than he was her.

“Isobel, there’s no blame involved.” He touched her arm tenderly.

Her mortified gaze met his for an instant as she backed away, clutching the blanket like a protective mantel. “I shouldn’t have left the bedchamber without my clothing and shouldn’t have encouraged your attentions. I knew better and am sorry my actions gave you the wrong impression.”

“Wrong impression? Sweetheart, we both want—”

“I shall retire now.” Chagrin and unshed tears thickened her voice.

He extended his hand. "Don't go. Your hair isn't completely dry and the chamber isn't heated. We can sit before the fire and talk, while your hair dries, if you wish."

He'd rather lay her before the blaze and explore every inch of her smooth, satin skin.

"No." A vivid blush swept her face, and she ducked her head. Shoulders hunched, she edged past him. She swiftly padded to the bedchamber, and a moment later, the door closed softly behind her.

What the bloody hell just happened?

Isobel had been a wanton siren one instant, and the next, frigid as Loch Arkaig in January. Plunging a hand through his hair, Yancy stared into the flames carousing in the hearth. A muted sound carried through the door separating them.

Sobbing.

Blast. Would he ever understand women?

A dram of whisky wouldn't be amiss right now. Who did he think he fooled? An entire bottle wouldn't cure the rod tenting his pantaloons or the guilt besetting him. A decent man would have proposed and wed her before taking such liberties, even if she had been willing and irresistible. And, God knew, he was no saint.

Yancy jammed on his boots, but ignored his shirt. He grabbed a whisky bottle as he stamped his way to the entrance. He'd already bathed, however another thorough dousing was in order—freezing well-water for his lust-ridden body and alcohol for his smitten heart.

The front door banging roused Isobel from weeping into the lumpy pillow. The fabric smelled slightly of Yancy. She flopped onto her back, an arm across her eyes.

Silly, becoming overwrought due to a few splendid kisses. *Fine*, a mite more than kissing had occurred, and perhaps the experience had been the most wonderful thing this side of heaven.

Sucking in a ragged breath, she swiped at the tears seeping from her eyes. She had acted a promiscuous tart with a man she knew full well couldn't offer her anything other than his protection. And worse, she'd been tempted to let him have his way, consequences be damned.

Then, her vexing conscience reared its prudent head with a litany of logical reasons why she needed to ignore her heart and the delicious sensations engulfing her:

You cannot throw your virtue away on a man who doesn't cherish it.

You'll never forgive yourself.

You'll be little more than a well-bred courtesan.

You won't have the remotest chance of making a respectable match.

Still, Isobel had been sorely tempted.

Until he so crassly mentioned an agreement.

That curbed her ardor faster than vermin in the sheets.

Yancy obviously wasn't as overcome with need as she since in the middle of their *interlude,* he could contemplate contract terms. He'd evidently assumed her responses meant she had agreed to become his mistress.

The devilishly handsome boor.

Tonight sealed her heart and her fate. She'd leave Craiglocky until Yancy departed. Then, in a year or two or ten, if she had a chance encounter with him, her emotions would be impervious to his charm.

He would likely have a passel of offspring with Matilda by then, and Isobel would either be a spinster, shriveled up drier than forgotten shortbread, or married with a brood of her own, the Good Lord willing.

They would simply smile and nod before passing one another as if this wretchedly wonderful attraction hadn't ever existed between them.

Burrowing deeper into the itchy blankets, she released a long, dejected sigh. Why had her feckless heart chosen Yancy?

Whit's fur ye'll no go by ye.

Tish tosh, Grandmother. What's meant to happen will happen, all right. And look what a colossal disaster everything has turned out to be.

A shuddery breath escaped her before she determinedly clamped her eyes shut. A visage of her and Yancy embracing finally enticed her into the arms of Morpheus.

Sometime before dawn timidly crept across the horizon, Isobel awoke with a cry. Rearing upward, fear choked her as she frantically searched the room. The moon's half-light filtering through the shutters lent an eerie glow to the chamber.

Where was she? And why was she naked?

"Isobel?" Yancy's shadowy form appeared beside the bed.

Memory flooded her. Gripping a blanket to her chest, she slumped in relief.

A dream. The attack had been nothing but a dream.

"Are you all right? You cried out in your sleep." Sitting on the edge of the mattress, he touched her shoulder. "And you're trembling."

"I dreamed Angus found me. Us." She brushed her hair away from her face, trying to breathe calmly. Terror's vise-like grip slowly let loose of her chest. "He stabbed you and put his hands on me intending to—"

She couldn't finish as a fresh wave of dread seized her. Squeezing her eyes shut, she fisted the blanket. Lord, the nightmare had seemed real. Yancy dead, a dirk impaling his heart. Tears oozed from beneath her eyelashes and tracked down her cheeks.

"Shh, sweetheart. I'm here." He draped an arm across her shoulders and pressed her head to his solid chest.

So nice and firm. The fine hairs tickled her nose. He smelled of strong spirits and the pleasant aroma she had come to associate with him.

"Scoot over and lie down. I'll stay with you until you fall asleep again." He bumped her slightly with his hip.

Isobel did as he asked. "Where were you sleeping? On the floor?"

He chuckled as he tucked her in. "Yes, outside your door."

"That must be awfully uncomfortable." She hadn't given a thought to where he would sleep. Selfish of her.

He shrugged, a boyish smile framing his lips. "I've slept in far worse conditions." He gave her a hip little squeeze. "Now, go to sleep. I would like to get an early start. I don't think we were followed, but I shall be more comfortable once we are on McTavish lands."

She settled against him, his shoulder pillowing her head. One of her arms rested on his chest, her legs flush with his. "Do you think Ewan raided Dounnich House?"

Yancy curved one of his arms underneath her nape. He lightly played with the tendrils there and settled his other hand atop her hip.

His voice thick with sleep, and perhaps a trifle too much drink, he mumbled, "I would bet on it. He'll have extra sentries patrolling his borders too."

"Hmm." Isobel yawned, nestling into his side. "That sounds like my brother."

Yancy kissed her nose and arched into her. His rigid length pulsed against her leg. "Now sleep, vixen, or I shan't be responsible for what happens next."

Chapter 23

Cool air blasted Isobel. Shivering, she snuggled closer to the warm body lying beside her. Awareness dawned. A firm, male body cradled hers from shoulder to calf.

Opening her eyes, her gaze collided with Yancy's languid green stare. She blinked sleepily and smiled.

His lips curled up lazily before his perusal moved to her exposed breasts. He touched one nipple with his fingertip.

Suddenly, she wasn't cold any longer. A delicious heat sang along her veins.

The door exploded open.

She shrieked and hauled the blanket over her breasts as Ewan, Father, Dugall, Harcourt, and several clansmen stormed into the miniscule chamber. They were packed tighter than biscuits in a tin.

Yancy surged upward, only to freeze as Ewan's sword tip pricked his Adam's apple. A dot of scarlet appeared.

"Do. Not. Move, Ramsbury." Ewan's savage expression nearly stopped her heart. He looked ferocious enough to kill.

She'd never seen this side of him, the side that earned him the reputation of an unparalleled Diplomatic Corp agent and unrivalled with a blade.

Hands splayed in surrender beside his head, Yancy sank onto his back. The rippled muscles of his abdomen bunched, as if lying submissive strained his endurance. Eyes wary, he met Ewan's enraged glower head on.

"Do you mean to run me through with your sister lying beside me?" His focus shifted to the Duke. "And Harcourt, thank you for defending me."

"Old chap, what would you have me do? You've been caught in the act red-handed—er, not *the act*, but I assume Miss Ferguson *is* naked as a plucked chicken under that blanket." Sporting one blackened eye, Harcourt rubbed the side of his nose. "Besides, I've not seen you in a predicament this interesting."

A sound, very much like a growl, accompanied the ugly glower Yancy sent the duke.

Harcourt chuckled wickedly. "I'm eagerly anticipating how you will extricate yourself. Should prove most entertaining."

"If you value your eyesight, I would advise you to stop ogling Isobel this instant, *friend*." Fire kindled in Yancy's eyes.

"Shut. Up." Ewan wedged the sword firmer against Yancy's neck. The scarlet grew larger.

Dragging the blanket with her, Isobel sat up. "Ewan, stop it this instant. Nothing happened. If you'd notice, he's wearing pantaloons."

She tried to ignore the awkwardness of the demeaning situation. Nonetheless, the men shuffling at the end of the bed and Harcourt's appraisal strained her composure. Pointing at the sword, she scowled. "Get that away from Yancy."

"I warned you, Ramsbury, not to trifle with her affections." Ewan sent her a glance filled with disappointed accusation. "I expected better from you, Isobel."

"*Aye*, it's shocked I be, lass." Father's usually jovial eyes brimmed with disapproval.

Pain welled within her chest, and she stifled a wounded gasp. Clasping the blanket tighter, she dropped her gaze as mortification surged from her bare shoulders to her hairline.

They blame me.

And Ewan had warned Yancy away from her? Tears pooled, but she refused to shed them.

Yancy shifted the tiniest bit, nudging her knee with his. "I suppose you wouldn't believe me if I told you I've every intention of marrying her."

Nearly letting loose of the blanket, Isobel swung her gaze to him. Had she heard him correctly? "Pardon?"

"Not the most romantic proposal, I know." A twinkle entered his expressive eyes. "A blade at one's throat does rather ruin the moment."

Father and Dugall appeared ready to pummel him. Ewan threatened with the sword tip, and the others' countenances were no less menacing, except Harcourt who seemed highly amused by the situation.

Her composure and patience at an end, Isobel jerked her head toward the door. "Leave. All of you, so I can rise."

"Not until we settle the matter." Legs spread, Father folded his arms, his expression unyielding.

Stubborn oaf.

Dugall mimicked their father's stance.

If it hadn't been for the seriousness of the situation, Isobel might have teased him. Instead, she flashed her father as stare meant to scorch his hair and blister his skin.

"Do you think to have this discussion with Isobel unclothed in full view of these men, Sir Hugh?" With a blade at his throat, Yancy dared challenge her father.

A rush of appreciation seized her. She might be able to pretend chagrin wasn't shattering her, but she wouldn't be able to continue the ruse much longer. Especially, with the curious and censured glances—and a few appreciative ones as well—covertly directed at her from the clansmen.

Everyone between here and London would know of her ruination within days.

Yancy's question took Father aback. His dark-brown eyes assessed the earl. "*Nae*. Clear the room. That be includin' ye, yer lordship."

Yancy patted Isobel's leg. "Everything will be all right. I promise."

As you promised last night?

Father lurched forward. "I'll thank ye to keep yer hands off me daughter."

Ewan stepped away and lowered his sword, though he didn't sheath the weapon.

As Yancy rose, the men ambled from the chamber except her father and Ewan who came up behind him.

"Father, wait." Isobel scooted higher, careful to keep the blanket secured over her breasts. "Where are Duncan and the twins?"

As one, the men turned to look at her.

A grimace settled on Ewan's face, and the scowl he leveled Yancy could have ignited tinder. "You didn't tell her?"

Yancy's fierce glower mirrored her brother's.

"No. She's been through enough, and I didn't think she needed any more worries at the moment. She was abducted, assaulted—in case her bruised face escaped your attention—held prisoner, and nearly forced to marry a crazed monster before she escaped and fled for her life. I'd say that was quite enough to endure."

Premonition slithered across Isobel's bare skin, and she shuddered. *Damned, rotten owl.*

"What has happened?" Isobel could barely form the words.

Ewan drew near again, his face lined with regret. "Gregor was shot. When we left Craiglocky, he fought for his life."

"Dear God, no." Isobel clapped a hand to her mouth, tears streaming from her eyes. She shook her head, her hair billowing about her shoulders. "No. No."

Not Gregor.

Yancy paused at the door, his features oddly tender. "I shall get your clothes. They should be dry."

The moment the door clicked shut, she buried her face in the pillow, sobs wrenching her. Dear Gregor had been wounded. Did he live? A wave of nausea slammed into her. *He must*. The gentle giant couldn't die. He couldn't.

She'd made a horrid cake of everything—caught bare as a bone in bed with Yancy by her father and brothers. Given Yancy's reputation, they wouldn't believe nothing happened.

How could she face them? Or Mother? Fresh shame engulfed her. To spare her family the disgrace, she'd go away, God only knew where, though.

Ten minutes later, hair plaited and eyes undoubtedly red and swollen, Isobel emerged. Only Ewan, Father, and Harcourt remained with Yancy. He had dressed and sat at the table, a guarded expression on his face. Tension firmed his mouth, and anger simmered in his eyes.

The fire had burned out during the night and no one had attempted to start another. They must intend to leave immediately.

Ewan stood near the windows, his back to the others.

The day promised a repeat of yesterday. Cold, dank, and miserable. Normal for Scotland, and a perfect description of her heart as well.

The door swung open and Dugall stamped inside. "It be a *dreich* day."

Yes, a dreadful day, indeed.

He shook off his wet plaid. "The beasties be ready."

Isobel advanced into the room and draped her shoulders with her cloak. "I take it we're to leave at once?"

Ewan turned from staring outside. "Just as soon as the vows have been spoken."

Isobel froze in fastening the braided cord at her throat. "Vows?"

She almost gagged on the croak that emerged. Determined not to glance at Yancy, she drew in a bracing breath. Nonetheless, she sensed his penetrating gaze willing her to look his way.

What of Matilda? She's ruined too.

"*Aye*, lass." Father strode to her. He touched her damaged cheek, compassion having replaced the wrath in his eyes earlier. "Ye've been compromised. I would save ye some embarrassment. Ye and the earl can exchange yer vows here. No one need know how we found ye before ye wed."

Except, everyone would in any event.

Attempting to stifle what the clan members witnessed in the bedchamber was as futile as trying to keep snow from melting over a blazing fire or damming the River Tay with a hairpin.

Nigh on impossible.

Father motioned to Dugall and Ewan. "Yer brothers and me be the witnesses. And the duke, too. I'll have the rector register the marriage when we get home."

Harcourt remained silent, his usual mocking expression gone sober.

What a confounded mess.

Isobel stepped away and continued securing her cloak. She examined each in turn, forcing a smile. "You've thought this through, it seems. And what if Lord Ramsbury doesn't wish to marry me?"

She bit the inside of her cheek, afraid of his response, yet knowing what she must do, no matter his reply.

Yancy rose and after a swift, guarded glance at Ewan, started toward her.

"That's far enough. You'll not touch my sister again until you are husband and wife." His countenance stony, Ewan fingered his sword.

A hungry bear proved more amiable.

"Oh, good heavens, Ewan. Leave off, will you, please?" Isobel felt rather like a cranky she-bear herself.

"Isobel, look at me." Though Yancy's tone remained gentle, she couldn't ignore his request.

To keep her features composed, she curled her toes in her half-boots.

He smiled that dashing smile of his, sending her silly heart into palpitations. "I want to marry you."

What did one threaten an earl of the realm and Britain's War Secretary to make him acquiesce to a forced marriage?

"Of course you do." She released a humorless laugh and fluttered her fingers in Ewan's direction.

Ewan regarded her warily.

"I am sure my brother's blade and whatever they threatened to do to you if you didn't make an honest woman of me has nothing to do with your eagerness to wed." She flinched at the shrill sarcasm in her voice.

Harcourt could take lessons from her today. She shot him a glance.

Compassion simmered in his silvery eyes, and he offered a kind smile.

Dugall couldn't hide his discomfit. Suddenly absorbed in the scarred floor, he wouldn't meet her gaze.

So, they *had* threatened Yancy.

No surprise, there.

They were Scots, after all. In addition to be ferociously protective and loyal, the Scottish weren't above using less than finesse means to obtain what they desired. Ewan had tricked Yvette into marrying him by similar means, albeit he had done so to keep her from certain ravishment.

Rather surprising His Grace hadn't objected or done something to aid Yancy. Perhaps he had tried, but to no avail.

"Isobel, I honestly do wish to marry you," Yancy said. "Nothing would make me happier."

So sincere were his voice and expression, she could almost convince herself he cared for her.

"Thank you, Lord Ramsbury. I am honored and humbled by your offer." She gave him what she hoped appeared a grateful smile. Quite difficult to do when her heart had been rent in two. "However, none of this muddle is of your making, and I take full responsibility for everything."

"Be that as it may, lass, he still be obliged to marry ye. He was caught in yer bed." His eyes bleary, Father held out his hand. "Let's be about it then, shall we? Yer Mother's frantic for yer return."

She stared at his large, calloused hand for a long moment then lifted her gaze. Surely, regret shone in them. Isobel shook her head. "No, I think not."

"What do ye mean, *nae*?" Brows wrinkled and lips pursed, Dugall appeared wholly baffled. He turned to their father. "Make her see reason, *Da*."

Father sighed and sympathy lined his craggy face. "Ye *dinna* have a choice, lass."

"You cannot be serious." Ewan planted his hands on his hips, glaring as if he would like to paddle her.

"I'll be tarred and feathered." Harcourt laughed. "Seems like you have escaped the parson's mousetrap, Ramsbury. By a whisker."

He chortled again.

"Why not?" Yancy angled his head, his gaze searching hers.

If she didn't know better, she would think him sincerely confused. Wounded, even.

She twisted her hands in the cloak. "My reasons are my own."

"You must marry. You're ruined twice over as it is." Ewan paced about the room, flinging her frustrated looks. "This is utterly ridiculous."

"I quite agree." Isobel angled toward the door. She had to escape before she ran screaming like a lunatic. Her reserve of dignity had depleted to a thimbleful.

Ewan swung to Yancy. "Ramsbury, will you take Isobel as your wife?"

She whirled to confront Ewan. "That is beyond the pale, Ewan. Just stop. Now."

If she had her parasol, she would whack him, the overbearing, interfering arse.

"I will." His unblinking gaze trained on her, Yancy stared into her soul. "And I do."

God, how she wished he weren't being forced to marry her, wished he'd actually chosen to ask her, wished he hadn't compromised Matilda and promised to marry the girl.

If wishes were horses then beggars would ride.

"Isobel, please, say you'll take Ramsbury as your husband." A pleading tone entered Ewan's voice. He truly was desperate to protect her. Her heart thawed a degree. Bless him and his misguided efforts.

All she had to do was say yes. Simple as that. Under Scottish law, she and Yancy would be legally married.

"I know what you are trying to do, Ewan, and though I appreciate the sentiment behind it, you overstep the bounds." Heavy of heart and foot, Isobel turned her back. She'd disappointed them and all but obliterated any prospect for her future happiness. Everything had gone to hell in a handcart.

She couldn't bear to glance Yancy's way, or she would burst into tears. At the off-kilter door, she held her breath, her eyes and mouth pressed into tight lines, as she struggled for control.

She didn't want the men outside to see her in a state, nor could she remain inside where any moment, her composure would crumble like a month-old ginger biscuit.

"Isobel?" Softly treading footsteps approached. Yancy turned her to face him.

No, don't say it. Don't ask me, I beg of you.

Don't make me deny the thing I want most in the world.

He cupped her face, forcing her to meet his troubled eyes. "Will you marry me?"

She swallowed as a tear seeped from the corner of one eye. "I cannot."

Bending nearer, he searched her eyes, his gaze tender. He caressed her chin with his thumb. "Why?"

The door burst open, smacking her hard and shoving her into Yancy's arms. His scent and arms engulfed her simultaneously.

Kinley, breathless, sweaty, and smelling of horse, tromped into the cottage. "Riders be approachin', movin' fast, and bearin' MacHardy's colors."

Chapter 24

"Please do exactly as I ask, Isobel. MacHardy is as ruthless as the men who took you." One hand on Isobel's elbow, Yancy led the group from the hut. He firmed his grip on her arm. "Do you understand? Promise me."

Her turquoise gaze probing, she scrutinized his face. What did she seek?

"I promise."

Easing from his clasp, she stepped away. A mantel of despair shrouded her, evident in her bowed head and slumped shoulders.

Drizzle seeped from the dreary morning sky, shadowing the glade laden in foggy grayness. Two score brawny Scots, heavily armed and alert, sat mounted and awaiting orders.

How the hell had he not heard *that* entourage arrive?

An entire bottle of whisky, that's how.

The crushing pain in his skull threatened to cross his eyes. No more than he deserved for such overindulgence.

Skye, along with several other saddled horses, shuffled restlessly. The horseflesh seemed as eager to be done with this business and return home as he.

And Isobel, for certain.

He ventured a glimpse toward her.

Regal as a queen, her delicate features outwardly composed, tumult simmered within the depths of her eyes. Placing her hood over her head, she shifted away from his scrutiny and stared into the mossy trees. She had fared the worst of all of them, and given this morning's ill-fated events, the conundrum hadn't fully played out.

By God, if she didn't accept his suit—

Not now.

Yancy shoved her rejection and his dismay accompanying her rebuff to an isolated corner of his mind. Later, at his leisure, he would examine them. More pressing matters demanded his attention. MacHardy's brazenness didn't bode well.

He sought the Scot who'd brought the news. "What are the baron's numbers, and how far away are they, Mister—?"

"Kinley, yer lordship." Hand on his belt, the Scot bobbed his head respectfully. "Fourteen men, and they be two miles, maybe a wee bit more to the northeast."

"Dugall, please help your sister mount." Yancy stopped himself short of ordering McTavish to put Isobel on Skye. "She's to ride with you."

Isobel hurried to do as he bid, a mite more eagerly than he liked.

Yancy turned to face Sethwick. "I trust you dealt with the Blackhalls?"

"Yes." Sethwick sent a guarded glance to his sister. "We won't have any more difficulties from that quarter."

He slipped a dirk into his boot. "Other than a few ambitious fools possessing more bravado than common sense, the rest dropped their weapons swifter than hot pokers pressed to their nether regions the moment we stormed the gates."

"The majority of the scunners be threatened and coerced into doin' Blackhall's biddin'." Sir Hugh stretched his arms overhead then flexed his wide shoulders. "They be havin' *nae* more desire for a conflict with other clans or England than we do."

"They were eager to cooperate, and in return, I gave them my word the Crown wouldn't seek retribution." Sethwick adjusted his plaid before tightening the belt at his waist.

Fingering the silver buttons on his coat, Yancy considered Sethwick. The man's diplomatic skills were legendary, as was his temper. "That was wise and a far better way to earn men's loyalty then trying them for treason. What of the MacGraths and Claustons?"

Sethwick actually smiled as he swept his dark hair off his forehead before placing his tam atop his head. "Except for a few rogue malcontents, the other tribes weren't involved in the unrest. Angus Blackhall and MacHardy contrived the whole scheme to get Tornbury lands."

"*Aye*. A few stolen plaids and strategically bandyin' some names about had people convinced the MacGraths and Claustons be aligned with Dounnich House." Sir Hugh hitched up his trews, his thoughtful gaze focused on Isobel. Lines of worry creased his forehead. He fretted for his daughter.

Sethwick grunted and kicked a pinecone. "Angus was an idiot for believing MacHardy would share an inch of Tornbury or that there'd be no reprisal if the baron had succeeded in marrying Miss Farnsworth."

Yancy rubbed his sore nape and smothered a yawn. He didn't favor sleeping on the floor and neither did his aching muscles. "You're saying MacHardy contrived the entire rebellion rumor so he could get his grubby hands on Tornbury's lands?"

Dammit, what kind of blind chucklehead didn't suspect that very thing? In hindsight, the ploy was as glaring as Prinny in his puce cutaway and breeches. A feudal baron, MacHardy's greed for land knew no bounds.

Had love done that to Yancy, distracted and jumbled his mind to the point he couldn't perform his duties? Self-castigation stabbed him.

Fool.

Both Sethwick and Sir Hugh nodded. A hint of

compassion shone in the latter's dark eyes, but Sethwick's gaze remained coolly aloof.

"What maggot got into MacHardy's head? To take that kind of a colossal risk for grazing land and pristine water?" Yancy snorted. "Bloody imbecile."

"Seems gold be discovered a wee while back." Pursing his mouth, Sir Hugh's face crinkled with a squint as if trying to recall when. "I heard rumors a year ago, meself. Farnsworth tried to keep it close to his chest, but news of that kind *canna* stay hidden *verra* long."

Gold?

All this chaos because of greed?

A muscle in Yancy's jaw jumped with suppressed rage. Men died yesterday, though the renegades deserved their fate. Gregor's life hung in the balance, perhaps had been forfeited, and Yancy's hope of winning Isobel may have been crushed to dust.

For what? So men could line their pockets?

"Our few wounded are en route to Craiglocky." Sethwick's announcement jolted Yancy back to the present.

"What of Angus and Dunbar?" Perched atop Dugall's massive beast, Isobel's quiet question echoed loudly through the clearing. Strain pinched her pretty face.

Every gaze swung to her.

Sethwick's features softened. "Dead. You've nothing to fear from them ever again, Isobel. Neither does Lydia."

Her countenance revealed neither relief nor joy at the news, but rather resignation. She idly toyed with the horse's mane. "Tasara and her brother and sister?"

"Safe and on their way back to the gypsy encampment with their father." Harcourt offered the information.

Something in his voice alerted Yancy. He eyed the duke. Harcourt appeared inordinately absorbed in a blob of mud on the toe of his usually shiny boot.

Sethwick grinned as if he was privy to an amusing secret. "There's a tale you must hear."

A flush stole up Harcourt's face, and the glower he shot Sethwick would have laid out a lesser man.

Several Scots snickered.

Yancy gave them a stern stare. "Another time, perhaps."

No *perhaps* about it. Harcourt didn't color. Come to think of it, he did seem rather subdued. Just how had he acquired his bruised eye?

That would have to wait. More important matters loomed. "Harcourt, take all but half a dozen men and conceal yourselves amongst the trees. Miss Ferguson goes as well."

Isobel opened her mouth, probably to protest, but snapped it shut at the severe look Yancy sent her. Good. She intended to keep her word.

He inspected Sethwick's men. Better trained than His Majesty's Army, he would wager. They might very well need to put their skills to use again. "Once MacHardy's party arrives, watch for me to mount. That's your cue to surround them."

With a stiff inclination of his head, Harcourt wordlessly slung onto his steed then led the others into the surrounding wood. Within moments, they had vanished into the grayness.

The day's gloom and poor visibility provided a perfect covering. MacHardy wouldn't realize he was outnumbered and entrapped until too late. Likely the sod hadn't figured on Sethwick outriding him and overtaking Yancy and Isobel before the baron did.

Sethwick must have ridden throughout the night to reach them—a testament to his tracking skills and devotion to his sister.

Five minutes later, the baron thundered through the forest and into the opening. With a cruel yank on the reins, his horse skidded to a stop, spraying Yancy with globs of filth.

Eyes rolling, the bay flicked his ears and swung its head, mouthing the bit. MacHardy had hurt the animal, the cawker.

Upon seeing Sethwick and the McTavish clansmen assembled, MacHardy's bushy eyebrows launched to his hairline. He schooled his features and pointed at Yancy's mud-splattered clothing, guffawing. "Ye should have moved, yer lordship. Yer natty togs be ruined."

"What brings you to these parts, MacHardy?" Giving the Scot a cursory glance, Yancy brushed a speck of muck off his forearm. "And why the large escort?"

He motioned to the motley men accompanying the baron.

MacHardy's crafty gaze roamed the area. A sneer bent his mouth, and he rested his elbow on the saddle. "I came to find ye. To demand justice."

"Justice? I find it rather odd you would seek me here"—Yancy jabbed a thumb at the hut—"and not at Craiglocky. Why, pray tell, is that?" He quite enjoyed baiting the liar.

"Cause yer that fat, royal turd in London's lackey, that be why." Hatred etched across the planes of his face as the baron pointed a grimy finger at Sethwick. "McTavish attacked Dounnich House, killin' several loyal Scots. I had me spies embedded there aidin' in catchin' the Blackhalls, MacGraths, and Claustons conspirin' to revolt against the crown."

Yancy slanted his head and crossed his arms. "Are you claiming to be an agent provocateur, that you've compiled evidence against the disgruntled Scottish clans for His Highness, 'The fat, royal turd?'"

The glade erupted in hearty laughter.

Yancy gathered Skye's reins and clicked his tongue. "And here I naïvely assumed you pursued Miss Farnsworth and had no idea Sethwick arrived before you."

"What game be ye playin', Ramsbury?" Reaching

beneath his kilt to rearrange his privates, the baron surveyed the clearing again. "Where be the chit?"

Yancy shoved his foot into the stirrup, and with a curt nod, swung into the saddle. "Lydia Farnsworth never left Craiglocky lands."

Let the bastard stew on that.

Except for the barest flinch, MacHardy remained stoic.

Sethwick and the others mounted. They pointedly encircled MacHardy, isolating him from his men.

"Your hirelings made a grave error. Have you any idea what that might have been?" Sword drawn and daggers shooting from his eyes, Sethwick edged his stallion forward.

"No, I can see by your face, you haven't a clue." With his sword tip, he deftly severed a button from the Scot's coat. "The lackwits you hired abducted *my sister*."

MacHardy gave his reins a reflexive jerk, and his mount sidestepped nervously. The baron's shrewd eyes thinned to slits as he exchanged a speaking glance with his second in command. A chorus of swords swished from his soldiers' sheaths.

"That be a grave accusation, and I be takin' exception to such a foul charge. I had nothin' to do with any abduction." Rage contorted MacHardy's features as he shook his fist. "I should call ye out, McTavish."

"But you won't." Sethwick's silky tone belied the wrath in his eyes. He rotated his sword in a small figure-eight. "We both know I would choose swords, and my skill with a blade is far superior to yours. Besides, if anyone is a hoggish piece of *shite*, it's you. I wouldn't give you three minutes against me, MacHardy."

The baron's jaw worked for moment. His fists clenched as he met Sethwick and Yancy's sardonic grins. He spat and wiped his mouth with his forearm then stiffened as Sethwick's men emerged from the woods.

"What be the meanin' of this?" The baron's vulture-like eyes narrowed. "Ye be in this together, Ramsbury? The Regent would be interested to hear ye be exploitin' yer position and power."

Yancy rubbed his nape again. "Actually, that sounds rather like what you've been doing, MacHardy. I doubt Prinny will be eager to hear of your treachery."

"Ye have *nae* proof." Some of MacHardy's swagger evaporated. He licked his lips, and his gaze darted about the clearing. "There's *nae* a man alive who can speak against me."

"Perhaps, no man can, Sir Gwaine, but I most assuredly can." Riding behind Dugall, Isobel's high color added to her exquisite beauty. She speared the baron with an unpitying glare. "And have no doubt, I shall, with pleasure."

MacHardy snorted and gave a dismissive flutter of his fat fingers. "The word of a tarnished wench? Worthless."

Yancy sidled his horse nearer. If his position as War Secretary didn't demand he act with judiciousness, he'd spit the bugger where he sat. Instead, he planted MacHardy a solid facer, knocking him from his saddle.

Yancy guided Skye to the prone bastard.

The horse quivered and raised his head, curling his lip. He blew out a breath. Seemed he didn't care for the baron's putrid stench either.

Sir Gwaine struggled to a sitting position and using the back of his hand, daubed at the blood trailing from his split lip.

Yancy leaned over. "Oh, I believe Prinny will be most interested in hearing what Miss Ferguson has to say. She is, after all, the sister of one of his favorite peers and my intended."

Chapter 25

Two days later, using her hood and Dugall's wide shoulders as buffers, Isobel avoided glimpsing the frequent, troubled glances Yancy directed her way.

He ought to be bothered, the dunderhead.

Riding left of the path's center and a horse's length away, he'd positioned himself in her direct line of vision. Her perfidious gaze kept slinking in his direction until she turned her head the opposite way and laid her cheek against Dugall.

She fully intended to complete the journey to Craiglocky and not speak a word to Yancy. That he blatantly manipulated the circumstances to his benefit peeved her no end. Matters were complicated enough without adding the betrothal lie to the mix.

Had he forgotten about Matilda? What was she to do if he threw her over? If he tossed the girl aside so readily, how long could Isobel expect faithfulness from him if he wedded her?

About as long as a stallion corralled with a herd of in-season mares.

She drew her cloak tighter, chilled both in body and spirit.

Marriage to a rake promised a lifetime of misery. For that reason alone, she wouldn't touch matrimony to Yancy with a barge pole. Besides, everyone she held dear had found true love. Her parents were devoted to each other, as were Ewan and Yvette and Adaira and Roark. She could add Flynn and his new wife and Lord and Lady Warrick to the list too.

She'd aspired to the same.

Given her limited alternatives—a faithless jackanape or a loveless union—spinsterhood might hold some appeal, after all.

Flimflam and claptrap.

Scalding tears filled her eyes again, and she ducked her head deeper within the hood's protective folds.

Grayness blanketed everything: the pewter sky, which promised more rain before they made the keep, and the narrow, muddy track they plodded along.

The bleakness encompassing my downtrodden heart.

Even the silvery squirrels scooting up the tree trunks and the smoky-brown hares springing to take cover in the dense charcoal shadows of the underbrush.

Everything—colorless and bland.

Ewan had probably prodded Yancy into making the betrothal announcement. Just like her brother to do something of that nature—under the guise of protecting her, of course.

Men.

She was well and done with the blasted lot of them. Maybe she'd enter a convent. And die of boredom.

"Leave off jabbing me, ye bloody sod." MacHardy's petulant complaint sent a frightened squirrel scampering for the nearest pine and a trio of hoodiecrows to wing. The birds' raucous cries echoed long after they had disappeared.

Yancy had taken MacHardy and his men into custody with astonishing little resistance. Wise on the part of the surly Scot since to a man, Ewan's dedicated clan would have splayed the baron open and danced a jig afterward.

He would fare scant better in prison, unless the gibbet saw him dancing instead. His singular reprieve lay in deportation to Australia, and his lands would be forfeit to the crown.

Upon hearing the news of Angus and Dunbar's deaths, relief swept through her for herself, Lydia, and the Faas children.

Harcourt cantered past, giving Isobel a jaunty salute. He truly was a rogue, but a charming one. She would give up clooty dumpling for a year to know who had darkened his daylights. Even with the bruised eye, and every bit as disheveled as Yancy, the duke appeared rakishly handsome.

Her gaze skittered to Yancy speaking to His Grace in low tones, and her pulse and stomach joggled peculiarly.

Most annoying. And disturbing.

She firmed her lips into a thin ribbon, determined to erect a protective wall against him and the havoc he wreaked on her emotions.

Singing and occasionally humming a bawdy Scottish ditty beneath his breath as he had for the past several miles, Dugall guided his horse around a moss-covered boulder.

Isobel released a trembling sigh. Oh, to be as lighthearted as her younger brother.

He turned his head and scrutinized her over his broad shoulder. "It *canna* be as bad as all that, lass."

"Yes, it is. I am fair disgraced."

"Why *dinna* ye marry the earl, then?"

"I cannot."

"Why not?"

The same thing Yancy had asked.

She frowned, and Dugall faced frontward.

He hadn't finished prodding, though. "Ramsbury not be hard to gaze upon, and he be a chum of Ewan's for more than a decade. He seems a good sort, and he be taken with ye. It be plain as the tail on a hog."

"Dugall, it is impossible." She shook her head against his back, needing to share the truth. "He is promised to another."

Dugall stiffened and threw her a shocked glance. "Be ye certain?"

His muscles flexed beneath her fingers as the horse plodded onward, every step reminding her of the excessive time she'd spent astride a horse of late. Her thigh muscles screeched for reprieve, and her battered buttocks ached.

"I'll bloody rearrange his pretty face, if that be true."

"You will do no such thing." She tightened her arms about Dugall's waist, a silent warning to behave. "And yes. I am certain. His intended made a point of telling me at Adaira's Yuletide ball."

"Why did he ask ye to marry him then?"

"Dugall, we both know Ewan gave him no choice."

"*Aye*. That be true." Dugall lanced Yancy with a searing glower and heaved a gusty breath. "God rot the bugger. I be sorry, Isobel. What will ye do?"

"I don't know." Tears trickled from her eyes. "I just don't know," she whispered into the folds of his plaid. "Go away, I think."

What would she do? Where could she go?

Hopelessly in love with Yancy, she couldn't seize her happiness at the expense of someone else's ruination. Truth to tell, her trust had been eroded to a needle's point, and his reputation as a rake and a scoundrel precluded placing further faith in him. In any event, she wasn't certain Yancy or her feckless heart deserved another chance.

Emotional and physical weariness weighed heavily upon her. She let her eyelids lower and allowed the memories of last night to come, relishing the few moments of bliss she had experienced within Yancy's arms.

She'd slipped into a fitful doze and awoke when they stopped beside a stream. While the clansmen watered the horses, she forced herself to eat a small repast, though she had no appetite and the stale bread stuck to her tongue.

Yancy attempted to waylay her as she returned from seeking a spot of privacy in the shrubberies. Legs spread-eagled, he blocked her path and gently placed his palms atop her shoulders.

She didn't recall him ever having appeared vulnerable before, but marked uncertainty shone in his observant eyes and his mouth turned down as if he, too, suffered.

"Isobel, we must talk before we reach the castle."

That he dared call her by her given name said much. She should object, but after all they experienced together in the past day, the breech of propriety seemed insignificant.

Her gaze firmly affixed to the droplets of water meandering the length of a fern frond, she shook her head. "No, there's nothing to say."

"Perhaps you have nothing to say, but I have a great deal." Anger's steely edge sharpened his words as his hold on her shoulders tightened a fraction. "I care for you, very much in fact. You've been compromised through no fault of your own. I would consider it the most profound honor to make you my wife."

What an ironic paradox.

His valor could save her virtue.

He tapped the end of her nose. "Wouldn't you enjoy being my countess?"

With the alacrity of one of the black slugs creeping along the ground, Isobel's gaze traveled from Yancy's muddy boots to the stained buckskin covering his thighs, skittered past the bulge at his loins and his impossibly muscled chest, and settled on his throat.

Whatever happened to his cravat?

Whyever do I care at a moment like this?

A pulse beat steady and hypnotic at the juncture of his neck and collarbone. She had the oddest urge to place her mouth there, to feel his heartbeat beneath her lips.

"Isobel?" Yancy possessed the patience of a saint; she would give him that.

Thick stubble covered his lower face. A memory sprang to her mind, the sensation of those whiskers scraping across her breast. Had that been just last night? It seemed an eon ago.

Isobel crossed her arms against her traitorous nipples' puckering. No other man caused her body to respond, so intense and uncontrollable, the way she did with him.

And no one else ever would.

She lovingly roved his features with her gaze. Yancy did have the most beautiful lips, and his high cheeks and aristocratic nose portrayed the blue blood thrumming in his veins. But his eyes, those mysterious green orbs, had always been her undoing. She could become lost gazing into them, her soul touching his.

"Isobel?" A soft rasp of yearning, he whispered her name and touched her unmarred cheek.

Of their own volition, her feet inched ahead, and she leaned toward him, her gaze locked on his mouth.

Dugall laid a heavy arm across her shoulders and maneuvered her from Yancy's grasp. "Isobel, Father wants a word with ye."

Dumping a bucket of freezing water from Lake Arkaig upon her head couldn't have been more jarring. She blinked, trying to collect her thoughts. She'd nearly kissed Yancy. Right here in full view of everyone. Her fate would have been sealed.

"Isobel, he be waitin'." Dugall squeezed her shoulder.

Giving herself a mental shrug, she forced her gaze from Yancy. "Yes, of course. Thank you, Dugall."

"Would you give us a moment more, please?" Yancy's touch to her elbow stayed her.

Dugall's hesitant gaze shifted between Isobel and Yancy. A shuttered mien descended, and he shook his raven head. "*Nae*, me lord. Me sister's made her position clear. Ye'll need to speak to our father if ye have more to say."

Isobel's heart wrenched at the expression of desolation puckering Yancy's face. Could he care for her, or did Ewan's threats cause his despair?

Determinedly keeping her attention on her father and Ewan, she hurried in their direction before she flouted good sense and bolted into Yancy's arms.

His muttered, "Bloody, maggoty hell," spurred her footstep a mite faster.

Afterward, she remained near her male relatives, giving Yancy no opportunity to catch her unaccompanied. She sensed his and Ewan's growing frustration.

Too bad. She would not be manipulated into marriage.

Dugall must have warmed their father's ears with her sad tale. All solicitousness, Father had once again become the great protector from her childhood. The man who, when she'd fallen and scraped a knee or had a splinter in her finger, had swept her into his embrace and tickled her tears away.

If only her waterworks and heartache might be eased that simply today.

"Mount up, and be quick about it. I mean to make Craiglocky by nightfall." Already seated on Skye, Yancy gave the order.

Dugall waited for her by his horse.

She picked her way between the slugs littering the ground. Gads, the rain had brought the horrid, slimy beasts out in droves. They quite reminded her of the revolting mushrooms in the mash Sorcha served with beef fillet.

A God-awful stench wafted past, and Isobel pressed the back of her hand to her nose. She examined the bushes. Had something died nearby?

"I'd be thinking twice, lass, about speakin' against me."

Isobel's attention lurched to MacHardy slouched atop a horse, his hands tied to the saddle. Unease pricked her, but she quashed it. He could do her no harm now.

Covered in reddish hair, his trunk-like legs poked from below his grungy plaid. The putrid reek emanated from him. The man proved foul in every regard.

She suppressed a gag. Pulling her cloak aside, she eyed him coldly. "I shall tell the truth, sir. It is up to the courts to decide how to act upon my testimony."

A sly smirk contorted his lips, revealing a row of brownish-black rotting teeth. "Do ye think I acted alone? *Nae*, I would be looking closer to me home, if I be ye."

Chapter 26

As night claimed the last vestige of daylight, Yancy led the fatigued company across Craiglocky's drawbridge. The thunder of over two hundred and fifty hoofbeats reverberating atop the wooden panels roused those in the baileys and keep.

Excited clan members surged from doorways and lean-tos. Holding lanterns and rush torches, they soon flooded the courtyard with light, and people eager for news of Isobel.

Yancy dismounted, and after handing Skye's reins to a stable boy, he stretched, easing the stiffness the lengthy hours in the saddle caused. "See he's rubbed down well, and given an extra portion of grain. He has earned it."

Skye pressed his nose to Yancy's chest and issued a low nicker.

"I'm grateful to be back too." He patted the horse's wither. "Well done, old friend."

Skye responded with another gentle whicker.

"Sir, might I wait until I hear the news of Miss Isobel? Did Laird McTavish find her? Did he bring her home?" Eyes round and anxious, the boy shifted from foot to foot, his gaze repeatedly flitting to the mounted riders.

The lad's devotion to his lady earned Yancy's admiration.

"Yes, he did." He stifled a yawn. "I haven't met a braver, more intelligent woman in my life."

"*Aye*, that she be." The whelp puffed his scrawny chest out, a grin splitting his freckled face. "She be of the clan McTavish."

"And you have every right to be proud." Yancy handed the lad a coin. He hadn't thought the youth's eyes could grow larger, but the astonished, saucer-like gaze gawking at him proved him wrong.

Yancy maneuvered his way through the throng. He needed a moment with Isobel before she fled into the house and escaped into her family's care.

He grimaced. *Fled*? *Escaped*? What, had she become his quarry? No, though he had every intention of snaring her.

"There be Miss Isobel." At the front of the crowd, an eager man holding a curly-haired toddler pointed to the new arrivals.

"Where?"

"I *dinna* see the lass."

"She be sittin' behind Dugall."

The horde spotted her, and a roar loud enough to shake the stars from the sky rose heavenward.

"Isobel?" Lady Ferguson's soft cry carried across the night air.

Sandwiched between Lady Sethwick and Miss Seonaid, Lady Ferguson hovered at the top of the gatehouse stairs. To her left stood Miss Farnsworth and Ross, in addition to Warrick and Bretheridge beside their wives. A rotund, elderly maid who kept dabbing at her eyes with her apron, and the McTavishs, save Gregor, had positioned themselves on Lady Ferguson's right.

A passel of dogs lumbered, *en masse*, down the steps, a monstrous gray boarhound in the lead, loping straight at Isobel.

Lady Ferguson and her daughters rushed into the crowd as Sir Hugh, Harcourt, and Ewan dismounted. The rest of those assembled on the steps hastily followed.

The crowd shushed and respectfully parted to let the women pass. Their pallor and tautness of their frames spoke of the anguish they endured in Isobel's absence. Several onlookers sniffled, and more than one clansman's eyes held a suspicious dampness.

Sir Hugh engulfed his wife in a bear-like hug then pulled Miss Seonaid into his arms.

Sethwick encircled Yvette in an embrace no less fierce.

A wave of envy washed Yancy. He would give up his earldom to know that kind of love with Isobel. Yet, she'd spurned him once again.

He would have the why of it this time. He deserved to know her reasons at least. No woman—nude as a water nymph and in bed with a man she obviously found attractive—when discovered by her father and brothers, would refuse to marry the man without damned good cause.

Yancy would hear the excuse from her lips before hauling MacHardy to Newgate to stand trial.

Lady Ferguson rose on her tiptoes and kissed her husband's cheek then disengaged herself. Her eyes shiny, she approached Dugall holding his stallion's halter. She gave him a swift hug. "Thank you, son, for bringing your sister home safely."

Though she had lived at Craiglocky almost three decades, her musical voice held traces of her French heritage.

Across the distance, Dugall's gaze locked with Yancy's. "I *canna* take the credit, Mother. Lord Ramsbury rescued our Isobel."

The whispers of the crowd drifted throughout the courtyard, a low buzz of praise and questions.

"*Non,* he did?" Lady Ferguson turned as Yancy reached her side and graced him with a radiant smile. "You have my deepest and most sincere appreciation, my lord."

"Please believe me, my lady, when I tell you that bringing your daughter home safely has been my greatest pleasure." Bowing over her hand, he brought his gaze even with Isobel's. "I've never been more compelled, nor have I ever done anything as worthy, in my entire life."

"Isobel, do let Lord Ramsbury assist you from the saddle, and then give your mother a hug." Lady Ferguson opened her arms wide. She glanced to Yancy. "Such a fright I've had. And trust me, Lord Ramsbury, with this family, there is always something afoot."

She released a tinkling laugh.

Yancy advanced until he stood directly beside Isobel. "Swing your leg over, and then put your hands on my shoulders. I shall lift you to the ground."

Weariness etched her features, and she stared at him for an extended moment. A haunted glint lingered deep within her beautiful eyes. Inclining her head, she complied without protest or speaking.

His hands at her waist, Yancy whispered in her ear as he lowered her from the horse. "We shall have that promised conversation. I shan't depart until we do."

Isobel stiffened and clutched his shoulders, her fingers biting into his flesh through his coat. Her eyes bored into his. Desperation and something deeper lurked there. Her adorable chin jutted upward. "I told you. I've nothing to say."

"Oh, I think you have plenty to say, and I am going to find out exactly why you've treated me as a leper for months now."

"Why won't you leave me be?" Defeat darkened her expression and sorrow weighted her words.

Yancy squeezed her waist. "I cannot, Isobel."

Her mother and the rest of her family swooped in with tears and murmured words of comfort and joy.

Yancy stepped aside. *Devil it.* So much for a few quiet moments with her.

Surrounded by her family, she smiled through her tears. Her eyes met his over Seonaid's shoulder. A shuttered mien settled on Isobel's face, and she shifted her attention to Lady Ferguson. "Mother, please tell me how Gregor fares. I've been terribly worried."

"He is sitting up, *chéri*, and his appetite has returned."

Her mother propelled her in the gatehouse's direction. "The doctor expects him to make a full recovery."

Before disappearing underneath the arched entrance, Isobel tossed a glance over her shoulder. The woundedness in her gaze lanced Yancy, rapier sharp. Pure gibberish, all her proclamations of indifference. She was no more immune to him than he to her.

Sethwick, Harcourt, and Sir Hugh approached.

Yancy pulled his attention from the gatehouse and the intriguing woman within.

"I shall have them locked in the dungeon until you're ready to set out for London." Sethwick motioned to MacHardy and his entourage. His keen gaze roved the bailey. "Do you want me to send a contingent of my men as escorts or will you send a courier to White Hall requesting English soldiers journey here?"

Sethwick remained reserved and none too pleased with him. Perhaps Sethwick's latter suggestion was borne more of his desire to see Yancy remain at Craiglocky and make an honest woman of his sister than a desire to be helpful.

Nevertheless, Yancy rather liked the idea.

The trip to London would take at least three days, another to gather the soldiers, and then three more to return to Craiglocky. He would have another week, possibly a mite more to win Isobel's favor.

God shaped the entire world and all of creation in seven days. In comparison, Yancy's feat of winning a wife should be simple as buttering bread.

If wishes were horses.

A blast of damp air heralded another approaching gale. Yancy rested his hands on his hips and made a slow, thorough sweep of the bailey with his gaze. A trio of speckled hens cackled and fluffed their feathers before scurrying to their coop for the night.

Most of the clan members had retreated into their homes after Isobel disappeared inside the keep. A few lingered outdoors, chatting. Others went about completing their evening tasks. A pair of swarthy-skinned grooms led several horses to the stables, while Sethwick's kinsmen corralled MacHardy and his riffraff.

Yancy rubbed his bristled jaw. A bath and shave topped his list of priorities. "Isobel said someone at the keep helped the Blackwalls."

"The devil, you say?" Sethwick's black brows swooped downward in outrage. He sent a stern glance about the courtyard.

A scowl creased Sir Hugh's craggy features, as he too surveyed the square. "Did she have any idea who?"

Yancy shook his head. "No, at least she didn't say if she did, but we hadn't an opportunity to discuss it."

They'd been too busy fleeing for their lives. "Isobel did mention she saw two travellers with the curs who abducted her. And I met a tinker in the forest, outside Dounnich House."

Sethwick's gaze shot to his. "The woman and children rescued from the Blackhalls were also travellers, Balcomb Faas's children."

"Yes, he's the man I sent to find you." Yancy rubbed his nape, the muscles stiff from the couple of hours he'd spent sleeping on the cottage's uncomfortable floor. "I believe someone in that tribe is our connection."

Nodding slowly, Sethwick narrowed his gaze at the gypsies gathered near the stables. "I shall question the travellers in the morning. Right now, all I want is a hot bath, something decent to eat, and to spend some time with my wife and son."

"I'll second that. Not the wife and son." Harcourt, silent until now, shuddered theatrically. "But the food and bath sound marvelous. I wouldn't say no to a finger's worth or two of Scotch or cognac and a bracing cup of coffee either."

Finger's worth or two?

Yancy would need an entire bottle to get a wink of sleep tonight. Visions of Isobel naked in his arms had tantalized him the entire day. His loins contracted. *Again.* Riding had been like sitting on a pouch of granite that repeatedly pounded his nether regions.

Maybe he'd make that a cold bath, or better yet, he would strip naked and soak in the loch until his swollen flesh hung puckered and limp.

Harcourt, his eye more discolored than earlier, yawned.

Yancy gestured at the bruise. "You must tell me how you came by that. It's a beauty. Some hamfisted behemoth must have caught you off guard."

Sethwick and Sir Hugh let loose with hearty guffaws.

Harcourt dredged up a feral scowl and attempted to straighten his hopelessly wrinkled coat. "I shall tell you—when a woman sits in Parliament."

Giving them another irritated glare, he marched to the keep, Sethwick and Sir Hugh chuckling at his retreating form.

Yancy pulled his ear. "You must tell me what is so amusing about Harcourt's, er, unfortunate visage."

Sethwick shook his head, an outlandish grin on his face. "No, the story is his to tell."

"If His Grace ever be getting over the humiliation." Sir Hugh's shoulder quivered with mirth once more.

Sethwick's men ushered MacHardy and his cohorts past.

"Think he knows who the collaborator here is?" Yancy jerked his thumb at the sneering Scot.

Sethwick turned and examined MacHardy before his gaze rested on a few gypsies scurrying into the stables. "I would bet on it."

Eyes heavy from lack of sleep, and bone-tired, Yancy accompanied Sethwick and Sir Hugh to the gatehouse.

"Welcome home, sirs." Usually stoic, a beaming Fairchild greeted them enthusiastically at the door. "I've taken the liberty of ordering baths and dinner trays for you."

He directed his attention to Yancy. "Lord Ramsbury, two correspondences arrived for you during your absence. I had them placed in your chamber."

"Thank you." Prinny no doubt, squawking about Yancy's resignation. Too blasted bad. The Regent would to have to find another War Secretary. Yancy had an heir to beget.

An hour later, having bathed and eaten a hearty meal in his bedchamber, he sat before the roaring fire nursing his third glass of Scotch since dinner.

Clothed in an emerald brocade banyan trimmed at the collar and wrists in black velvet, he stretched his legs before him and wiggled his toes, grateful to be free of his boots. He let his eyelids flutter shut, dual mantels of fatigue and liquor jumbling his mind.

He cracked an eye open, taking in the turned down bed.

No. Too much effort to walk that far.

Maybe he would sleep right here. His gaze lit upon the short stack of missives placed atop the cumbersome night table. None bore the Regent's telltale gold-trimmed, beribboned stationery. Who had written then? Was something afoot at Bronwedon Towers or Yancy's house in Mayfair?

He yawned, not bothering to cover his mouth. The letters could wait. He'd deal with them in the morning. If the matter had been urgent, a messenger would have been sent.

Yancy took a hearty sip of the spirit despite being a trifle disguised already. He'd eaten little for days and had indulged in a generous glass prior to dining and several more since. His thoughts kept turning to Isobel, a revolving cadence of frustration, adoration, and confusion.

The letters drew his consideration once more.

His curiosity wouldn't let him ignore the confounded

things. Heaving a sigh, he rose. The room wavered for a dizzying moment.

"I'm half-sprung." He chuckled and after a mocking salute with his nearly empty glass, finished the Scotch.

Turquoise eyes swirled to the forefront of his mind as he crossed the Axminster carpet patterned in rich shades of brown and beige.

"Better plan on drinking the whole damned bottle."

Julia Cambrill's sultry, doe-like eyes suddenly plowed into his brain, much like a runaway carriage tumbling off a cliff. And about as welcome. The familiar humiliation thoughts of Julia usually brought failed to rear its ugly head. She couldn't compare to Isobel in either appearance or in his affections.

Without a jot of regret, Yancy shoved her image aside.

He picked up the two letters atop and squinted to read the words, deuced difficult to do when foxed. The first was from Bronwedon's steward. A quick perusal revealed the man had at last acquired a villa in Spain Yancy had visited and become enamored of while on his grand tour years before.

The second bore Cecily's spiraling strokes. He held the paper between his thumb and forefinger as if pinching a long-dead rodent's tail. He eyed the letter with distaste. Cecily correspondences seldom bore good news.

Damned curiosity.

He cracked the seal and scanned the short missive. "Bleeding hell."

Evidently, Matilda and the vicar's pimply-faced son had been dallying. Caught coupling in the conservatory by none other than Lady Clutterbuck—one of the *haut ton's* most notorious gossips—a frantic Cecily begged Yancy to bestow a substantial dowry on Matilda to entice the cur to marry the chit.

Ramsbury, you've always shown Matilda the greatest kindness and respect, much like that of an adored older brother.

Please, if you can find it in your heart to bestow a generous dowry on her, so that she might marry and escape the scandal to some small degree, I shall be forever grateful, as I know would Matilda.

Yancy snorted.

Doing it up a bit brown, aren't you, Cecily, especially with that adored older brother balderdash?

She'd been shoving her niece beneath his nose for years, hoping Yancy would marry the chit. He had long suspected the girl wasn't Cecily's niece at all, but rather her illegitimate daughter. They bore too great a resemblance to one another.

Nonetheless, he would do as Cecily asked in a heartbeat if it meant he wouldn't have Matilda underfoot. She undressed him with her eyes whenever he chanced to be in the same room as she.

Most discomfiting since he hadn't regarded her as anything more than a bothersome child. She'd probably seduced the poor sot— had his trousers circling his ankles and his cock in her palm before he knew what she was about.

Now, if he could only rid himself of Cecily's troublesome presence. If he married, he could banish his stepmother to the dower house or send her on an extended holiday to the continent.

Yawning, he tossed the letter onto the bed, and after stretching, sauntered back to the fireplace's warmth. Yancy poured the last of the Scotch—scarcely more than a swallow. He took one, quick swig, downing the amber liquid.

He glared at the empty bottle.

Won't do at all.

A swift glance at the mantel clock had him donning his trousers. Likely everyone was abed at half past midnight. However, venturing below stairs, his long shanks bared for all to see, was beyond the pale, even for him.

After tucking his feet into a pair of slippers, he nabbed a candleholder and marched to the door. Sethwick's study boasted a sizable assortment of first-rate spirits.

Stepping into the corridor, he plowed full on into Isobel.

Chapter 27

For the second time in scarcely more than week, Isobel planted her face in Yancy's wide chest. Only this time, soft hairs tickled her nose and warm flesh met her cheek. Both sensations caused her knees to weaken, silly things. Or perchance, that he smelled positively delicious could be blamed.

To steady her, he circled her waist with an arm, holding her snugly against him, thigh to chest.

The urge to cuddle closer tempted stronger than the reek of spirits permeating him. Zounds, how much had he consumed?

"Careful, we don't want to take a tumble holding candles." His words, though pronounced perfectly, seemed too clipped and precise.

She studied his face.

A shock of unruly hair lay across his high forehead, and a silly smile molded his mouth. His forest eyes glowed with that same dangerous look that had gleamed in them at the cottage. He gave a lazy wink before his gaze sank to Isobel's lips, and his nostrils flared. He pulled her closer. "I love your hair down."

He's foxed.

She tried stepping away, but Yancy didn't relinquish his tenacious hold. She checked both ways along the hallway. Lord, all she needed was for someone to come upon them in their nightclothes while embracing.

Well, she wasn't embracing Yancy, but he most definitely held her, and quite intimately too. His maleness pressed insistently against her belly. Only a numbskull could mistake the hard bulge for anything other than arousal.

His large hand skimmed her bottom, giving it a tiny squeeze. A squeeze that caused several naughty ideas to spring to mind. *Blasted books.*

"My lord, cease this instant." Trying to wriggle away, Isobel kept her tone quiet. "Let me go."

"But you feel good." Yancy sniffed her head then nuzzled her neck.

Most assuredly, ape drunk.

"You smell"—he licked her ear—"and taste so sweet."

Isobel stifled a gasp and clutched his shoulder with her free hand. She must put an end to this, and swiftly, before she found herself in the same compromising situation as in the woodland cottage.

She painted a stern expression on her face. "Lord Ramsbury, how much have you had to drink?"

He lifted his head and frowned at her. "Only one bottle of Scotch."

"One bottle? The entire thing?" She shook her head as she examined him, clamping her teeth to keep from smiling. "Yer oot yer face."

"*Oot yer face*?" He squinted, the corners of his eyes crinkling. "What does that mean?"

She steered Yancy toward his chamber. "It means you're very drunk."

"I like it when you speak Scots." He grinned again and wiggled his eyebrows. "Say something else. How do I tell you, you're beautiful? I can say it in French, *tu es belle,* and Spanish, *eres hermosa*, and Latin, *pulchra es.* But I don't know how in Scots or Gaelic, except whisky—*uisge*."

Yancy proved a silly drunkard, and Isobel smiled, despite herself.

"Come now, my lord." She tugged him another foot.

"All these years you've spent time in Ewan's company, and you haven't picked up any Scots?"

"But I never wanted to tell Sethwick he was beautiful."

Yancy appeared so perplexed, a giggle escaped her.

He caressed her bum again.

"I said, stop that." She slapped at his hand.

"Tell me how to say you are beautiful, and I love you." His voice dropped to a gravelly timbre, and he nibbled the sensitive flesh along the juncture of her neck and shoulder.

Another jagged crack rent Isobel's heart, even as pricks of arousal sprang to life. Such sincerity rang in his words, yet nothing could come from it.

Foolish man.

Foolish me.

Yancy's choices had brought him to this place, and though a part of her yearned to throw love in the face of good sense, another was piqued at his thoughtless selfishness.

"We shouldn't be having this conversation, my lord." Pushing into his side, she turned him to the door standing wide open. "Let's get you to bed, shall we?"

He gave her a devilish smile. "Only if you join me."

"That is not going to happen." Though, Lord help her, she wanted it to.

He trailed a finger across her jaw. "You would enjoy bedding me, I promise."

I have no doubt of that.

Arm about his waist, Isobel guided him into his chamber. She set her half-burned candle on the drum table beside the door, and then urged him to the side of the bed nearest the entrance.

He stumbled and tottered for a moment. Eyes shut, he chuckled.

She snatched the candle from his hand. "My lord, may I suggest you not go doddering about drunk as a wheelbarrow while toting a candle? I am fairly certain my family wouldn't be pleased if Craiglocky went up in flames."

"Happened once already, didn't it?" Apparently, trying to focus, Yancy peered at her, his nose mere inches from hers. The flecks of gold in his eyes stood out brightly against his oversized pupils.

Firming her arm at his back, Isobel urged him onward.

He cupped her bottom once more. "But someone took a second chance and rebuilt. 'Cause they thought it worthwhile, to make the effort. When something's important, a person doesn't give up. They keep at it. Until they succeed. It becomes a quest. A mission."

His odd ramblings had her eyeing him curiously.

He regarded her innocently, the barest hint of a smile arcing his mouth. "Didn't the first castle burn?"

"Yes, in the twelfth century. The old castle ruins are on the other side of Loch Arkaig." She had imagined his subtle double entendre.

Gripping his waist, Isobel placed his candleholder on the night stand. Pushing his shoulders until he sat upon the bed, she scanned the room.

For a decade, he'd used this chamber when he came to visit. It held touches of his presence: boots lined up neatly beside the wardrobe; a short stack of rather ominous-looking volumes and several rolled documents topped the writing desk. His riding crop, sword, and a silver-topped cane stood, wedged beside the drum table, upon which a pair of gloves had been tossed.

Isobel had been an awkward, pudgy girl of nine the first time she'd laid eyes on Yancy. Even then, one look from him had sent her schoolgirl heart a-pattering.

Never mind that.

She bent to untie his sash, and her hair swung about their heads, creating a curtain.

His warm breath, heavy with spirit, whispered across her face.

After gathering her hair and tossing the strands behind her, she edged the material off his shoulders. Her fingers skimmed his flesh as she shoved the satin down his arms.

He tensed and inhaled, a sharp, swift gulp of air.

Drat.

How naïve can you be, Isobel?

She hadn't undressed a man before. How was she to know how sculpted his muscled torso would be, or how the curly hairs on his chest disappeared into the waistband of his trousers, or how his muscles would ripple from her touch even as their breathing quickened?

Or how my knees and insides would turn all quivery?

Biting her lower lip, she dared peek at him.

His eyes hooded, he regarded her, the sharp lines of his face strangely tense.

Isobel tugged at his banyan, and he lifted a hip allowing it to slide free. He was magnificent and only sheer stubbornness kept her from gawking and feathering her fingers across his chest and shoulders. She swallowed a gulp and flung his robe to the end of the bed.

He could sleep in his trousers.

Forcing a calm façade, she lifted the covers. A piece of paper floated to the floor. "Here, get in."

Yancy dutifully lay on his back and angled his long legs beneath the bedclothes.

She drew the sheets and counterpane to his chest then smoothed them.

One hand behind his head, the other draped across his waist, his penetrating gaze didn't waver from her face.

She brushed the strand of hair off his forehead. "There you are. Now go to sleep. You will have a devil of a headache in the morning."

"Can I have a kiss goodnight?" Yancy's focus dipped to her mouth, and he exhaled a ragged breath.

Isobel pursed her lips. "I don't think that would be wise."

Not that she didn't trust him to give her a single kiss. No, she would be the one to lose the tenuous grip she had on her control.

"Come now, a little peck, so I might dream of you? What harm could there be in one kiss?" His eyelids drooped, and he slurred his words.

Liquor or exhaustion? Probably both.

He really did have a lovely mouth.

"If you won't marry me, Isobel, at least gift me with your sweet lips."

His softly uttered words enveloped her heart. She made a pretense of straightening the counterpane across his chest. Another opportunity to see him thus or kiss him again wouldn't present itself.

"One chaste kiss is all I ask," Yancy mumbled, half-asleep. His eyes shut, a nascent smile curved his mouth, and his chest rose and fell rhythmically.

"Fine, so you will hush and go to sleep." Bending, she braced her hands on his shoulders and touched her lips to his in a tender kiss.

A soft snore escaped him.

Asleep? He fell asleep?

Isobel straightened, unsure whether to be piqued or amused. Giving in to the urge, she kissed him again, committing the moment, his taste, his smell, his beloved features, to memory. Her breath caught in sorrow, a painful lump where her heart should be. She forced herself to turn from Yancy and collect the candle. Something crinkled under her foot.

Bother.

She'd forgotten the paper that fell to the floor when she

tucked him in. Retrieving the crumpled page, her gaze sank to the elaborate script. One word stood out from the others.

Matilda.

Isobel shouldn't read the letter. She wasn't given to snooping, yet her blasted eyes refused to leave the foolscap. She read the missive in its entirety, not once, but twice.

Yancy wasn't now, nor—at least from what she gleaned from the letter—had he ever been involved with Matilda Darby. The girl was to wed another. He was free to marry, had been all this time.

Isobel hurried to the entrance and, after a swift perusal of the hallway, closed the door. Before she could change her mind, she peeled off her robe and slipped into bed.

Chapter 28

A warm, rounded bottom pressed into Yancy's loins, and he cupped a bountiful breast in one hand. Soft hair caressed his nose as he breathed in a woman's subtle fragrance.

No, not just *a woman's*.

Isobel's.

He remained perfectly motionless, unwilling to waken from the delightful dream; so real, he imagined he heard her soft breaths and felt her ribs rising and falling as she slept.

Gently squeezing the supple softness in his palm, he prodded her bum with his penis, bidding entrance to the sweet sanctuary of her womanhood.

Murmuring his name, she sighed and nestled closer.

Yancy's eyelids sprang open the same instant the chamber door did. Awareness crashed upon him. The woman in his arms proved no more a phantom than the crushing pain behind his eyes.

Ah, bloody hell.

Had he been so confounded foxed last night, he'd forced Isobel to his bed? He remembered nothing after she tucked the blankets about him. His head felt nigh on to disintegrating if a mouse so much as twitched a whisker.

"Good morning, my lo—" His shocked gaze riveted on the feminine lump lying beside Yancy, Swanscott stuttered to a stop. The valet's attention dove to his polished shoes. "Er, I wasn't aware you were, ah, *entertaining*, my lord. I shall return later."

Red-faced, he spun to the door and careened headlong into Sethwick.

"Good morning, Yancy."

Isobel's quiet greeting yanked Yancy's attention to the nymph lying beside him. Eyes sleep-laden, her cheeks pink, and almond-brown hair tousled, she appeared to have been thoroughly made love to.

She smiled, seemingly unperturbed by her abrupt awakening or her brother and the valet gaping like twin stuffed boars at the end of the bed. The warmth in her blue-green gaze caused another painful surge of blood to his aroused member.

"Good morning to you, my sweet." He touched her cheek. "Forgive me, but I cannot recall how you came to be in my bed."

"I'd bloody well like to know how that came about as well." Sethwick stood beside the bed, his nostrils flared, fists clenched, and eyes narrow slits of fury.

Isobel didn't spare her brother a glance, but continued to gaze at Yancy like a woman in love. *In love*?

"This is twice I've found my sister abed with you, Ramsbury." Sethwick gave Yancy a terse prod in the shoulder. "I demand satisfaction."

Shit.

"Don't be a bird-witted bore, Ewan." Shoving her glorious hair over one shoulder, Isobel scooted to a sitting position.

Thank God she wore a nightgown, though if one looked closely, the dark outlines of her perky nipples showed through the gossamer fabric.

Yancy tugged the sheet upward, covering her chest.

Gracing him with a breathtaking smile, she tucked the edges beneath her arms. "Thank you."

His cockstand stood taller, quite obvious below the sheets. To hide his arousal, he, too, maneuvered into a sitting position.

Sethwick's scowl deepened until he spied Yancy's sword near the door.

He wouldn't.

A calculating expression settled upon Sethwick's features, and his gaze shifted between the blade and bed.

Yes. He would.

Yancy feared his longtime friend might be on the verge of running him through.

"Isobel, remove yourself from this scunner's bed and this chamber immediately." Hands fisted, Sethwick's expression portended violence. "You and I shall discuss this matter after I've dealt with Ramsbury."

She settled further into the pillows. "You're not my father, Ewan, nor do you have the right to order me about."

"I am your laird," he said between clenched teeth, clearly on the verge of losing the last vestiges of his control.

"Pooh." Isobel fluttered her dainty hand dismissively. "That has no bearing in this situation."

If he weren't sincerely concerned that Sethwick meant to murder him with his bare hands, Yancy would give vent to the laughter bubbling in his chest.

Calm as a pond on a windless day, Isobel folded her hands in her lap and eyed her infuriated brother.

"Yancy is not to blame at all. I took horrid advantage of him, Ewan. Far into his cups, he was in no condition to resist my advances. I came to be in his bed quite willingly."

Ewan and Swanscott gawked at her as if she'd announced she was an East End harlot. Yancy didn't doubt his face reflected the same flabbergasted expression.

Her lips curved sweetly, and she gazed at Yancy in adoration.

I must still be soused.

He shook his head, *hard,* to clear his muddled imaginations but stopped as agony ripped from his forehead to the rear of his skull. Served him right for downing a bottle of Scotch.

No more spirits for him.

He sliced Isobel a sidelong glance. Yes, her eyes held an enraptured glint.

What happened to the Isobel adamant she wanted nothing to do with him? What changed her mind? *Had* she, in fact, changed her mind? Maybe he was bosky. Or maybe this was a damned realistic dream.

He pinched his thigh. No, he wasn't asleep.

By God, could things possibly get worse?

Harcourt strode into the chamber.

Harcourt's inquisitive gaze swung between Yancy and Isobel, before a mischievous grin split his face.

"Seems like I've arrived right on time." He wiggled his fingers toward the bed's occupants. "Crack on. Pretend I'm not here."

"What has my chamber become, a cheap theater?" Yancy swept his arm in Isobel's direction. "Are we the entertainment lined up for today?"

Combing a hand through his messy hair, he shot an angry glare to the entrance. "Can I expect anyone else to make an appearance? Is Prinny prancing about below? Have, perhaps, Lady Jersey or Countess Lieven, or another patroness of Almack's come to call?"

Isobel pointed at Harcourt's bruised face. "Your Grace, my abominable curiosity won't leave off. How did you come by your damaged eye?"

Her abrupt, and likely deliberate, change of subject defused the tension markedly well. Every eye turned to Harcourt.

He heaved a hefty sigh then hunched a shoulder. "I tried to steal a kiss from a gypsy wench I rescued at Dounnich House."

"Tasara Faas? You didn't." Isobel giggled. "And she gave you that?"

"Indeed, I did," Harcourt confessed, "though it was meant to be entirely innocent, a token of her appreciation."

"I'll bet." Yancy grinned, despite the severity of his situation.

Harcourt's shame must be monumental.

He touched his eye. "That black-haired virago can pack a wallop."

His martyred expression brought on another bout of giggles from Isobel and a chuckle from Yancy.

Swanscott struggled to keep his features impassive.

"Can we get back to the matter at hand? My sister's ruination?" Sethwick's angry voice cut through their mirth. "Name your seconds, Ramsbury."

Harcourt stepped forward. "I'd be honored to act—"

"Stubble it, Harcourt." Prepared to stand, Yancy shoved the covers aside. "Sethwick—"

"Ewan, do leave off." Isobel gave Yancy another blinding smile. "I have agreed to marry Lord Ramsbury."

Isobel held her breath, terrified to look at Yancy after her brazen declaration. His sharp intake of breath didn't help her already-cavorting nerves. She prayed she would be able to leave the chamber somewhat composed if he denied her statement.

The moment she discovered Yancy hadn't been a philandering cur, that he had been trying to court her these many years, she'd made her decision. Another night wouldn't pass without her sleeping beside the man she loved.

"Aren't you going to wish us well, brother dear?" She laced her fingers with a silent Yancy's. He looked utterly flummoxed, poor man. "After all, you were most insistent we wed."

"Why the abrupt reversal?" Ewan eyed her suspiciously and scraped his hand through his black hair, leaving several strands standing on end. He paced back and forth at the foot of the bed. "Yesterday, you refused to entertain the notion."

"A woman's permitted to change her mind, isn't she?" Isobel plucked at the counterpane's edge, not quite meeting Ewan's eyes.

Disentangling their fingers, Yancy edged from the bed. He should be the one to hear her reasons. Not bothering to don his banyan, he crossed to the door. "I need a few moments alone with my intended, gentlemen. Swanscott, I shall break my fast below stairs."

"Yes, sir." After a swift dip of his head, the valet beat a hasty retreat.

Uncertainty flickered within Ewan's eyes, no doubt torn between defending her honor and relief he didn't have to meet one of his dearest friends on the dueling field.

"I'll give you ten minutes. There'll be no more of this nonsense"—he waved at the rumpled bed—"until after the vows are spoken. I'm sending for Reverend Wallace the moment I leave this room."

Harcourt winked at Isobel. "Sethwick, why don't you let me send for the cleric and inform the others of the wedding while you tell Yancy why you barged into his bedchamber at this ungodly hour to begin with?"

She nodded. "That's a marvelous idea, Your Grace."

"I'd say it's most fortuitous that everyone has arrived for Lady Sethwick's birthday celebration. Bet my morning coffee, they'll be cackling like hens raiding a strawberry bed upon hearing the good news." He gave her a teasing smile.

Isobel grinned in return. She would have to pay Tasara a visit and discover precisely what occurred between the gypsy and the duke. Harcourt hadn't shared the entire tale.

"Thank you. That would be most helpful. Please tell the

others the wedding will take place . . ." Ewan hesitated, his gaze seeking Isobel's. "What time would you like to wed?"

She dared meet Yancy's eyes. Only tender warmth showed in their depths. "My lord? Have you a preference?"

"Call me Yancy, or if you insist, Bartholomew, though I'm afraid I won't know you're speaking to me, but don't address me as *my lord*, Isobel. You are my equal." He turned to Ewan. "I would like the ceremony to take place as soon as possible, if my betrothed agrees."

"Isobel?" Ewan waited, the signs of his prior anger gone. Instead, a merry twinkle flashed in his eye. It seemed all was forgiven. "Can you be ready within the hour?"

She considered Yancy's muscular chest. No, she had something else she wanted to do first. She glanced at the bedside clock. "It's just past eight. Let's plan the ceremony for eleven. That is, if the time is convenient for Reverend Wallace."

She swiped at a stray curl teasing her cheek.

"Eleven it is. I shall notify the others." Harcourt gave them a brash grin and whistling, marched from the room.

Yancy closed the door behind the duke. "You had something of importance to tell me?"

Ewan scratched his chin.

"Yes, I wanted to return this"—he held up Yancy's signet ring—"and also let you know, we've discovered Craiglocky's traitor. A gypsy stable hand Jocky hired on a couple of weeks ago is the culprit. Last night, he sneaked into the lower chambers by way of an exterior door."

Yancy slipped on his banyan and Isobel hid a disappointed sigh.

"Did he think to help MacHardy escape with your men standing guard?" He knotted the robe's belt. "Not terribly bright of the fellow."

"Desperation has made many a man a fool. He's kin to the gypsies the Blackhalls held captive, and those filthy Scots curs"—Ewan cast Isobel a guarded glance—"threatened to *misuse* his family if the travellers didn't aid in Miss Farnsworth's abduction. Once he learned the Faas family had been rescued, he confessed and begged for forgiveness."

"What will you do with him?" Yancy sat on the edge of the bed and took Isobel's hand in his.

Not caring Ewan looked on, she laced her fingers with Yancy's again. "Can you be lenient, Ewan? His fear and concern must have closely mirrored yours when I was captured."

"I've already sent him on his way, after a stern warning, naturally." Ewan turned to the exit then faced them again. "Oh, and I sent a messenger to request soldiers to accompany MacHardy and the rest of those vermin to London. Lydia and Ross are packing as we speak."

Disappointment swept Isobel. She'd wanted an opportunity to speak with Lydia. "They're not staying for Yvette's birthday?"

"No, Ross insists they leave for Tornbury tomorrow. He's most adamant on the matter."

Unlike Lydia's, his presence wouldn't be missed.

Ewan opened the door. "Yancy, I shall see you in my study at ten to discuss the marriage settlement terms. I'm sure Hugh will wish to participate in the conversation as well."

His face brightened. "Let me be the first to offer you felicitations."

After Ewan left, Isobel stared at the door, rather surprised he hadn't left it open. Unnatural silence permeated the bedchamber.

Cupping her cheek, Yancy turned her face to his. His gaze unreadable, he traced her lip with his forefinger. "What changed your mind?"

Chapter 29

Isobel swallowed her sudden nervousness. "I . . ."

Dash it all, she might as well tell him the truth.

"I read that letter." She pointed to the wrinkled paper lying beside the clock.

"And something therein convinced you to marry me?" Yancy's brow furrowed. "What, pray tell?"

A hot flush stole from Isobel's chest to her hairline. "Well, I had thought you practically betrothed to Matilda, and—"

He made a crude noise in the back of his throat, clearly horrified by the notion. "By all that's holy, not as long as I draw a breath. Why would you think such a thing, Isobel?"

The truth hit her with enough force, her breath hitched.

The chit had lied. And Isobel had been too naïve to realize or suspect it. She'd treated Yancy like a blackguard, and he'd done nothing wrong. Jealousy and fear had blinded her to the truth this entire time.

Chin tucked to her chest, she withdrew her hand from his. She fiddled with the sheet, afraid and embarrassed to meet his eyes. "She told me you'd been intimate and that when she was of an acceptable age, the two of you would marry."

"Blatant lie. Why didn't you ask me?" Yancy laid a hand on hers and gave it a gentle press. "Haven't I always been truthful with you?"

The pain coloring his voice brought tears to her eyes.

"I should have. I was a complete idiot," Isobel whispered. "I know that now." Eyes awash, she lifted her gaze to his. "Can you forgive me?"

He swept her hair from her neck and bent to place a kiss below her ear. "Of course, I can. I love you."

"And I love you." Tears crept from her closed eyes, and she buried her face in his shoulder. "And I almost lost you because of my foolishness."

"Well, you have a lifetime to make it up to me, and I can think of several intriguing ways you might do that."

The tone of his voice caused a delicious frisson to skitter across her flesh. "And what might those be, my lord?"

"I told you not to call me my lord." He growled and pounced on her. Pushing her into the bedding, he tickled her ribs. "I would be happy to begin your instruction before our vows are spoken."

Laughing, Isobel tried to wriggle from underneath him. Something flexed against her thigh, and her breath left her lungs in a rush.

Feeling brazen, she trailed her finger along Yancy's collarbone. "Why don't you give me my first lesson? Besides, I didn't thank you for your valiant rescue."

He angled onto his elbows then shot a glance to the closed door. "Now? Your brother is expecting us below."

"He can wait." Isobel drew his head downward as she lifted her mouth. "I'd like to show you how sorry I am for not trusting you."

"In broad daylight?" A devilish smile curved Yancy's mouth. "Who am I to deny my bride?"

In one swift motion, he rose. Stripping off his banyan, he then locked the door before heaving the robe onto a chair. Without a jot of chagrin, he peeled off his trousers.

Isobel almost licked her lips in anticipation.

His penis stood proud and stiff, as bold and impressive as the rest of the man.

Sitting upright, she lifted her nightgown over her head. There would be no pretense of shyness. She wanted him as he obviously wanted her.

Yancy's gaze slid to her breasts. In three elongated strides, he stood beside the bed.

Isobel opened her arms in welcome.

He bent over her, his thumbs burning trails of desire as he circled her breasts. "I want you so badly, I may not go as slowly as I should."

"I don't want you to go slowly. I've ached for your touch for years." She traced his lips with her tongue as she encircled his length with her fingers.

His breath hissed between clenched teeth. "Keep that up, and I shall be spilling my seed into your hand."

"Is that possible?" She raised her head to examine his manhood cradled in her palm.

Yancy scooted onto the bed. "Yes, it's possible, but that's for another time. For our first time together, I intend to be buried deep within your sweet folds when I find my release."

Lying atop her, he took her nipple in his mouth, grazing the tip with his teeth.

Isobel groaned and arched into him. She spread her legs and gripped his buttocks, urging him closer. She needed something, she didn't know what, but a hunger had been awakened deep within her woman's center.

His hands and mouth were everywhere, stroking, igniting.

She returned his caresses, instinctively comprehending if she enjoyed a certain touch, he would too.

"Yancy, I cannot stand much more." She ran her hands up and down his spine, scraping her fingernails. Pressing her face to his throat, she nipped his neck.

His muscles bunched and flexed beneath her inexperienced hands.

He trailed a hand to the curls between her legs. A spasm of pure bliss shot to her core. She moved against the rhythm he introduced her to with his skilled fingers.

"It will hurt a little the first time, sweetheart." Yancy settled his hips between her thighs.

He took her mouth in a searing kiss, his tongue sweeping hers, as he eased into her tightness.

Isobel hadn't expected the stretching, the fullness. The unfamiliar sensation made her want to move her hips. She tested the urge, tilting her hips upward at the same instant Yancy surged downward.

A strangled cry escaped her.

"I'm sorry, my love. The worst is over." Yancy tenderly kissed her while rocking his hips the merest bit.

Moaning, Isobel wiggled beneath him. "That feels good."

"Just you wait." He chuckled and lifted her hips, sinking deeper.

He rocked her again, and soon she caught the rhythm. Yancy increased the tempo, his breathing raspy.

Meeting him stroke for stroke, Isobel touched his face.

"I love you." Gasping, she crested the glittering wave, spiraling on a rainbow of sensation beyond time and words.

"And I love you." Yancy groaned against her throat as he stiffened and tremendous shudders shook his body.

Isobel lay with her head on his shoulder, more replete and content than she'd ever dreamed possible. She yawned, not the least interested in moving. "I suppose I ought to bathe and get dressed. Those below expected us quite some time ago."

"I suspect they know exactly what has caused our delay." Caressing her from shoulder to hip, Yancy seemed as disinclined to move as she.

She propped her chin on his chest, running her fingers through the crisp hairs. "Too bad we don't have time for me to show you my remorse again."

A movement caught her eye, and she turned her head. The sheet above his groin twitched.

Sliding up his chest, she arched an eyebrow and gave him a seductive smile. “We’ll be late.”

“Who cares?” Yancy settled Isobel on his lap, and by the time he’d finished, she didn’t care either.

Epilogue

South of Naples
May 1819

"Will you look at that?" Isobel angled her parasol and pointed to the remains of Paestum's amphitheater. "However did they manage to build such astounding structures?"

"Come along, sweet. I'm afraid our driver is becoming impatient." Yancy grasped her elbow, guiding her toward the waiting open-top carriage.

She offered the olive-skinned man standing before the door an apologetic smile.

"I suppose he has grown rather used to all of this. I never could." After a final reluctant glance, she hurried to the conveyance.

"We've been here six weeks, my love, and we were in Spain two months prior to that. I don't believe you would ever grow bored, and you've two chests packed with artifacts and mementos to remind you of your time here." Yancy helped her into the carriage before taking the seat beside her.

Isobel couldn't suppress a wistful sigh. Tomorrow they sailed for England.

Placing her hand on his thigh, Yancy gazed at the passing scenery. "What's to be our next adventure? France? Egypt? Russia?"

She shivered. "No, not Russia. Much too cold, although the country is rich in history. I had something of a different nature in mind."

"Oh, and what might that be?" Yancy glanced at her, a smile playing about his mouth.

"Motherhood." She cradled her flat belly.

His jaw sagged, and so did his gaze, straight to her stomach, before leaping to meet her eyes. "Are you . . ."

She nodded then squealed as he pulled her onto his lap. She almost dropped her parasol and accidentally clouted the driver on his back. "I'm so sorry."

He turned around and grinning, pointed to her lap. "*Bambino*?"

"*Si, bambino*," she said, patting her tummy.

The driver faced frontward once more, and Yancy kissed her full on the mouth.

"How long have you known? When will the child arrive?" He placed his palm on her middle. "Should you be traveling?"

"Darling, I just became aware myself. Our babe will arrive early next year, and yes, I am perfectly fine to travel. I haven't experienced a jot of malaise."

She rested her head against his chest. "We are very blessed."

"Indeed, and to think, I almost told Sethwick no when he invited me to Craiglocky those many years ago." Yancy hugged her closer and kissed her forehead. "Not a day goes by that I don't thank God I said yes."

"That makes two of us," Isobel whispered against his lips.

If you enjoyed *Virtue and Valor*,
be sure to read Collette Cameron's
Castle Bride Series,
now available from
Soul Mate Publishing at Amazon.com:

HIGHLANDER'S HOPE

Not a day has gone by that Ewan McTavish, the Viscount Sethwick, hasn't dreamed of the beauty he danced with two years ago. He's determined to win her heart and make her his own. Heiress Yvette Stapleton is certain of one thing; marriage is risky and, therefore, to be avoided. At first, she doesn't recognize the dangerously handsome man who rescues her from assailants on London's docks, but Lord Sethwick's passionate kisses soon have her reconsidering her cynical views on matrimony. On a mission to stop a War Office traitor, Ewan draws Yvette into deadly international intrigue. To protect her, he exploits Scottish law, declaring her his lawful wife—without benefit of a ceremony. Yvette is furious upon discovering the irregular marriage is legally binding, though she never said, "I do." Will Ewan's manipulation cost him her newfound love?

Buy now at:
http://tinyurl.com/pq4dhds

THE VISCOUNT'S VOW

Half Romani, noblewoman Evangeline Caruthers is the last woman in England Ian Hamilton, the Viscount Warrick, could ever love—an immoral wanton responsible for his brother's and father's deaths.

Vangie thinks Ian's a foul-tempered blackguard, who after setting out to cause her downfall, finds himself forced to marry her—snared in the trap of his own making. When Vangie learns the marriage ceremony itself may have been a ruse, she flees to her gypsy relatives, declaring herself divorced from Ian under Romani law. He pursues her to the gypsy encampment, and when the handsome gypsy king offers to take Ian's place in Vangie's bed, jealousy stirs hot and dangerous.

Under a balmy starlit sky, Ian and Vangie breech the chasm separating them, yet peril lurks. Ian is the last in his family line, and his stepmother is determined to dispose of the newlyweds so her daughter can inherit his estate. Only by trusting each other can Ian and Vangie overcome scandal and murderous betrayal.

THE EARL'S ENTICEMENT

She won't be tamed.

A fiery, unconventional Scot, Adaira Ferguson wears breeches, swears, and has no more desire to marry than she does to follow society's dictates of appropriate behavior. She trusts no man with the secret she desperately protects.

He can't forget.

Haunted by his past, Roark, The Earl of Clarendon, rigidly adheres to propriety, holding himself and those around him to the highest standards, no matter the cost. Betrayed once, he's guarded and leery of all women.

Mistaking Roark for a known spy, Adaira imprisons him. Infuriated, he vows vengeance. Realizing her error, she's appalled and releases him, but he's not satisfied with his freedom. Roark is determined to transform Adaira from an ill-mannered hoyden to a lady of refinement.
He succeeds only to discover, he preferred the free-spirited Scottish lass who first captured his heart.

Also read the first book in the
Highland Heather
Romancing a Scot Series:

Triumph and Treasure

A disillusioned Scottish gentlewoman.

Angelina Ellsworth once believed in love--before she discovered her husband of mere hours was a slave-trader and already married. To avoid the scandal and disgrace, she escapes to the estate of her aunt and uncle, the Duke and Duchess of Waterford. When Angelina learns she is with child, she vows she'll never trust a man again.

A privileged English lord.

Flynn, Earl of Luxmoore, led an enchanted life until his father committed suicide after losing everything to Waterford in a wager. Stripped of all but his title, Flynn is thrust into the role of marquis as well as provider for his disabled sister and invalid mother. Unable to pay his father's astronomical gambling loss, Flynn must choose between social or financial ruin.

When the duke suggests he'll forgive the debt if Flynn marries his niece, Flynn accepts the duke's proposal. Reluctant to wed a stranger, but willing to do anything to protect her babe and escape the clutches of the madman who still pursues her, Angelina agrees to the union.

Can the earl and his Scottish lass find happiness and love in a marriage neither wanted, or is the chasm between them insurmountable?

CPSIA information can be obtained
at www.ICGtesting.com
Printed in the USA
BVHW09s2220111018
529909BV00001B/212/P